Empty
Hearts

ALSO BY JULI ZEH

PUBLISHED IN ENGLISH

Eagles and Angels
In Free Fall
Decompression

Empty Hearts

A NOVEL

Juli Zeh

TRANSLATED FROM THE GERMAN
BY JOHN CULLEN

 NAN A. TALESE | DOUBLEDAY
NEW YORK

Translation copyright © 2019 by John Cullen

All rights reserved. Published in the United States by Nan A. Talese/Doubleday, a division of Penguin Random House LLC, New York, and distributed in Canada by Random House of Canada, a division of Penguin Random House Canada Limited, Toronto. Originally published in Germany as *Leere Herzen* by Luchterhand Literaturverlag, a division of Verlagsgruppe Random House GmbH, Munich, in 2017. Copyright © 2017 by Luchterhand Literaturverlag, a division of Verlagsgruppe Random House GmbH, Munich, Germany.

www.nanatalese.com

Doubleday is a registered trademark of Penguin Random House LLC. Nan A. Talese and the colophon are trademarks of Penguin Random House LLC.

Book design by Pei Loi Koay
Jacket design and illustration by Emily Mahon

LIBRARY OF CONGRESS CATALOGING-IN-PUBLICATION DATA
Names: Zeh, Juli, 1974– author. | Cullen, John, 1942– translator.
Title: Empty hearts : a novel / Juli Zeh ; translated from the German by John Cullen.
Other titles: Leere Herzen. English
Description: First American edition. | New York : Nan A. Talese/ Doubleday, [2019] | "Originally published in Germany as Leere Herzen by Luchterhand Literaturverlag, a division of Verlagsgruppe Random House GmbH, Munich, in 2017"— Title page verso.
Identifiers: LCCN 2019002645 (print) | LCCN 2019013474 (ebook) | ISBN 9780385544542 (hardcover) | ISBN 9780385544559 (ebook)
Classification: LCC PT2688.E28 (ebook) | LCC PT2688.E28 L4413 2019 (print) | DDC 833/.92—dc22
LC record available at https://lccn.loc.gov/2019002645

MANUFACTURED IN THE UNITED STATES OF AMERICA

10 9 8 7 6 5 4 3 2 1

First American Edition

There. That's how you are.

Full Hands Empty Hearts
It's a Suicide World
Baby

—Molly Richter, "Empty Hearts,"
from her 2025 debut album

**Empty
Hearts**

1

Knut and Janina come over at five.

The weather's splendid. For several days now, the sun has shown the kind of strength you would hardly have thought it capable of after a typical Braunschweig winter and the drizzly first weeks of spring. The light lies like pale yellow chiffon on the smooth surfaces of the furniture, sparkles in the glasses on the table, penetrates into the remotest dust-free corners. Three times a week, Britta has Henry, a young man from Laos, make the house spick-and-span. Unfortunately, the picture windows always exhibit a couple of smudges that Henry has missed.

With the children, daily routines have changed somewhat. Before, the adults would have met at dusk for the first aperitifs, not in broad daylight for dinner. But that's normal, it's the same for all of them, the whole army of parents with only children. Britta used to work until midnight, sleep until noon, and ingest the first solid food of the day in the early afternoon, when Babak, no morning person himself, would come to the office with something—usually a sandwich—for her to eat. The arrival of baby Vera seven years ago put an end to all that. Only sometimes Britta still feels a slight dizziness and something akin to alarm, symptoms of existential jet lag.

"This mess keeps falling apart," Richard calls from the kitchen, addressing no one in particular. Out in the hallway, Britta accepts the bottle of red wine that Knut has brought, a nice gesture, even though they have a whole cellar full of Luis Felipe Edwards Cabernet Sauvignon, a 2020 Chilean she and Richard like and have grown used to. She'll regift Knut's Rioja, a bottle with a ribbon around its neck, when the opportunity arises.

"Sticky fingers." Richard laughs as he raises his gummy hands in the air and greets his guests with his elbows. "I'm following the recipe exactly, but the stuff still looks like biowaste."

Before him lie shreds of seaweed and clumps of gooey rice, the results of his wrapping experiments. Richard has got it into his head to make his own sushi this evening, and Britta never interferes in such plans. The kitchen is Richard's domain. She'll keep the guests entertained and make sure the children eat something, it really doesn't matter what, by seven o'clock or so.

"Man, it looks great. We'll get some flat spoons and eat it directly off your granite countertop," says Knut.

It's actually polished concrete, but Britta keeps her mouth shut. Knut's kind of a wimp and probably not even particularly intelligent, but Britta likes him anyway, because he's good-humored and because his daughter, Cora, gets along so well with Vera. Seven years ago, Janina and Britta met at baby swim class, each with a screaming bundle on her arm; after that first day, they spent many a long, sluggish afternoon together. At first, they'd indulge in reciprocal venting about their troubles; later, they'd enjoy an hour or two of relative peace by the side of a play area while the two little girls kept them-selves busy. This play-date friendship has even withstood their decision to send Cora and Vera to different schools. While Knut and Janina's daughter goes to a children's music school where piano lessons are compulsory and smartphones pro-hibited, Vera is receiving a normal, Silicon Valley–influenced education, and is certainly no worse off for it. Cora's practic-ing "Faster, Faster, Little Snail" on the xylophone; Vera has just written her first program, which causes a fish to swim back and forth across her computer screen and snap at a baited hook when it's dropped into the water.

The two girls have already disappeared into Vera's room, while the adults are still occupied with standing around, which is apparently a phase that must be endured at every such gath-ering. You lean in a doorway or support yourself with both hands on the back of a chair and laugh in one another's faces until everyone is finally relaxed enough to sit down. Britta's house has a spacious living-and-dining area with big, glazed windows; nevertheless, everybody always squeezes into the kitchen and insists on sitting at the much-too-small breakfast table. She's given up wanting to do anything about this.

Britta pricks up one ear and aims it at Vera's room across the hall until she hears the usual Mega-Melanie sounds. The girls are wholly in love with Vera's Mega-Mall, a multilevel plastic monstrosity that has Wi-Fi, several electronic screens, and a programmable sound track. When Cora comes for a visit, she always brings some of her Glotzis, cuddly little aliens with three big eyes, currently all the rage. They constitute the driving force of a complex Martian attack on the Mega-Mall, which must be repulsed by Mega-Melanie, Mega-Martin, and their Mega-Friends. Most of the time, after various complica-tions, the members of Mega-SWAT start shooting wildly in all directions, killing not only the Glotzis but also all the customers in the Mega-Mall. Then the adults hear dramatic music and synchronized whoops of "Collateral damage!"

While the Edwards is breathing in the decanter, Britta opens the refrigerator and takes a moment or two to enjoy the sight of perfectly presented food. A stick of butter in a glass butter dish. Little vegetarian sausages, two eggplants, three tomatoes, a pitcher of milk. She takes out two different bottles of beer and hands each of the men his favorite. She opens a bottle of prosecco for Janina and herself.

"How was the showing?"

"Fabulous."

Janina clinks glasses but doesn't drink from hers, puts it down, and straightens her upswept hairdo. With her flowered dress and romantic coiffure, she presents a stark contrast to Britta, who wears her light hair straight and chin-length and prefers plain pants in gray or pale blue and tops that appear inexpensive except to a practiced eye. All the same, looking at Janina gives Britta pleasure. When Janina had her daughter, she was in her early twenties—having children while you're still young is back in style these days—and it often seems to Britta as though her younger friend comes not only from another decade, but also from a different planet. Janina is comfortable adapting to circumstances, whether it's a matter of her wardrobe or her hairstyle, her tiny apartment, her family, or her girlish dreams. For the past few weeks, she and Knut have been looking for a house in the country, a project that strikes Britta as rather absurd. She herself has known for fifteen years that big cities are passé, but also that provincial life cannot remedy metropolitan mania, since no evil can be cured by its opposite. Towns of medium size and medium importance, towns that obey the laws of pragmatism down to the smallest detail—those are the urban centers most appropriate to the twenty-first century. They have everything, but not too much of anything, enough of a few things, and in the midst of all that, affordable housing, wide streets, and architecture that leaves you alone.

Years before, while the people she knew were still busy renovating old farmhouses in Brandenburg and growing organic tomatoes, Britta used the first income from The Bridge to buy a house in a peaceful neighborhood in Braunschweig. A concrete cube with a lot of glass, practical, roomy, easy to clean, just like Braunschweig itself—straight lines, smooth surfaces, doubt-free. So completely thought through that each piece of furniture has only one possible location. There's a cellar, a child's room, a guest room, a sufficient number of bathrooms and storage spaces, a low-maintenance garden, and built-in household electronics that regulate room temperature, make coffee at scheduled times, and sound a warning when the refrigerator door stays open too long. Britta loves her house. If you have no desire to indulge in any self-deception about the times you live in, then polished concrete is exactly what you can still love.

"To be totally honest, I think we've found it." Janina raises her prosecco glass and clinks with the others again, and this time she drinks too. Her enthusiasm fascinates Britta. Janina loves peeling paint on old wooden doors, wheelbarrows planted with colorful flowers, and a big sheepskin rug in front of the fireplace. An anachronism that cries out to heaven. Complete ignorance of the fact that things have changed.

"The old people who own it just moved out. It was awful for them, leaving their house. All their lives, it was their home."

"So why do they want to sell it?"

"Not want to, have to. Out there, once you're old, you're not very well protected anymore."

"Old folks? Protected?" says Richard. By now, three more or less complete maki rolls are lying before him, slightly curved, like dog shit. "What's this about, palliative real estate?"

Britta laughs. She loves him for his quick wit, and she loves laughing at Janina's house-buying plans.

"Admit it," Britta says. "It's a perfectly run-down old dump, probably with wood stoves and straw mattresses, and when you want hot water, you put a kettle on the boil. Impossible to clean, because dust is constantly drifting down from the ceiling. And fat spiders in every corner."

"Sounds about right," says Knut, laughing good-naturedly.

"O-kaayyy." Richard stretches out the word in a tone that's supposed to mean, "No accounting for taste."

"The house is fabulous," Janina reiterates. "You have to come out with us sometime and see it. Cora's all enchanted. Imagine, she could keep a horse out there."

"Does Manufactum have horses in its catalog?" asks Richard.

"Seriously, it's just what we want. No electronics, wooden floors, clay plaster walls. A big garden with old trees. We'll invite you out and build a bonfire."

"Wearing full-body hazmat suits to ward off the ticks," says Britta. "So how much is this going to cost?"

Slightly exaggerating her discomfort at this question, Janina makes a face.

"Too much," says Knut. "But we've decided not to think about that."

"An outstanding financial strategy," Richard jokes. At this point, he's moved on to portioning out the pressed rice for the nigiri and is slowly gaining control of the sushi situation. Everyone present knows that Knut and Janina can't afford a house, or even a garden shed, regardless of whether the government's negative interest rate policy is extended indefinitely. As a playwright, Knut's still waiting for his breakthrough, and Janina's start-up, which she calls "Typewriter," and which offers secretarial services for writers, painters, and other freelancers, suffers from the fact that her clients have no more money than Janina and Knut themselves. Nevertheless, what they do have can suffice for the three of them to live a modest life, assuming that someday Knut becomes an earner, but the whole process will require time to develop. That Janina, in spite of this, is on the lookout for a house in the country strikes Britta as both touching and courageous. She decides to set aside her antipathy to self-constructed idylls and to let Janina know, as soon as possible, that if she has problems with the bank, then she, Britta, can help with the initial funding. Janina is, after all, her best friend, and besides, Britta has more money than she knows what to do with. The Bridge has done so well in the past year, what with Frexit, Free Flanders, and Catalonia First!, that now it's high time for her to start paying attention to financial strategies again. As she refills the prosecco glasses and opens two more beers, she makes a mental note to discuss her options with Babak tomorrow.

Britta emerges from her thoughts to find that Richard has already produced sixteen little rectangular blocks of rice. The topic of conversation has shifted from houses to something about politics. While Knut stares spellbound at his phone screen, Britta stands up and removes a bowl of last night's pasta and a couple of veggie sausages from the refrigerator. She knows few people who don't feel awkward taking out their smartphone nowadays. Whoever does so undaunted either has permanent employment or votes for the CCC, the Concerned Citizens' Crusade. Knut fits into neither of those categories, and yet he reads the "Snaps" posted by Regula Freyer and her associates. Years before, Babak developed a hack that allowed smartphone users to delete factory-installed apps. He passed the tool on to Britta and Richard, but Knut didn't want it.

"The CCC is introducing Efficiency Package Number Five," says Knut. He looks around, as though all present must now express an opinion in turn. "After it's in place, there'll be no more regional inquiry commissions or parliamentary advisory boards or oversight committees."

Janina clears her throat. If this sound doesn't induce Knut to restrain himself, then either he didn't hear it or didn't understand it.

"Do they want to do away with federalism altogether now?"

"It's possible," answers Richard serenely. "I wouldn't put anything past these CCC nutcases."

Britta gently shoves him and his sushi rollers to one side, puts the induction wok on the stove, and pours in a little oil and the pasta; then, while that's heating, she chops the veggie sausages into small pieces.

"They're giving the whole country a makeover."

"That's what they ran on doing. Lean and fit, into the future."

"Remind me, what kind of committees were those?" Janina asks.

"The budget cuts they're making, the amounts of money they're saving, are certainly enormous." Knut looks at his phone again. "It's the taxpayers' money, after all."

Britta doesn't believe that Knut has ever in his life paid taxes.

"In actual fact, nobody knows what we need federalism for," Janina says.

"None of us voted Concerned Citizens," says Richard. "So what are we even talking about?"

"Efficiency Package Number Five," Knut persists.

Britta is slowly getting irritated. Even though she is, for professional reasons, forced to keep up with politics, however superficially, she thinks people have no obligation to speak about politics in their private lives. It's all too obvious that Knut has yet to understand that politics is like the weather: it happens, whether you watch it or not; your attention makes no difference; and only idiots complain about it. She has a dim memory of having felt differently, once upon a time. She sees herself standing in a voting booth and marking her ballot with great conviction. She knows that in days gone by she would discuss the question of whom to vote for with other people, and she remembers that the answer seemed important to her. She's no longer so sure exactly when that was; definitely before the refugee crisis, Brexit, and Trump, and long before the second financial crisis and the meteoric rise of the Concerned Citizens' Crusade. In another time.

"Collateral damage!" The jubilant voices come from the children's room, accompanied by Mega-Music, which stamps loudly across the hall.

"Calm down in there!" Janina calls out. "Your dinner's almost ready!"

When Britta adds the sausage to the wok, the concoction begins to hiss. She stirs the ingredients thoroughly and switches on the exhaust hood over the stove.

"That smells pretty damn tasty," says Knut.

"I'm almost ready too." Richard opens some vacuum packs, takes out pieces of raw fish, and garnishes his sushi-rice blocks with them. Square plates are already on the table, along with pairs of chopsticks resting on little porcelain holders and bowls of soy sauce, pickled ginger, and wasabi paste.

"The hellacious part is, nobody has any idea what might come of all this," Knut says, returning to his topic. "I mean, the CCC simply won't do, that much is clear. But just for an example, who would have thought at the time that idiots like

Trump and Putin would put an end to the Syrian war? That's some post-factual politics."

Britta hates expressions like "post-factual" and "post-truth" and "post-reality." For years they've been flooding blogs and media outlets, which use them to make stupid people feel that actual political analysis is going on. As if politics were ever "factual." What was factual? Absolutism? Imperialism? National Socialism, the Cold War, the disintegration of Yugoslavia, or September 11? Britta has a great appetite for the truth. And the truth is that it's been years since anyone has known what to think.

With Knut still absorbed in scrolling on his smartphone, Britta turns on some music to signal that the conversation is over. Molly Richter's soft voice fills the room. This singer is the phenom of the season. Twelve years old, buzz-cut hair, the body and clothes of a little scamp, and a voice like Josephine Baker. *Full Hands Empty Hearts / It's a Suicide World Baby.*

Britta opens a can of peeled tomatoes and pours them into the wok. The hissing turns to bubbling, and the sautéed sausage pieces and pasta disappear in the red liquid. She mashes the tomatoes with the tip of her cooking spoon until the mixture takes on a mushy consistency. A cup of cream turns the red into a brownish pink and the mush into sauce. The children call the result "sausage goulash," a dish they both love.

"Looks good." Knut is standing next to her. He dips a spoon in the wok and tries some. "Tasty."

"Five minutes to sushi," says Richard.

"Sushi is for the eye, this here is for the belly." Knut holds out a square plate to Britta. "Much too good for the children."

She exchanges a look with Richard, who rolls his eyes but smiles, and so she doles out a portion of goulash. Janina appears with two more plates—one for herself, one for Britta—takes some spoons from a drawer, and sits at the table.

"Vera, Cora," Richard calls. "Your parents are eating up your sausage!"

"So, everyone dead?" asks Janina, tousling the girls' hair as they come running into the kitchen, carrying Mega-Melanie, Mega-Martin, and two Glotzis. They place them next to their plates before they fall upon the sausage goulash. Richard divides the sushi and sashimi into equal portions, places them on wooden boards, and serves them. The food looks better than expected; everyone claps and yells and calls out *"Arigato!"* before starting to eat everything indiscriminately, sausage and pasta and raw fish. Britta jumps up from her chair because she's forgotten the wine. They clink glasses yet again and the Edwards tastes fantastic, even though it pairs well with neither the sushi nor the goulash. The general mood is buoyant—a really nice evening.

There are strawberries for dessert, picked by Vera with her own hands in the neighbors' garden. Everyone gets a small portion. Britta watches Janina turn down sugar and whipped cream and smiles silently to herself. It's a good thing that problems are, at least to some extent, equitably distributed. Britta often considers herself a bad mother because she secretly loves her work more than her family. On the other hand, she can eat whatever she wants.

At seven forty-five, Vera—as she does every evening—wants to watch an episode of her favorite series on Netflix. A little drone named "Featherweight," which has escaped from its owner, helps a girl solve everyday problems.

While Vera and Cora stare at the screen, Janina and Knut have already begun to thank their hosts and to propose some ideas for a reciprocal invitation. Britta and Richard assure them that they need no help cleaning up, that it's been a super-nice evening, and that they'll gladly drop over to their place with Vera for a meal sometime—or maybe it would be better to go to the park for a cookout, because Knut and Janina's apartment is pretty small and, as Britta secretly thinks, not particularly clean either.

"Wow! Awesome!" cries Vera in the living room.

"Collateral damage!" Cora shouts gleefully.

That sounds too violent for Featherweight. Britta, followed by the others, crosses the hall.

The girls have switched to television mode, one of the few things that Britta rigorously forbids. Television is out of the question. She's about to launch into a scolding rant, but she's distracted by what she sees on the screen. The eight o'clock news.

"What the hell is that?" she whispers, or rather hears herself whisper, for her lips have moved without her say-so.

The others have stopped in the doorway, still discussing the proposed cookout. Britta's standing in the middle of the room, by chance exactly in the center of the star-shaped rug pattern, looking at the TV. Washed-out images, a forty-five-second report, the first half of which she's already missed. Nonetheless, she grasps the situation at once. Black uniforms, operations officers speaking into two-way radios, circling helicopters, tear gas, flash grenades, the works. If she's not completely mistaken, the culprit, who has been brought to the ground, is wearing an explosive belt, but the picture quality is very bad, like a cell phone video taken from a great distance.

Britta's knees get weak, and she flops onto an armchair. The girls are tussling on the couch. Richard cries, "Turn off that blasted television, right now!" Janina says, "We're leaving!" Knut has likewise stepped in front of the television set; he's looking at the news anchor, a woman, part of the whole cheesy eight-o'clock shtick, including a candy-colored suit and blow-dried hair, how amazing that this hasn't stopped, that it simply goes on and on, as though absolutely nothing has changed in the past twenty years. Terror attack, says the anchor. Leipzig/Halle Airport, cargo area, attackers thwarted at the last moment. One suspect dead, the other in custody. Thus far no indication of what group, if any, is responsible; ongoing investigation; information blackout. Britta has the impression that she's taking part in some surreal film. Any second now, the woman will take off her mask and turn into Featherweight, or in any case, that's Britta's hope.

"What's wrong?" asks Knut.

The newscast has moved on to another story, this one about a new, genetically modified plant, due to be patented soon: a corn-pumpkin hybrid, extremely large, extremely nutritious, and possibly the end of hunger in the Third World, as the spokespersons for the government and Google maintain at a joint press conference.

"Oh, nothing."

"They were shooting everywhere, it was really cool, the guys in black had flash crenades and smoke bombs and giant guns."

"Mama, was that a SWAT team? Or the secret servant?"

"Grenades," says Knut. "And secret service. And shooting everywhere isn't cool."

Britta surreptitiously reaches into her pocket, takes out her smartphone, and unlocks it; when she realizes that Knut has seen her, she puts the device away again.

"What's the matter, sweetie?" calls Richard from the kitchen. "Is it one of your patients?"

Richard and the others know that occasionally one of The Bridge's clients "does something stupid," as Britta puts it. When that happens, she acts devastated for a couple of days, while the other three strive to console her, assuring her that she bears no guilt, reminding her that her therapeutic success rate is higher than ninety percent. "They're just people," Richard usually says in such cases. "You can try to help them, but there's only so much you can do."

"I thought so for a second, but I was wrong," says Britta.

"Kids, we're going now," says Knut. "Cora, where are your Glotzis? Put your shoes on."

About what she saw with her own eyes, Britta can speak to no one. Except to Babak. If she could, she'd call him up at once. Ask him for facts. He must have gone through the available information quite thoroughly by now. Then again, she needs, urgently needs, time to think; her head's about to explode.

Instead, she must bid farewell to her guests and put Vera to bed. After that, Richard will want to drink one more glass of wine and engage in a detailed discussion of the evening with Knut and Janina. Their house-buying plans. Their disastrous jobs. Britta's thoughts are on a roller coaster in her head, but she pulls herself together, stands up, smiles at Knut, takes the wriggling Vera by an arm—at seven years old, she's already quite a heavy little person—thinks, *Cargo area, why the cargo area,* and says things like "Stop it now, no drama, you promised," while they stand around a little longer in the hallway until Knut and Janina have got themselves organized, thanked their hosts for the third time, and said good-bye as often; until Cora is finally dressed and ready; and until the unwieldy family unit has been maneuvered out the door. *Who comes up with the idea of attacking pieces of luggage? Because they're easier to get to?* So long, so long, the automobile starts, it could really use another visit to the car wash, they wave until their visitors have disappeared around the next corner.

Richard goes to the kitchen to clean up; Britta goes to the bathroom with Vera. Once visitors have left, she's always tormented by the urge to clean the whole place immediately, top to bottom. *Henry's coming tomorrow;* the thought soothes her. Everything's organized, everything's taken care of. When she sees her face in the mirror, she feels nauseated.

Not now, she thinks, *please,* and the nausea goes away.

How had the authorities arrived on the scene so fast and so heavily equipped? Who shot the video and gave it to the media? Why did one suspect survive?

She and Vera are in negotiations about the length of time, in minutes, prescribed for the little girl's toothbrushing when Britta's phone rings. Unknown number. She accepts the call and admonishes herself to speak softly. The bathroom and the kitchen share a wall, and Richard might hear her.

"Good evening," she says.

"Who is it?" Richard calls from the other side of the wall.

"Babak!" she calls back.

"Best regards!" calls Richard.

"Just take it easy," says Babak.

"Have you found out anything?"

"Found out what?" asks Vera, her mouth full of toothpaste.

"Let me talk to Babak for a minute," says Britta. "It's about business."

"No talking, not now. I'm calling to tell you to stay calm. This probably has nothing at all to do with us."

"Didn't you see that—"

"Of course, it's possible I saw a suicide belt, but I'm not certain. The news reports aren't clear. Stay calm, spend your evening with your family, don't log on to the Internet. Everything the same as usual. Okay? We'll talk tomorrow."

"Okay."

"Until morning, then."

"I've definitely brushed enough now." Vera spits out toothpaste foam and runs into the kitchen. "Night, Papa! Kisses!"

she says, and darts across the hall to her room. Britta follows more slowly, taking deep breaths, and feels professionalism flowing back into her body, like the effect of a mild drug. In the kitchen, Richard has again turned on some music, and she can hear Molly's voice through the wall. *Full Hands Empty Hearts / It's a Suicide World Baby.*

Chapter

The next day is also radiant and sunny, the sky a bright, polished surface garnished with freshly washed clouds. There's a light wind, unusually warm already, though it's still early morning. Since Richard's taking Vera to school today, Britta goes to work on her bicycle. She pedals as little as possible, opts for a zigzag route through the neighborhood, peers over fences and hedges into gardens, occasionally greets a neighbor who has decided to spend his unconditional basic income on lawn mowing and tree pruning. Lehndorf is a quiet district, one- and two-family houses built by the Nazis back in the 1930s, perfect for children and as ugly and practical as the rest of the city. Precisely because Britta has slept very little, waiting all night for the moment when she would finally be able to talk with Babak, she forces herself to go slow. Mental control; the boss in her own house.

When she crosses under the autobahn, she starts pedaling a little faster, enjoying the ride along the wide lanes, beautifully straight and bordered by king-size sidewalks that look as though they were built for a tank parade. In the city center, the streets are still wet from the cleaning brigade's water cannons. There are some days when Britta loves Braunschweig as much as though it were her own creation. The chunky pomposity of totalitarian luxury buildings, which look like palaces and in reality are only shopping malls. The Deutsches Haus hotel, where she occasionally puts up clients and whose corridors somehow smell like socialism. The city's nonexistent aura, a result of having eliminated, in deference to vehicular traffic, any sort of aesthetic appeal. This all represents something of a relief compared to the claustrophobic pluralism of the metropolises. After graduating from high school in the 2000s, when it was still relatively chic to move to Berlin, Britta felt little desire to live in the capital. TV commercials featuring young, unshaven types who rented apartments in Prenzlauer Berg were all the rage. Britta moved to Leipzig to study and later to Braunschweig to work, and in the meanwhile, changing trends proved her right. Independent professionals left Prenzlauer Berg in droves to move to medium-size cities that had been destroyed in the war and were still being rebuilt in the spirit of rationalism—function, construction, and form.

While Britta's waiting for the bicycle light to change, she looks at the display screens on the traffic poles and reads the headlines.

Fine weather to continue—Efficiency Package Number Five on the way to the Reichstag—Spelt & Sesame Slice named Bread of the Year—Regula Freyer on a visit to China.

Braunschweig suits Britta so perfectly because here, somehow, you fly under the radar. Well-thought-out mediocrity, inconspicuous muddling through. Britta wants a peaceful existence for herself and her family; she wants to do work and to take on responsibility, but only for things she's capable of handling. Why should she feel responsible for the rest? These days, nobody knows what to be for and what to be against anymore. Of course, the Concerned Citizens are dismantling one hard-won democratic achievement after the other. But even so, people are doing well, maybe even better than before. When Trump was inaugurated, there was talk of the Decline of the West, and then, after forming an alliance with Putin, he quite casually put an end to the Syrian Civil War. American isolationism halted Israel's settlement policies and as a result almost inadvertently brought about a two-state solution and a peace treaty between Israel and Palestine. The economic war between Europe and the U.S. transformed the Middle East into a lucrative outlet for American products, and this in turn caused the whole region to flourish. Practically all at once, Islamic terror stopped being a global problem, and now ISIS has dwindled from the Western world's scariest nightmare to a handful of decadent warlords.

Meanwhile, people have given up political speculation. They live their lives and stick their heads in the sand, because in a world where someone like Trump can be accepted as anything other than a shit, they can think of nothing better to do.

Britta operates under no illusions. She doesn't think she understands ongoing developments, and she doesn't try to know any better. She lives in a tidy house in a tidy city and runs a tidy company. That's her contribution. Once—a long time ago, before founding The Bridge—she read a sentence that made an indelible impression on her: *Morality, the compulsory part of the program, is for the weak; the strong excel in the free skate.*

As she nears the main railroad station, her heart starts beating fast again. Ever since the previous evening, she's been repressing the desire to pull out her smartphone and look for more information. Instead of doing that at breakfast, she picked up the local newspaper, the *Braunschweiger Zeitung,* which is still being printed in small editions for nostalgic ironists like Richard. She found a report on the events in Leipzig, a brief article obviously squeezed onto page three just before the edition went to press. There was also a photograph, which she recognized from the television news she'd seen: black uniforms in a large, hangar-like space, and a long, narrow shadow on the ground. The copy revealed as little as the picture. The previous evening, two suspected terrorists, apparently carrying explosives, had forced their way into the cargo terminal at the Leipzig airport. Acting on an anonymous tip, the security service was able to intervene quickly and prevent the worst from happening. One suspect was shot dead, the other is in custody. Interior Minister Wagenknecht reacted to the incident by declaring that Germany remains a target for terrorists, and that there is cause for heightened vigilance, but not for panic. The government is doing everything it can to ensure the safety of the people. An example of this commitment can be found in the measures granting wider powers to the police and the secret service that, along with federalism reform, are included in Efficiency Package Number Five.

While Britta is racing down Kurt Schumacher Street, she raises her head, delighting in the way the wind blows back her hair. She's grateful to her mother, from whom she inherited that hair: thick, straight, wheat-blond, perfect for short haircuts; a bit of tousling is all it needs to look good. Hair you don't need to brush, shirts you don't need to iron, vacuum cleaners you don't need to push around—Britta likes such things. She also likes having a coworker willing to stay up all night long to compile the latest news for her. Smooth operation is for Britta the highest principle.

The Kurt Schumacher Apartment Blocks on the northwestern side of the Braunschweig railroad station are part of an odd sort of neighborhood, tidy but featureless. Apartments stacked high; on the balconies, laundry; on the ground floor, storefronts and offices, mainly doctors and dentists of Arab origin, Nabils and Sahids and Jawads, who X-ray, massage, peer into mouths, noses, and ears, drill into teeth, and cut away liver spots. A clump of dreariness in an excellent central location. An example of ghettoization, which the CCC steadfastly maintains does not exist.

There's a passage between the blocks, an accumulation of low-rise buildings, gray and inconspicuous, as though built for badly performing businesses of all kinds. Britta pushes her bicycle into a bike rack and opens a door with her own name on it: "The Bridge, Britta Söldner and Babak Hamwi." Under the names, in smaller lettering: "Medical office. Licensed healing practitioner. Psychotherapy and applied depth psychology, self-managing, life coaching, ego polishing," and a few other terms that have nothing whatsoever to do with the practice's real activities. In the dental laboratory across the hall, the pony-tailed blonde at the reception desk keeps her eyes fixed on her computer screen, doesn't greet Britta, and doesn't budge. Every morning, Britta wonders whether the girl is real.

The practice smells like coffee; no trace of Babak.

With the surrounding high-rise buildings, it's dark in The Bridge's offices. The ceiling lights are on, as always, dim fluorescent tubes set in square fixtures and glowing overhead at all times, in all seasons. The Bridge's rooms are extremely unsuitable for a healing practice; its display windows are too big, and its atmosphere is too murky; a tattoo salon would have made a better fit, or a dog-grooming service, or the next Humana Second Hand store. There's a brownish carpet on the floor; the reception counter was held over from the previous owner, even though the practice has no need for it at all. Other amenities include a living room suite where Britta sits with new candidates for their initial conversation, and a large worktable for Babak's sole use. Everything's well-worn but clinically clean; after all, Britta personally handles the housekeeping duties in the office. The uninviting atmosphere is purposeful; walk-in business must not be encouraged.

Britta leans over the worktable, to which a sheet of paper two square meters in area is fastened with special clamps. Babak has the paper custom-made and gets it directly from the manufacturer. One corner of the sheet looks dirty, but if you gaze more closely, you can see that innumerable little differently colored dots cover it so thickly that there's hardly any space between them. The Bridge experiences long lulls in activity, no cause for alarm, just a part of the normal work rhythm. While Britta uses such phases to catch up on paperwork, fetch Vera early from her after-school day care center, putter in her garden, and—on hot days—inflate the wading pool, Babak holds down the fort in the office and passes the time making dot pictures. In leisurely fashion, he removes the cap from a felt-tip pen, adds a couple of dots, puts the cap back on, and opens the next pen. There's something meditative about the clicking of the pen caps. Months can pass before such a picture is finished. Britta must admit that she admires the results. They display indistinct gradations, the colors bleeding, oscillating from red through purple to blue and back, moving in waves, like rain veils or sand whirls the eye can scarcely perceive.

Noises come from the basement. Like all the commercial spaces in the Kurt Schumacher Passage, the practice has an underground floor, windowless rooms level with the nearby expressway and the traffic roaring past on it. Coffee cake can be found down there, along with toilets, a tiled multipurpose area, and the well-secured server room, where Babak spends the greater part of his working time.

Now he mounts the spiral staircase at a rapid clip, carrying a stack of documents that he drops on the coffee table. Then he looks at them pensively and wipes his brow with his forearm. He and Britta know each other so well that they forget to say hello. Even when they go a few hours without seeing each other, they never feel separated. Twelve years ago, when they first met, Babak was fat, gay, nerdy, and Iraqi. These days he's not fat anymore, and as for the other things, he's no longer ashamed of them. In his view, Britta saved his life, and therefore he idolizes her like a big sister. Whenever he's agitated, as he is today, it's not because he's confounded by events, but because he's worried about Britta's state of mind.

"What have you got there?"

"Dossiers. All the information on the attack."

"In quadruplicate?"

"One for you, one for me, one for the files, and one just in case."

Britta can't help laughing. Babak has spent the entire night in front of the computers; she can tell from the bluish circles under his eyes, even though he took an early morning shower in the office and put on a fresh shirt. Since starving himself down from 250 to 165 pounds, he handles his body like an object of great value. When he comes over for dinner, he and Richard can discuss Scandinavian gentlemen's outfitters for hours, bemoan the persistence of "hipster fashion," and philosophize over the shape of a perfect shoe toe cap. On such occasions, Britta listens in silence and remembers how women used to be ridiculed because fashion was their sole topic of conversation.

"Sit down. Here's some coffee."

Babak brings a tray with two little cups and a small copper pot, in which he prepares the coffee Turkish-style. When he fills the cups, Britta sees his hands shaking.

"Let's hear it. What have you got?"

"Markus Blattner and Andreas Muradow, twenty-one and twenty-five years old, automobile mechanic and chemistry student."

"Chechens?"

"Germans. The name Muradow isn't all that rare."

"Which one's dead?"

"Andreas."

"And which one is the convert?"

"Probably neither."

"You can't be serious."

"An overview of the situation indicates that we can't assume an Islamist background."

"Hasn't ISIS claimed responsibility for the attack?"

"They claim responsibility for every overturned watering can."

Britta sighs. "Just the facts, please."

"Two men forced their way into the sorting center in the freight terminal at the Leipzig airport yesterday evening around nineteen hundred hours."

"Shift change?"

"The freight hub operates twenty-four/seven, but the big crush takes place in the evening. Markus and Andreas were dressed in DHL uniforms and carrying fake ID cards."

"So their handlers were professionals."

Babak shrugs. "Or ecstatic amateurs."

"I thought I saw a belt on the TV screen."

"You thought right. They were both wearing explosive belts."

"Shit."

They fall silent. Britta finishes her coffee; Babak pours her some more, adds a bit of sugar, stirs it in for her. Of course, she's known the whole time that the disastrous operation was a suicide attack. Her gut feeling was unequivocal. No heavy weapons, no resistance. But there were two of them, side by side, and that had given her a little hope. Most suicide bombers act alone.

"We knew this would happen one day, didn't we?" says Babak, and Britta nods.

"It was only a matter of time. It's not really so bad."

Britta nods again. Then her rage comes welling up. "Who was it, dammit?" She strikes the table with both fists, capsizing the freshly filled coffee cup and turning the contents of the pretty sugar bowl into a brown slurry. When she realizes that Babak doesn't need to run downstairs for cloths and sponges to clean up the mess because he already has them ready under the tray, she lets herself sink back into her chair. "You're incredible, Babak."

"How so?" He puts on an innocent expression. "We've always worked with prognoses."

They grin at each other.

"Stop worrying," Babak says. "We'll get a handle on this."

She lifts the tray while he wipes up. Although the dossiers have escaped unstained, Babak runs a dishcloth over their protective covers. Britta picks up her copy. Biographies and metadata, page after page printed too small for her to read without glasses.

"You were thorough."

A smile makes a brief appearance on Babak's face and immediately vanishes. He doesn't want to show how happy praise from her makes him.

"Unfortunately, there's not much we can use in there. No traffic within the groups, no videos, nothing in preparation. Andreas had been active on Facebook during the past few weeks, even with some Arabic-language contacts; a little *insha'allah* and *alhamdulillah*, along with mountains of emoticons. The usual rubbish from people who don't know the language. He'd also posted videos of a couple of preachers, including jihadi stuff."

"So Islam, after all."

"I don't know. Pretty superficial, all of it."

"Death to the infidel?"

"Sure."

"And who did the tip come from?"

Babak shrugs. Britta looks at him thoughtfully.

"You don't like it."

Babak raises his hands defensively. "I'm just putting pieces of information together."

"What do your instincts say?"

"That it had nothing to do with Islam. Maybe it was supposed to look like it did. But that's all."

Britta nods. "Has there been a press conference yet?"

"They say they'll hold one today. But in any case, they don't know anything. We can skip it."

As they say nothing for a while, a noise moves into the foreground, a sound that Britta up to now has been only half-conscious of. It's an electrical buzz, accompanied by the humming of a large fan. It climbs up out of the opening to the spiral staircase, it seems to set floor and furniture vibrating, it fills the entire space, familiar and soothing; it's the operating noise of their shared existence.

"Lassie's running," says Britta.

"Been running all night."

"When will we have results?"

"Any minute now."

Britta leafs through her dossier. She's been hoping for more photographs. The two on hand have been greatly enlarged; they're pretty blurry and not very informative. Nevertheless, Britta thinks one of the two men looks familiar.

Babak holds up the palms of his hands. "I couldn't find better pictures. You can see the belts, but you can't tell how they're packed."

"TATP?"

Babak shrugs again.

"What about the store receipts?" asks Britta.

"Cheese slices and dental floss. Neither of the two bought anything relevant."

"Acetone and hydrogen peroxide are in every drugstore."

"Right, but generally people do some web searches first."

"Well, the dead guy was a chemistry student."

"Suicide-belt construction isn't part of the curriculum. You have to have a little electrotechnical knowledge too."

"Could they have brought the system in from abroad?"

"They weren't abroad. Besides, TATP is much too explosive to transport over any significant distance."

"Or they mixed some kind of stuff together themselves. After all, nothing got blown up."

"I think they were intercepted before they reached their target. They didn't get far enough to do anything serious."

"Babak, you're getting on my nerves."

"Sorry, Britta, I know what you want to hear."

"But you don't want to say it."

"We can only speculate at this point."

"You don't think they were acting on their own. You think they had help. They were sent."

Before Babak can answer, the printer in the basement begins to hum.

"Lassie's delivering."

Britta forces herself to remain seated while Babak runs down the stairs to get the printout. But when he comes back, she gets up anyway, so that they wind up standing in front of each other as though they've met by chance, he with a single sheet of paper in his hand, she with a question mark on her face. Babak holds up the page.

"Markus: two-point-five. Andreas: two-point-eight."

"Say that again."

"Two-point-five and two-point-eight."

Britta feels herself turn pale. Babak's eyes seem fixed, as if the brain behind them has shut itself off. The moment passes, and they look at each other. It's Babak who finally finds his voice again: "Lassie thinks they didn't want to kill themselves at all."

3

Britta doesn't really like playgrounds. It makes her sad to see what becomes of people whose sole interest is their children. Fathers whose arms wear out from hours of swing pushing. Mothers who crawl on all fours, grunting like pigs, through big plastic tubes. Couples enthusiastically building a sand castle while their bored three-year-old stares into space. Britta dislikes sippy cups and rice crackers. She loathes listening to women who spend half the afternoon talking about what kind of extraordinary giftedness their offspring's whims might portend. Britta loves her daughter too. But unlike other parents, she doesn't try to replace, with Vera's help, what all of them have lost: politics, religion, a sense of community, and the belief in a better world.

Nevertheless, every few days she finds herself once again on the edge of the adventure playground in the city park, with Janina at her side and a green-tea go-cup in her hand. Richard often stays at work until late in the evening these days, and Britta gets bored alone in the house with Vera. Britta's not good at paging through picture books, changing doll diapers, or buying miniature loaves of bread in make-believe shops. Shooting at stuffed animals with Mega-Melanie and Mega-Martin is the very last thing she wants to do. She'd rather sit in the park with Janina, watching the two little girls romp and the other parents parent.

Janina's wearing her long hair loose and lying on the grass with her coffee cup, draped like a figure in a Klimt painting. Britta sits next to her, holding her torso upright so that as little of her body as possible comes into contact with the green blades. Behind her, a "Sport Is Public" group is practicing yoga. When they all raise their arms and bend forward at the same time, they look as though they're worshiping Britta and Janina.

"How are things with Richard?"

"He has a lot on his plate."

"Is his swapping venture doing any better?"

"Not really. Emil and Jonas continue to behave like little children."

Whereas Britta calmly pedals to work, where she drinks coffee with Babak—whom she's always glad to see—while they discuss the latest Silicon Valley gossip, Richard must spend every day with conceited venture capitalists, endure the marriage-like running battle his partners conduct, and not even make any money. In Richard's place she'd be envious. The fact that he's not counts for a lot in her eyes. He's happy for her success, even though in reality he has no idea what she does. It doesn't even bother him that she earns money and he doesn't; he's just as loving and funny as he ever was.

"I've got a couple of out-of-town appointments in the next few days. Can Vera come to your house after school?"

"Sure," says Janina, without hesitation.

In the meantime, Vera and Cora have called a halt to running around and moved on to building a large-scale sand castle. For this undertaking, they carefully wet sand and then, with the help of plastic buckets, shape it into the blocks that become the foundation. After Janina has watched them for a while, she sinks down on her back and stares at the sky.

"And you?" she asks.

"What about me?"

"How are things with your practice?"

"Fabulous." Which is no lie; they're only in the second quarter, and already it's clear that this year's income will almost double last year's.

"Really funny, isn't it?" Janina's voice sounds lethargic. "The worse off people are, the better you and Babak do."

A chubby little boy has appeared, and he's circling the girls' construction site. Britta's sitting too far away to hear what's being said, but it's obvious that Vera and Cora don't want to let the fat kid play with them.

Janina rolls herself up onto her elbows. "Actually, do you have an explanation for that? For the rising suicide rate?"

Entire walls could be papered with theories about the suicide phenomenon. Fear of the future. Burnout. The dissolution of gender roles. The second financial crisis. Europe's disintegration. The neglect of the underclass. Increasing discrimination against fringe groups. Poor nutrition. Growing isolation. Too little exercise. Decadence. Guilt complexes. The parents of the 1990s and their failure at child rearing.

"I think there's a hole in us, deep inside us," says Britta.

The chubby boy stomps over to the swing, unenthusiastically pushes himself back and forth a few times, and then returns to the half-finished sand castle. He watches as Vera and Cora tirelessly moisten sand, pack it into buckets, and place one block after another on the castle walls.

"We have no idea who we are. Or want to be. Or should be."

"I don't feel any hole."

"And therefore you'll never wind up in my practice."

Janina laughs. For a moment, Britta imagines what it would be like to put a woman like Janina through the program. In all these years, Britta has only ever worked with men.

The fat kid has started to throw sand at the sand castle. Vera tells him to stop, or something like that: in any case, Britta recognizes, even at a distance, her daughter's *No!* face. Then the boy kicks the outer wall, causing a large part of it to collapse.

"Mama!" scream Cora and Vera in chorus.

"Such a little asshole," says Janina.

The boy kicks again, then several times, one after another, and tramples what he's brought down into the ground.

"Mama!" Vera bawls. "He's ruining our castle!"

"Whack him one!" Britta calls back.

She can feel Janina's astonished look. Vera too is briefly startled before sizing up the boy, who's a good deal bigger than she is. Then—having apparently decided against punching and in favor of kicking—she springs forward and takes aim at her opponent's swinging leg. *Not bad at all,* Britta thinks, as the tip of Vera's sneaker bangs against the chubby boy's shin. He howls, more in disbelief than in real pain, beats a whiny retreat, and goes off in search of his mama.

"Hey, what are you thinking?" calls a woman who's sitting on the grass a few yards away and rocking a baby in her arms. "Is that what you want to teach your daughter? To resolve conflicts by force?"

"Have you got a better idea?" Britta asks in turn. "Shall I teach her to hold her tongue later on, when she's being raped?"

The other mother shakes her head, grabs her things, stands up, and looks around for another place to sit.

"Or maybe to keep her eyes on the train platform and do

nothing, along with ten other people, while a man's being beaten to death?" The farther away the other woman gets, the louder Britta shouts. "You think you're superior because you've been ducking all your life? You believe doing nothing makes the world a better place?"

When the other woman is out of earshot, Britta sinks back down, exhausted.

"What was *that* about?" Janina's sitting up and laughing.

"No idea. I have to stretch my legs." Britta gets to her feet. Often, walking around a little helps her overcome her nausea spells. She circles the playground, where Vera and Cora are busy rebuilding their ruined castle, and when she feels better, she goes back to Janina.

"You're not pregnant by any chance, are you?"

"Nonsense," says Britta. "Are you ready?"

"At your service, Madam."

They call this the dilemma game. One of them describes a difficult situation in which a decision has to be made; the other must say what she would do. Britta finishes her tea and throws the cup away. "Do you see that trash bin over there?" she asks.

Janina looks in that direction and nods.

"Inside it there's a bomb that's going to explode in five minutes."

This example is fun for Britta, because she knows with nearly one hundred percent certainty that the trash bin in question will not blow up, not today or tomorrow or in the coming weeks, because there won't be an attack anywhere in the whole country. At any rate, that's what she would have claimed to know for certain twenty-four hours ago.

"As it happens, you've observed the terrorist and captured him. He alone knows the code for defusing the bomb. What do you do?"

"I pull the bomb out and throw it in the pond."

"It's set to explode the moment anyone touches it. You'll die, and so will all the other people here."

Janina sighs. Britta invented this game, and Janina plays it for her sake, but the truth is, she finds it pretty exhausting. "I appeal to the terrorist's conscience."

"He laughs at you."

"I call the police."

"Not enough time."

"You want to know if I'd beat him until he defused the bomb?"

Britta shrugs. "What would you do?"

Janina reflects for a moment. "Honestly? I'd pick up Cora and Vera and run as fast as I could. Until we reached safety."

"And let the other children die?"

"I've answered the question. It's my turn."

Britta smiles and nods. She can take deep breaths now; the remaining traces of nausea have disappeared. The dilemma game brings her relief, every time.

"You're driving through the neighborhood when a cat suddenly runs in front of your car. You hit the little animal, but it's not dead."

"Didn't we have something like this recently, but with a dog?"

"The cat's lying on the side of the road, panting and whimpering. It's obvious that it has no chance of surviving. What do you do?"

"The same as the last time. I keep on driving."

"You don't even get out of the car?"

"What for?"

"You could get help."

"But you just said there's no chance the cat can survive."

"Suppose it belongs to a family? The children find their pet dying in a gutter."

"Then they'll learn never to run into the street. Who knows, maybe that lesson will save one of their lives."

"I don't know." Janina shakes herself. "I find that pretty . . . brutal."

Britta watches a grandma shuffling along the gravel path and pulling a tiny dog on a leash behind her, the sort of dog you acquire in life's last stage only so that you can still have someone to bawl out.

"But you ran away from the bomb, didn't you?" Britta says. "Spare me the hypocrisy."

It sounds harsher than she intended, which doesn't escape Janina's notice either. She looks pensively at Britta. "You seem odd today, somehow."

"I'm sorry. A bit of stress at work."

"Well, I know what that's like." Janina nods earnestly, even though both of them realize she hasn't the remotest idea what that's like. She's familiar with dwindling orders and extended slack periods. Stress at work is something people like Knut and Janina wish they suffered from. A sudden wave of affection breaks over Britta. She knows Janina's about to ask her a question, and she knows what that question will be. Britta herself is often astounded by the accuracy with which she can predict the behavior of others. It's as if a part of Lassie's abilities has rubbed off on her.

"If we really decide to buy this house," Janina says, twirling a strand of her hair around one finger and staring at the ground, "would you lend us some money?"

Chapter

They've had a quarrel. Babak insisted on one of The Bridge's fundamental rules: Travel rarely, and then only in extreme emergencies. And is this really an emergency? Britta had no good counterarguments. She herself doesn't know exactly what she aims to accomplish with the proposed visits. Maintain a presence. Look out for clues. Make it clear to her regular clients that The Bridge bears no responsibility for the disaster in Leipzig. Babak reminded her again and again that the Leipzig incident might well have been the work of two nutcases acting on their own and throwing in a bit of Islamist rah-rah to make the thing seem bigger than it was.

"With scores under three?" Britta asked, whereupon Babak fell silent.

Neither of them believes there's any possibility that Lassie has made a mistake. The algorithm is sophisticated, highly intelligent, self-learning, perfectly trained. Babak has been working on its continued development since The Bridge's very first days. He brought Lassie into the world, he feeds her, cares for her, trains with her, praises her when she does her job well, and corrects her when errors occur, which practically never happens anymore. Lassie's earliest results already exceeded all expectations. That was eleven years ago, and since then the algorithm has improved with each use. Lassie isn't the Google search engine, but in her own field, she's a solitary peak. She feels at home not only in the visible web, but in the dark web too. She runs on ahead, nose to the ground, sniffing the corners, both bright and dim, of human communication, establishing links. At the same time, she makes evaluations, assigning scores of between 1 and 12 on the suicidal tendencies scale developed by Britta. Numbers under 3 indicate insignificant levels of suicidality.

Basically, there are only two possible explanations. Either there's a competitor who wants to enter the market and is going about it in the stupidest way conceivable: sloppy casting, sloppy planning, sloppy briefing. Or—the "or" is harder. Or the two lads were maximally fooled.

Britta sticks headphones into her ears, listens to Molly Richter, and watches through the window as the landscape rushes by. A display above her head informs her that the weather will get worse, that Regula Freyer is traveling to Turkey again, and that the number of constitutional judges has been reduced, for reasons of efficiency, to three. Four hours later, the train pulls into the main station in Cologne, where she must transfer.

Britta arrives in the Bonn–Bad Godesberg train station with time to spare before her appointment, and so, deciding against a taxi, she proceeds on foot through the inner city. It's hard to believe how much Bonn has changed in the past few years. Around the time when Britta first started making the occasional business trip to meet clients in the big city, there were suggestions in the press that the municipal district of Bad Godesberg should be renamed "Klein-Bagdad," Little

Baghdad. All around the Theaterplatz, Bad Godesberg's central square, the boutiques had closed and been replaced by tearooms, which sprang up out of the ground like mushrooms. Bookstores were shrinking their inventories of literary works and putting copies of the Koran in their display windows. In the middle of the wide pedestrian zones, beturbaned men were taking their black-veiled wives on walks. The city had acquired an excellent reputation among medical tourists from the Arab Emirates, so billionaire oil sheikhs who could have afforded to lift entire peoples out of poverty traveled instead to Bonn with their royal households in order to purchase bypass surgery, titanium hips, or new teeth. On many street corners, the pavement was covered with burning candles, teddy bears, and bouquets of flowers, along with photographs of young men and handwritten notes—"I love you, Nils!" "We miss you, Amir!"—commemorating immigrants murdered by right-wing nationalists or privileged prep school students slain by North Africans.

But ever since Regula Freyer, with her tight pants and stylish hairdos, began her second term at the head of the government, the tearooms and Koran-selling bookstores have vanished. The pedestrian zones have been expanded and vehicular traffic in much of the city center restricted. The sidewalks renovated, the facades of the houses repainted, tasteful plantings arranged in tiered flower beds. The orange uniforms of the cleanup crews brighten every corner. Long files of people wearing red "Sport Is Public" T-shirts move through the narrow streets; the clicking of Nordic walking sticks fills the air. Britta doesn't know whether or not she liked Bonn better before. She never had a problem with burkas; on the other hand, the city is cleaner now. All she knows is that somehow things didn't turn out the way everyone thought they would, and that it's best to accept conditions as they are. Furthermore, given the existing situation, her business makes more and more money with each passing year.

The Dubai Lounge is a leftover from the old days, tucked into a corner of the old city center and perhaps simply overlooked during the recent cleanup operation. When Britta steps in, Hassan is already sitting—or rather lying—in his usual place, a deep basket chair that gives him a view of the carpetlike curtain covering the entrance. Judging from his posture, he's been in that chair for at least the past three days.

The lounge is windowless and so large that the rear regions appear hazy and indistinct. Dim lightbulbs under pseudo-Oriental shades create their own time zone, as though it were always two in the morning. A square bar occupies the middle of the room, a four-sided counter with a narrow opening in one side, a monstrous construction of dark wood and golden ornaments that looks strangely vacant: no kegs or taps for dispensing beer, no cocktail shakers, no wine coolers, no illuminated cases displaying expensive whiskeys, no schnapps glasses or shot measures hanging overhead. The whole place is so *halal* that—unless you were familiar with the concept of money laundering—you might wonder what they sell here.

There's a piece of living furniture, a heavily made-up waitress of the "disco-Islam" type, leaning behind the bar, wearing a pink headscarf and a fringed band, supposed to evoke the *Thousand and One Nights*, over her forehead. The bored girl is playing with her smartphone and doesn't even look up when Britta pushes the curtain to one side. Except for Hassan, Britta, and the waitress, the Dubai Lounge is completely empty.

Hassan's facial expression doesn't change when Britta walks over to his table, nor does he make any move to rise from his seat, but he says, "Hey, bitch, what's up?" and raises one languid hand, which in his case must be interpreted as a sign of particular fondness.

Britta has known him forever, since the beginnings of The Bridge. Back then, Hassan was just sixteen and the smallest fish in the pond, sent by some uncle or cousin to check out the situation. He acted as though he had a strong aversion to dealing with a woman. Although he peppered his speech with Arabic expressions, Britta was pretty sure he could barely speak the language. Nevertheless, when it came to a global enterprise like ISIS, you had to be glad to have any sort of personal contact at all.

At that first meeting, Hassan's response to Britta's business proposition had been a scornful shake of the head. Why should he give *her* commissions? They had their own people, there were no shortages in that area. Besides, The Bridge's rules contradicted ISIS's decentralized, pseudo-anarchic conception of violence. Hassan had wagged a hand at Britta, dismissing her. But when the Syrian peace had been negotiated and Assad sent into exile, Hassan was quick to contact her again. These days, ISIS is happy to be able—with the help of The Bridge—to carry out the occasional attack, a quick, clean strike just to prove they're still out there.

Hassan looks much the same as he did back then; the pimples haven't disappeared, the gym shoes are still red. Faded jeans, white T-shirt, and sunglasses, which he never takes off, not even indoors. A thoroughly average guy with a dreary job in his father's rug store in the old city center who has always been more concerned about his Netflix access than jihad. He's no fanatic, he's just someone who, from time to time, does the work. For what remains of a multinational enterprise that was once the scourge of the West.

"Do you have something for us?"

As always, there's a certain avidity in Hassan's question. His people are probably pressuring him—the last attack was, once again, a good while ago. To gain time, Britta gets the waitress's attention and orders a cup of tea. Until it's brought to her, she sits in silence and considers whether Hassan is bluffing. He seems to have no idea why she's here. The sunglasses don't make it any easier to read his thoughts. She decides to stay on the offensive.

"Was it you?"

"Huh?"

"You and your people."

"Nah."

"You claimed responsibility."

He falls silent for a while. The black reflective surfaces his eyes hide behind look on Britta without seeming to see her. He doesn't say what they both know, namely that ISIS exploits any occasion to claim responsibility for something or other.

"That's your question? Are you off your rocker?"

Britta dons her professional smile. "You're a regular client, Hassan. This is my job. Has The Bridge caused you some problem? Have we failed to fulfill your expectations? Were you dissatisfied with our past transactions?"

"What do you actually want?"

"Don't play dumb. I want to know if The Bridge has competition."

Britta's frankness makes him laugh. He shakes his head, but cheerfully.

"Do you know what this reminds me of, all this nonsense you're talking?" He sips his tea and makes a face, as though he'd rather have ordered a beer. "Season Four, Episode Three. When Tywin says to Tommen—that is, Cersei's second son, and Joffrey's already dead, murdered, actually, and so Tommen will succeed to the throne—and Tywin tells him that a good king doesn't need holiness and a sense of justice and strength, what he needs is to listen to the wisdom of his counselors. Epic shit."

Hassan has been addicted to *Game of Thrones* for years, and now he thinks he possesses global insight because he's spent half his life watching a crowd of actors stride around in medieval robes and men's fur coats.

"What does that have to do with me?" asks Britta.

"You should listen to Babak, you shouldn't be here."

Chapter **5**

Less than twenty-four hours later, Britta's sitting in a train again, this one bound for Leipzig. It's been raining buckets since morning. The world outside is a gray blur, undifferentiated except for the red warning lights of the wind turbines, which blink spookily through the haze. Contrary to her usual custom of dressing up to visit clients, Britta's wearing sturdy shoes, jeans, and a waterproof jacket with a hood; after all, she has to figure on spending some time outdoors. The train car smells of wet umbrellas and damp clothes, of drying hair and soaked shoes. The other passengers look more real today, less like actors impersonating people and more like genuine living beings, maybe because they're a little cold, maybe because they're sharing the contentment of knowing that others are worse off than they are, for example all those who are on foot right now, not hurtling through sheets of water in a dry, cozy train.

Shortly before the train departed, Babak called her and tried again to dissuade her from making the trip.

"This dashing around from place to place isn't smart," he said.

"Neither is calling a cell phone number," she replied.

He simply hung up on her. First time ever. Britta's not used to quarreling with Babak. The world feels wrong, like a tilted picture. In the group of four seats diagonally across the aisle from her, an elderly man is reading something on his smartphone to his wife. Apparently plans are afoot to raise the five percent electoral threshold for political parties to fifteen percent in order to make the parliament operate more efficiently. When the man begins to explain the advantages of this idea, Britta plugs her earbuds into her ears.

She watches the raindrops run a horizontal race across the window and thinks about Babak. Her trips to Leipzig always make her think about Babak, for Leipzig is the city where they met.

The first time she saw Babak, he was standing at the railing of an S-Bahn bridge in Leipzig. It was dark; the orange light from a streetlamp illuminated his massive body, his slumping shoulders and bent back. Britta was wearing running shoes, a tight-fitting sports outfit, and a fitness armband that displayed her vital statistics. She was crossing the bridge, following the route she usually took to Clara-Zetkin Park, where she would go at night to jog the boredom of her business administration courses out of her bones. It was autumn, and Germany was about to win the World Cup. The tsunami of refugees hadn't started yet, the United Kingdom hadn't left the European Union, unemployment and interest rates were at historically low levels. Germany was the most fortunate country in the world, without even noticing the fact.

There was something peculiar about the way Babak was staring down at the tracks. He was there again the next evening, and also the evenings after that. More than once, the mere sight of him made her furious. She considered taking another way into the park, but that would have meant running for a stretch along a main thoroughfare, an ordeal she hadn't the slightest desire to undergo. On the fifth night, she stopped directly behind Babak and addressed him: "Jump or walk away, whichever you want, just don't always be standing around here like that."

Babak cringed as though he'd been struck.

When Britta took off again, he simply went with her. She wanted to run; he was as slow as a snail. She adjusted to his pace without knowing why. Sprinting off and leaving him was somehow impossible. They trotted along side by side, two mismatched ramblers on their way through the night.

Clara-Zetkin Park already smelled like winter; although it was only the beginning of November, the weather was pretty cold. Britta, who was wearing thin jogging gear, started shivering. Babak took off his jacket and gave it to her without even looking in her direction. All he had on underneath was a T-shirt. The jacket smelled like cheap detergent and surely had not been fumigated for a very long time. Nevertheless, it was fun to wear—like a giant, protective tent.

The old-fashioned streetlights on the avenue, lined with large plane trees, cast the joggers' shadows in front of them and made those shadows shrink, grow, overtake themselves, and fall behind again. The moon painted white puddles on the park's lawns. The paths crunched under their feet; psychotic blackbirds sang at the illuminated intersections. All at once, Babak began to speak. The words flowed out of him, as though someone had removed a stopper.

As a small child, he had come with his parents to Germany, where his father, who actually was a physician, opened a greengrocer's shop, while his mother took care of the household and the children. Ever since God rescued them from the war, his parents had grown increasingly devout. They were always taking Babak to the mosque, where he was taught that love between men is a sin. At some point, he'd built himself a computer, and from then on, he'd lived in worlds that no one else understood.

A week ago, his eldest brother, Murad, had caught him visiting a gay dating platform on the Internet. Fearing any further contact with his brother, Babak had been spending half the days and nights wandering the streets. He avoided his mother, and he stopped showing up for work in the greengrocery because he didn't know what Murad had told their father.

Babak said he had no idea what to do with his shitty life, and no idea what to do with himself, a fat, queer nerd with a high school diploma who was neither a German in Germany nor an Iraqi in Iraq, and who had nothing, no money, no car, no friends, not even any interest in girls.

Britta let him talk. They crossed through the park and reached Gottschedstrasse, a street that featured one bar after another. Even in Babak's jacket, Britta had started to feel cold again, and so she opened the first door they came to and dived into warmth, light, and a confusion of voices. They found an open table for two and sat down. Britta ordered a green tea for herself and a beer for Babak.

"I don't drink alcohol," he said.

"Drink," said Britta, and Babak obeyed.

"So," she said, holding the hot teacup with both hands, "enough blathering."

Babak kept quiet and looked at her.

"No prospects, no identity, no money, and nobody to fuck," she said. "All ego-related stuff. Not valid reasons for making a final exit."

"Who says I want to kill myself?"

"I don't care whether you jump off the bridge or not. But if you do, then please do it with some dignity."

Babak, looking confused, took a sip of his beer. "I should kill myself, but you want me to please make sure it's done for the right reasons?"

"And done in the right way."

They looked at each other. Neither of them knew whether Britta was speaking in earnest.

"Consider for a minute," she began again, placing her hand on his forearm. "Such a suicide gives you incredible power. You can do things you will never be punished for. For a brief period of time, you can be whoever you want and do whatever you like. You're the king of the world. The most dangerous weapon there is."

As a matter of fact, Britta herself didn't know exactly what she was saying and why. It was as though she were holding the corner of something in her hands and pulling on it without any idea of what she was about to get a look at.

"You're pretty crazy." Babak shook his head but didn't protest when she ordered him a second beer. He drank it fast and ordered the third himself.

"So in your opinion, what should I do?"

Britta shrugged.

"Become a jihadi. You're an Arab, right?"

"Those boys are too crass for me."

"Separatism? Ecology? Occupy?"

"Nah."

"Maybe you just want to go back to your old school and shoot it up?"

"Most certainly not."

"You're a tough one."

Now they both had to laugh.

"So it's jihad, then." Britta leaned far back in her chair. "People say they pay really well."

"I could use some money. I'd leave it to my mother. Then she could buy a dishwasher."

"You don't have a dishwasher?"

"And a decent vacuum cleaner. And a good food processor, a Thermomix. Maybe even her own car. And new clothes from the shop where she always stands in front of the window but never goes in. I'd put the money into an account that only she could access. And I'd leave a will forbidding her to give the money to my father or Murad. She wouldn't dare disregard my last wishes. She'd have to buy all that stuff, because I'd be ordering her to buy it from beyond the grave."

When Babak smiled, you could just make out his real facial features under the fat. Again they looked at each other, for a long time, and in the end Britta recognized something in his eyes. An ache, a deep sadness, a loss; it seemed somehow familiar to her.

"I think I have an idea," said Britta.

"What's your name, anyway?" said Babak.

A conductor asking to see her ticket startles Britta out of her thoughts. The retiree in the quartet of seats across from her complains that it's too cold in the train, and the conductor promises to turn the heat up. After he's gone, the open car calms down, like water briefly churned up by the passage of a motorboat. The passengers sink back into their respective activities; Britta returns to Molly Richter and thinks that there would be even more violence in the world, a lot more, if headphones had never been invented.

. . .

They met again on the succeeding evenings. Britta drank green tea; Babak ordered his beers himself, even though she had to keep on paying for them. At the end of two weeks, the concept was in place, and then the work began.

According to statistics, in Germany alone around ten thousand people commit suicide every year, three-quarters of them men, and more than half by hanging. Babak set about developing an algorithm that—with the help of data mining, profiling, and stylometrics—would be capable of fishing for and identifying suitable persons on the Internet. At the same time, Britta created a series of behavioral and psychological tests, with the help of which she could thoroughly evaluate the candidates' will to suicide. A healing practice for suicide prevention. The majority of their clients would be released back into life, forever cured of suicidal thoughts through a hard confrontation with their own death wish. A few incorrigibles would remain. People who in any event wanted to die, one way or another. These would be passed on to organizations that would know what to do with them. That would give them a goal, a sense, something worth dying for. And would pay a good price for them. Clients could leave their share of the fee to a loved one if they wished.

Britta and Babak amused themselves by trying out names for their business—R.A.M., Rent-a-Martyr, or T'n'T, Therapy and Terror—and by drawing logos on beer coasters and napkins. It was Babak who came up with the name that stuck: The Bridge.

Britta stopped taking her business administration courses and started studying to become a *Heilpraktikerin,* a healing professional. She learned how eye movement can be used to overcome traumas; how human despair can be reduced to self-beliefs, negative or otherwise, that can then be worked on;

how the application of pressure to specific body parts and the recitation of mantras can increase self-confidence. None of this was needed for her later work. During her preparations for the final examinations, the beta version of Babak's algorithm spat out the first names. Britta contacted them and wrote invitations, repeated two or three times when necessary, in which she substantiated her credentials with references forged by Babak. She termed initiating contact this way "proactive client recruitment" and designated what she was offering as a "method of confrontation." Not all the targeted persons reacted; however, a great many of them did, and of those responders, a smaller number declared themselves prepared to come in for a first interview. Britta didn't ask for a fee, but candidates were required to bear their own travel expenses. Should they be satisfied with The Bridge's work, they had the option of paying a sum of their choosing.

Some clients left the program after a short time and disappeared, never to be seen again. Others were officially discharged after the fourth, fifth, or seventh stage of the evaluation. Those who had been cured paid fees. Many clients were so filled with gratitude for their positive outcomes that they dug deep into their pockets.

The first candidate to pass through all the evaluation stages was Dirk, a pedophile tired of living with his inclinations. Britta and Babak fished him out of a suicide forum, where he'd been wrangling for months over the question of what would be the surest way to leave the world. Right from the start, Beta-Lassie had assigned him a coefficient of 10.4, the best result they'd obtained so far. Dirk was so set in his purpose that he positively flew through the evaluation process, ending with a score over 11, which according to The Bridge's bylaws was more than sufficient.

When Britta offered to work out all the suicide logistics for him—settling of personal affairs, planning and execution of the act itself with a one hundred percent guarantee of success, middle-class funeral and burial arrangements—and moreover suggested the possibility that he could end his life in the service of a higher goal, he wept for his good fortune. She placed him with Green Power, an environmental organization convinced that the planet would be significantly better-off without people. The organization had chiefly made its mark through an ongoing series of spectacular operations against the whaling industry.

Green Power proved to be enthusiastic about The Bridge's new business model, and Dirk was enthusiastic about the idea of sacrificing himself for the survival of the whales. An agreement was reached in the twinkling of an eye, and after everything was arranged, Britta and Babak had but one thing to do: wait.

Babak, who had already lost more than forty pounds while programming Lassie, now lost an additional six or so. Britta stopped drinking green tea when the caffeine jitters in her hands moved to her arms. At last, news portals began reporting the breaking headline: an environmental activist group classified as a terrorist organization had sunk a Norwegian whaling vessel on the high seas; one of the activists had died in the attack. The YouTube video that Green Power posted shortly afterward showed a rubber dinghy racing at top speed toward the gigantic whaling ship and then exploding immediately in front of the bow. Within a few hours, the clip recorded a million views. Britta and Babak celebrated late into the night.

Dirk had insisted that The Bridge should receive not just the agreed share but the entire sum paid by Green Power for the operation. Furthermore, he'd bequeathed his not inconsiderable personal fortune to Britta and Babak and left behind a letter in which he expressed deep gratitude and the hope that their commitment, in equal measure passionate and professional, would work to the benefit of many other people in the future. With this money, Britta and Babak moved to Braunschweig, leased the commercial unit in the Kurt Schumacher Passage, and bought Lassie her first large server.

Since that first operation, Britta has taken great pleasure in her work. She interacts with many people, lives an independent life, and does a great deal of good. The rescue of potential suicides constitutes by far the lion's share of her activity. In the instances when The Bridge procures suicide attackers for other entities, it adheres to a strict code—limited number of victims, careful avoidance of escalation, no collateral damage. Its clients have gradually adjusted to these conditions, and by now there's practically no one else organizing such operations; collaboration with The Bridge is the only way. Since the triumph of the CCC, terrorist organizations have grown weaker, their goals have lost their magnetic appeal, and they themselves are scarcely still capable of recruiting martyrs. As the first and thus far only terrorist service provider in the Federal Republic, The Bridge has pacified and stabilized the sector. The company takes great care to keep the sense of imminent threat, a feeling that every society needs, at the proper level. And it has made Britta and Babak fairly rich.

In the end, though, it's something else that fills Britta with pride and joy. Since the founding of The Bridge, she has lived in complete harmony with the Zeitgeist, the spirit of the age. If she didn't feel sick so often, she'd probably call herself a lucky woman.

Britta takes her time getting off the train and then stands unmoving on the platform. When the train has departed again and the arriving passengers have scattered, she looks around, mentally divides her surroundings into grid squares, and scans them with her eyes. Leipzig's central railway station, with its impressively vaulted glass roof, is always worth taking in, but Britta's interest is trash bins. On each platform, there are about ten such bins, set far apart, big stainless-steel containers with deposit holes for glass, plastic, paper, and miscellaneous other garbage. As long as no train is pulling in, she has an unobstructed view of four platforms on either side, and she'd be able to spot anyone hanging around one of the bins. Nevertheless, the platforms are too long for her to see all the way to the end, so she'll have to do a good deal of walking on each one in order to check all the bins, and since there are twenty-one tracks, she's in for a real workout. Furthermore, there are garbage cans both on the concourse and on the two basement levels, where the usual retail shops and food stalls can be found, so there's no guarantee she'll find G. Flossen this way; the station's big enough for them to miss each other all day long.

Britta sighs and tells herself that despite the odds, this method has always worked in the past. Flossen possesses neither a cell phone nor an e-mail address, and if he's got a mailing address, she doesn't know what it is. At any rate, with this bad weather, it's fairly likely that he's somewhere in her vicinity.

Just as she's about to set out on her quest, two men in uniform start moving in her direction. The security staff has her in their sights, and it's too late to elude them.

"Can we help you?" The men have stopped directly in front of her. Each rests one hand on his pistol and the other on his truncheon.

"With what?" Britta asks back.

"It's not clear what you're doing here," says the second man. "The next departure from this track isn't until forty-three minutes from now."

"I'm looking at the roof," says Britta. "Aren't these reinforced concrete arches incredible? Not to mention the glass. More than a hundred and seventy thousand square feet of glass."

"We have to ask you please to leave now. This is a transit area."

Through controlled breathing, Britta subdues her rage. She tells herself that the security guys want nothing from her, it's not personal, they have no idea who she is and what she does, they're just doing their job. Besides, it's her own fault. It should have occurred to her that the recent attack would put everyone on edge.

She manages a smile and a no-problem gesture, to which the cops respond with a we're-keeping-an-eye-on-you look. In any case, this level of security makes it a pretty sure thing that G. Flossen isn't loitering on any train platform.

It's still raining. It's raining not like weather, but like apocalypse. Although it's unequivocally daytime, it's dusk in the streets. The streetlights have come on, tinting the deluge orange. Cars are cleaving forks in the flooded thoroughfares; the sewers don't stand a chance. Leipzig has disappeared behind a curtain, from which people emerge and run crouching toward the station entrances. Inside stand the indecisive, not yet daring to dash out and wondering whether they can wait out the rain, even though it's plain to all that it could go on like this for hours.

Britta has no choice. Normally, she'd walk—Rosental Park is barely ten minutes away. But in weather like this, every second counts. She pulls her hood over her head, opens her umbrella, and presses her shoulder bag against her body. In the lee of the station wall, she runs to the cabstand on the west side. When she climbs into the taxi, her pant legs are wet to the knees.

Very soon after the taxi drops her off at the park, Britta realizes she's going to get a lot wetter. Instead of running over the open lawns, she opts for a path on the edge of the woods, where the rain isn't falling quite so heavily. But the ground is soft; within minutes she's got water inside her soaked shoes, and even her jacket proves to be less waterproof than she thought. Already the first drops are running down her back. But the worst part isn't the cold and wet; it's the gnawing question of whether what she's doing here makes any sense. G. Flossen is a nutcase. But is he nuts enough to stay outside on such a day? Be that as it may, Britta remembers that she has no choice but to go on. A second trip to Leipzig in the near future is impossible. If she wants to talk to Flossen, this is her only chance. She throws an inner switch, chucks her useless umbrella into the bushes, and marches on. She wants to circle the Rosental once and then to check two more parks before yielding to the worst possible outcome and going home with her purpose unfulfilled.

Despite her fears, she seems to be in luck. On the other side of the vast lawn, not far from the Zooschaufenster, the "window to the zoo"—from which today there is certainly no animal to be seen—Britta spots a slowly moving blue tent. At once, she steps off the path and heads directly for the tent. Soon she starts to run, even though the tent makes no move to flee; on the contrary, it has stopped altogether, and now it's looking at her.

Up until the last second, she's not sure whether it's really Flossen. Only when she's standing directly in front of him does she recognize the bearded face with the slightly confused eyes under the hood of his huge poncho. Under the poncho there's also a bicycle, on the sides of which, as Britta knows, big saddlebags filled with plastic bottles are hanging.

"Hey," says Flossen. "There you are."

"Did you wait for me?"

"I thought you were coming and so I hung around inside the station, but that sort of thing's rather difficult now."

"So I noticed."

"Have you got something for me?"

As a matter of fact, she does: two empty soda bottles with especially high deposits. When she pulls the bottles out of her shoulder bag, Flossen's whole face lights up. He takes the bottles from her, lifts his poncho, and stashes the booty in his saddlebags. She has never asked him why he spends his days rummaging through the city's garbage bins in search of bottles with refundable deposits. She's come to believe that he simply lives off them. Maybe, she speculates, G. Flossen hates society so much he can't in good conscience perform a job that's of any use to other people.

"But you haven't come here just to hand over a couple of empties. Ask your question."

"Okay," says Britta. "Was it you?"

"No. You?"

"No."

Flossen sighs. Then they fall silent for a while, each of them dwelling on what this double *no* means. Neither doubts that the other is telling the truth. Britta doesn't find Flossen very congenial and is glad she doesn't have to like him. He's got arrogant nostrils and a voice better suited to a carping woman than to a man in his seventies. In an earlier life, he studied social sciences and then made himself an important figure at a Berlin university for decades, before something happened that threw him off course, something to do with a wife and a child and a stretch in prison. Since then, he's devoted himself body and soul to eco-activism. Green Power's antiwhaling campaign receives the most notice, but G. Flossen's specialty is blocking infrastructure development. In the past, with the collaboration of Britta's candidates, he's succeeded in blowing up the main piers of a bridge that was under construction over the Elbe River, the borehole for a city tunnel, and several half-finished wind-power farms. Personal reservations aside, Britta does enjoy their professional collaboration; something ingenuous in his character elicits her trust.

"You have no idea what's going on?" he asks.

Britta shakes her head.

"No doubt you've already asked the Muslims?"

"They say it wasn't them."

"I didn't think so. Why would they target a freight terminal? We'd be more likely to go after something like that—a hub for meat transport, that sort of thing."

"Have you got any ideas?"

She's never stopped addressing him with the formal *Sie,* even though when he talks to her, he obstinately uses the informal *Du.* Now he looks at her thoughtfully, perhaps even a little worriedly.

"Not really," he says. "But there's something brewing."

"What's that supposed to mean?" asks Britta harshly.

"I have no clue. Just a feeling, that's all."

Britta can't stand vague hints, but she has to admit that she herself made a similar remark to Babak: *No idea, but I've got a bad feeling. Something's up.*

"You dominate the market," says Flossen. "Any competitor would have to offer more than this airport crap."

"People are often amazingly irrational."

He laughs, blowing air through his nostrils. "Nevertheless. The thing smells bad."

Britta feels a sudden, strong desire to go home. Under her jacket, she's shivering with cold.

"Maybe somebody's trying to draw you out," says Flossen. "Maybe they've got their eye on you somehow."

"Who's *they*? What's *somehow*?" The anger in her voice is impossible to ignore. Flossen shakes his head.

"Look, my child. The world's big and complicated. Just be on your guard."

His poncho rustles and sends little waterfalls in all directions while he slips under the polythene sheet, climbs onto his bike, and prepares to pedal away. "Thanks for the bottles," he says, and off he goes, heading not in the direction of the city, but over there, where the woods begin.

Chapter 7

Walk-in business. Something that essentially never happens at The Bridge. The young woman gives the office sign a brief glance and then without hesitation opens the door.

Babak calmly replaces the cap on the felt pen he's been using to work on a section of his dot picture. Britta is likewise calm as she closes her laptop and remains seated in a corner of the couch. Both of them look at their visitor in a friendly way, as though it were completely normal for someone to drop into the practice.

"Greetings," says Britta. "How may we help you?"

The young woman looks around and gives no answer.

"Coffee?" asks Babak.

The woman shrugs her shoulders, shakes her head, and then immediately nods. Babak disappears down the stairs to the kitchen. With a hand gesture, Britta invites the visitor to have a seat and gives her time to take in her surroundings. The girl observes the seldom-used reception counter, the cheap carpet, and Babak's dot picture. Britta observes the girl. Early twenties, anorexic. Dark curly hair, equally dark eyes, big and innocent. She is, without a doubt, unusually beautiful. But Britta's fascinated by something else. As if it were too big to find room in the young woman's slender body, her personality seems to overflow her corporeal boundaries and fill the room. As Babak comes upstairs with the coffee tray, they exchange looks. Britta's eyes say: *We don't take women.* Babak's eyes reply: *But this one's a 12.*

The previous day, they had a bad quarrel. Britta wants to start, with Lassie's help, a large-scale search operation in order to pull as many candidates as possible up to the surface in a short time. Babak refused to see what good that would do. They still knew no more than before about how to classify the airport attack.

"If you know nothing, you have to keep a low profile," Babak kept repeating.

But Britta insisted on being prepared. She quoted G. Flossen: *The thing smells bad* and *Be on your guard.* She said, "It can't hurt to put as many candidates as possible in place."

If they really have competition, she went on, wouldn't it be best for them to defend their territory? With a spectacular operation, for example, something to make it clear that they operate on a higher level than the people responsible for the ridiculous Leipzig attack.

"What's wrong with that?" Britta asked.

"The dust we'd kick up," Babak replied.

It went back and forth for a while; Babak accused Britta of mindless activism, she accused him of cowardice, until finally she was angry enough to convert her request to an order. Ever since then, Lassie's been humming without pause, Babak has made good progress on his dot picture, and Britta and Babak have hardly spoken.

After Babak has filled the cups, Britta starts the conversation once again. "Is there something we can do for you?"

"I'm interested in your . . . work."

The hesitation between the last two words serves to confirm what Britta already suspects: the young woman hasn't come here by chance.

"We're pleased that you're interested. The Bridge is an alternative medical practice dedicated to working with people in difficult predicaments. In the past, using our special confrontation method, we've been able to help countless at-risk individuals out of desperate situations. Indeed, we normally take a proactive approach to our work. Which is not to say that we prowl the city's bridges, on the lookout for potential suicides." Britta smiles suavely, like a museum guide who always cracks the very same joke in the very same spot. "We utilize the most up-to-date technology to generate digital prognoses."

The young woman has closed her eyes. She sits motionless for a long time, as though she's fallen asleep. When she finally says something, she keeps her eyes shut and moves only her lips, like a person in a trance. "Spare me the drivel. I know what you do." It sounds like a threat.

"How?"

"From the web."

"There is no information about The Bridge on the Internet. Healing practices are subject to an advertising ban, which we comply with."

"There's a deeper level."

Britta can actually see Babak's ears prick up. He's sitting with them, holding the coffee cup in front of his face and blowing uninterruptedly on the hot liquid. The deep web is his element. It's accurate to say that The Bridge is mentioned there;

word-of-mouth propaganda, as it were. But there aren't very many people in a position to notice that.

"And what is it we *do?*"

Now the girl opens her eyes. Britta feels her gaze like a physical touch.

"There's a guy buzzing around the Darknet who talks about you."

"If he's buzzing, that means he's still alive."

"Of course."

"I'm glad to hear it. The Bridge's method is considerably more successful than classic psychotherapy."

The young woman twists her mouth into a grin her eyes don't share. Her dark gaze deepens and generates a silent incandescence. Babak stares at her as though she were an abyss into which one might fall.

"I like success," she says. "That's why I'm here."

Now Britta's staring too. "What do you mean?" she asks cautiously.

"Scrubbing down. Sweeping out. Major cleanup." The young woman's grin widens. Her canine teeth are a bit longer than the others.

"Do you take us for some kind of janitorial service?"

Now the girl laughs. She raises a hand and lets it fall on her thigh. Like the gesture of a mechanical doll.

"I absolutely do. And I admire your broom."

The ensuing silence becomes complicated. Britta mentally counts to five, picking the perfect moment for a surprise attack.

"This is no game, you understand me?" she says, suddenly fierce. "We're not putting on a play!"

The visitor flinches only slightly before regaining control of herself. "You're looking for people," she says.

"What we're looking for is none of your business." Britta gets up. "I don't believe we can do anything for you."

The Bridge runs on rules. Rules are the practice's capital, its real substance. Lassie's search parameters. Rules for establishing contact with candidates. Strict rules of evaluation. Rules for traveling and for communicating with clients, rules for placing candidates and for carrying out operations. The true significance of a rule always first manifests itself when the practice ventures upon shaky ground. Normally, candidates don't come ambling through the door; normally, they aren't women; and normally, their behavior is not so offensive. It's almost as if the girl were throwing down a gauntlet in front of them, and Britta feels a strong temptation to take it up. But the first rule of the evaluation process is couched in no uncertain terms: frustrate the candidate, send him away, and wait to see if he comes back.

"Okay," the young woman says. "Let's start over. I'm quite serious about this." She reaches out a hand. "My name is Julietta."

"Stop!" Britta raises an index finger. "We don't want to know your name. Please leave this office. At once." With a sidelong glance, she checks to see whether Babak is as stony-faced as she is. He's set his cup down and is looking absentmindedly at a corner of the coffee table; his lack of interest seems total. *Good,* Britta thinks, suppressing a relieved smile. When the chips are down, they function as a team.

"That's bullshit." Julietta strikes her chair's armrests with both hands. "You're supposed to be . . ." She leaps to her feet, stares at Babak as though she wants to punch him, and turns away. As she goes, she runs into a leg of the coffee table.

"Like I give a shit. Fuck."

She steps quickly to the door, puts one hand on the handle, and turns around once again. "What's this droning sound I hear?"

"Freezer," says Babak. "Not the newest model."

"Fuck you," says Julietta, and she disappears.

Chapter **8**

"Are you in competition for the Supermother of the Year medal?"

Janina's wearing one of her flowered dresses. Her hair is carelessly, artfully pinned up, and she's surrounded by all sorts of gear: a large picnic basket, a cooler, a colorful blanket, a child's bicycle, sand-digging toys, and an umbrella, together with a backpack that probably contains sun hats, sunscreen, wet wipes, insect spray, and other useful accessories. Nobody can get past this accumulation of obstacles on the sidewalk, which is why Cora (on the picnic basket) and Knut (on the cooler) have made themselves comfortable.

Britta springs jauntily out of the VW bus while Richard electronically opens the side door and the tailgate and then runs around the car to greet their friend. Britta has entered into the spirit of the occasion by putting on gym shoes and a denim skirt, whose rough fabric feels daring against her legs. "Maybe an electric blanket too? A pressure cooker? A robovac? How long do we plan to stay? A week?"

Janina laughs, catches her in her arms, and hugs her tight.

Today Britta not only tolerates the embrace, but she even returns it, and heartily.

"The people who make fun of picnic baskets are the same ones who eat the most chicken thighs afterward," says Janina, and it occurs to Britta, not for the first time, that her friend, in spite of her mommy look, is as sly as a fox.

They roar merrily out of the city on the A 392, an autobahn spur. The multivan is relatively new and well equipped, with movable seats, individually adjustable air-conditioning, and a Bose sound system. Richard's behind the steering wheel and Britta's next to him, so that at any time she can put her hand on his knee and look at him from the side. They're both wearing sunglasses. It feels good to be traveling along under the broad, bright sky with two high-spirited children and a couple of good friends in the rear seats; they go on a weekend outing all too seldom. It was Britta's idea to make the house viewing a two-family excursion, and when Richard turns on some music and the soft piano sounds and subdued beat of "Suicide World" come trickling out of the speakers, Britta thinks that her idea was a damn good one.

In the back, Vera and Cora are enthroned on their raised seats, chattering and giggling without pause, while Knut and Janina have rotated their own seats so that they can look at the girls while traveling backward, as in a train compartment. The autobahn turns into Celler Heerstrasse, and Vera begins to rave about her first field hockey practice, where she—in her own opinion—was greeted like a superstar and subsequently streaked around the field like a fireball. Richard smiles broadly, observes his excited darling in the rearview mirror, and quotes a couple of remarks made by the coach, who proved to be quite taken with Vera's talent.

"Have you heard," Knut asks, "that the UN is going to be dissolved?"

"UNO? Why? It's a super card game."

"Not the game, sweetie," Janina replies. "The UN, the United Nations. It's an organization."

"The U.S. and Russia are in agreement. France, Germany, the UK, Turkey, and a few others are invited to meet for consultations."

"Well, the UN has already been invisible for a long time," says Richard.

"The notion of international law sounds kind of twentieth-century anyway," Janina opines.

"What are you working on at the moment, Knut?" Britta asks loudly.

Outside a billboard in the middle of a field flashes by. "You are you!" it says, without any reference to a product.

"Oh, an interesting project." Knut sticks his smartphone back in his pocket and turns around in his seat so that he's better able to speak forward. "Kind of like Handke's play *Offending the Audience*."

"Knut's got this theory," says Janina. "About the way people feel these days, about why they're so miserable."

"This will interest you, Britta," says Knut. "In a certain sense, it concerns your line of work."

Britta doubts this and wishes she'd chosen to change the subject with a question about Janina's order situation instead.

"Modern man suffers from the claustrophobia of his cosmic inner space, of his place on the space-time continuum," Janina announces.

"Huh?" says Richard, with a laugh.

"Globalization means there's nowhere you can escape to anymore," Janina explains. "Because everything's already everywhere. So suicide becomes the last remaining emergency exit."

"Actually, the important point is that capitalism of the body is ultimately communism of the soul." Knut adds extra force to his voice, getting himself back into the conversation. "An actor stands on the edge of the stage and tells his life story in such a way that everyone in the audience thinks he's talking about them."

"Bam!" Vera screams. "Problem solved!"

"Dead!" Cora rejoices.

Mega-Melanie and a Glotzi have made it into the Volkswagen bus. Britta thinks that maybe a play could be made out of the Megas, an exciting theater piece, even though the word "theater" sounds rather twentieth-century too. Her good mood evaporates. She feels vaguely sad. The VW bus passes a long file of "Sport Is Public" participants on bicycles. Britta concentrates on the landscape, which looks wonderfully neat. The straight line of the horizon, the regular right angles of the fields. The polished, cloudless sky, the waving surface of young wheat.

"So it gets fairly intense in the end." Janina's sticking straws into little triangular containers of cherry juice. "The actor asks the audience to take him home with them."

" 'You've made me,' " says Knut, quoting himself. " 'Now take me with you. Dress me like a human being, set me in a chair, don't let me stick anything in my eye.' "

Knut and Janina exchange a kiss, and then he too gets a little pack of cherry juice. Britta forces herself to make an appreciative sound. She knows that this time will be no different, that Knut's play will not receive a spectacular premiere in a great playhouse, but at best a barely noticed mini-premiere in some artsy Austrian barn. Knut's problem isn't lack of talent or laziness, but simply the fact that he's not a winner. He's a guy whose friends inadvertently call him "Kurt" from time to time. Destiny has taken stock of him and decided it's not interested.

"Hey, Britta," Janina calls from the back. "Here's a dilemma for you. A woman makes fun of her friend's picnic basket. Does she still get a turkey sandwich?"

"By all means," says Britta. "She even gets the biggest one as a reward for her critical awareness."

Janina laughs and hands a wrapped sandwich forward. Britta gives Richard a bite and then takes one herself.

"Now it's my turn," Britta says with her mouth full. "A woman finds herself in a difficult position, but she already has a plan that she wants to put into action. Her best friend advises against it. What should the woman do? Should she do what she herself thinks is right, or should she yield to what her friend thinks?"

"Which of the two is smarter?" Janina asks.

"No idea." Britta feels caught somehow. "The woman, I suppose."

"Then she should listen to her friend. People who think they're smart are usually wrong."

Bam, Britta thinks.

"Are you having problems with Babak?" Richard asks, speaking so softly that she can pretend not to have heard him.

"More!" Vera screams.

"If you two keep this up, the picnic basket will be empty before we get there," Janina says.

"The same as always," says Richard, laughing as he flips on his right blinker to give the SUV that's been crowding him room to pass. "Let me have another bite."

Because Richard doesn't turn his eyes away from his outside mirror, Britta has to lean far over toward him, sandwich in hand; mayonnaise runs down Richard's chin.

"Is he going to pass or not?"

Knut and Janina look through the rear window; Britta turns

around too. The SUV is so close on their tail that they'd be able to identify the driver's eye color if half his face weren't hidden by sunglasses, a visor cap, and an old-fashioned mustache.

"What does this guy *want?*"

"Just don't hit the brakes."

"I'm already driving faster than I like."

"Such a jackass."

"Why is he driving so close behind us, Mommy?"

"He's after Knut."

"Why after Daddy?"

"Why after me?"

"Because you're writing a play full of social criticism. The CCC isn't crazy about that sort of thing."

"Richard's only joking, Cora. The truth is, some drivers just aren't playing with a full deck."

"He's playing cards?"

"Can you make out his license plate?"

"He doesn't have one. At least, not in front."

"When will self-driving cars finally be available?"

"Slow down," says Britta.

"What?"

"Turn on your hazard lights and get off the gas."

They've crossed under the A 2 and passed the turnoff for Hillerse, and they're traveling on a two-lane highway, the B 214. There's some oncoming traffic, not very heavy. As the multivan loses speed, the SUV falls back. "Now he's calming down," says Richard. He sounds relieved.

"Step on the brake. Stop."

Richard gives Britta a sidelong glance she doesn't return because she's concentrating on looking behind them, and then he does what she said. The VW bus comes to a stop on the shoulder of the road. The SUV seems to hesitate; farther back, other cars start blowing their horns. Suddenly the SUV driver accelerates, taking advantage of a break in the oncoming traffic to surge past the unmoving Volkswagen.

"Eyes on the license number! Can anybody read it?"

"The plate's completely dirty."

"He wasn't playing cards."

"Sure, he doesn't want to be lasered."

"It was a pickup."

"That's just a figure of speech, sweetie."

"What make?"

"Toyota, I'd say. White."

"He's way down the road now."

"What a sociopath."

"All right, let's go on."

Britta lets herself fall back into her seat. Her forehead is so tightly furrowed that it hurts. Her heart's beating fast. She thinks about what Janina said. That the smart woman should have listened to her friend. Then she forbids herself any more thoughts on that subject and does some stomach breathing.

"Get a load of this! A thousand windmills!"

"Are we there yet?"

"Where are we going, actually? Denmark?"

"Since when is the chauffeur allowed to ask questions?"

"Think about this: every kilometer, the price per square meter goes down. Look around and watch the houses get cheaper."

"Anybody want any more cherry juice?"

Not fifteen minutes later, they reach the municipality of Müden an der Aller. Small villages zip past the windows—a lot of half-timbering, large roofs, planted front gardens. An even narrower road branches off the narrow road they're on; the road sign for Wiebüttel is for the most part covered up by a lilac bush. The asphalt ends, and they follow a bumpy cobblestone road through a piece of woodland. Bright yellow shafts of sunlight pierce the foliage; Britta can practically see how it smells here: like rotting wood and earth and mushrooms and wild boars, and a little like childhood. How long has it been since the last time she was in a forest? Her parents used to take her with them on long hikes. They would gather fir cones and acorns and beechnuts and make animals out of them. At some point, the woods became too dirty for Britta, and from then on, she'd stay at home when her parents went hiking.

"That's it," Janina says reverently.

"What a dump!" Richard says merrily.

Britta slides off the passenger seat and stands on the broken pavement, gazing in bewilderment at the Object. It's there, half-hidden behind an exuberant growth of trees, a squat brick building with dark brown wooden trim and melancholy shutters. Small bay window, clay pantiles, historic satellite dish. In front of the elevated entrance, a formerly paved and now half-overgrown entryway. There seem to be neighbors on only one side; the lot is located on the outskirts of the village. Britta takes a few steps and looks past the house into the garden, which is surrounded on three sides by an untrimmed hedge over two meters high. Still more trees, doghouses, an old rotary clothesline. The high grass says "ticks," the loamy soil "tetanus." It's a nightmare of a house, escapism made stone, an outdated parody of the dream of an open fire, basket chairs, and bouquets of dried flowers. Not even Britta's parents would have ever come up with the idea of moving into such a shack.

"Isn't it beautiful?" Janina asks.

"It's beautiful," says Britta, a little rattled to discover that she's only half lying. Janina's joyous beaming strengthens Britta's wish to waste no time in getting the hell out of here.

Embarrassed, she pulls out her cell phone as though checking her e-mail. However, as she never writes e-mails, she doesn't receive any, not even from Babak. She finds, oddly enough, that her device has shut itself off and is currently in the process of powering up again; in the center of the screen, the flower-shaped symbol turns around and around. Irritated, Britta shoves the phone back in her bag.

The real estate agent comes, affable, crafty, in a big hurry. The children play in the garden, with much shrieking, as though they were performing in a Bullerby film set in Noisy Village; the grown-ups visit every room in the house. Britta takes deep breaths through her mouth and is careful not to touch anything. The whole place is incredibly filthy. Many windows are almost opaque. Masses of dead flies lie on the windowsills. The layer of dust on the floor is so thick that other potential buyers' footprints can be seen. When they enter the kitchen, two cats sleeping in a patch of sunlight on the floor spring up, dart away, and disappear through the front door, which is standing open. Britta imagines spiders in the cellar and the color of water flowing through rusty pipes. She feels Richard's sidelong glance and forces herself to smile. She tells herself that she's encountering nothing that can't be washed off and disinfected as soon as they get home.

Knut and Janina listen closely to the agent's explanations, offer some invented expertise of their own, and act as if they are weighing pros and cons even though their decision has long been made. The price is low, and Janina's in love. She'll buy the house, and The Bridge will pay for it. No interest on the loan, no lease or leasehold—some legal arrangement will be reached. The agent gives them permission to spread their picnic blanket in the garden, locks up the house, reminds himself, yet again, that there are a great many other parties interested in the property, and drives away, heading back to the city.

During the picnic, Britta, in a surprise fit of hunger, consumes three cold chicken thighs, one after another, indifferent to her companions' loud laughter. Vera and Cora climb trees, pick flowers, and throw sand at each other. Richard and Knut discuss a new Ego Adventure, which looks better and is more intelligently designed than ever before. Janina leans back on her elbows and gazes rapturously at the house. Britta knows exactly what she sees: a place where the rest of the world will definitely not matter anymore. Where she can raise her child and live a life moving from breakfasts in the garden to midday picnics to evening barbecues. Of course, Britta knows that's a complete fiction. But she envies Janina her ability to believe in it.

She looks at her smartphone once again. Only now, when everything looks the way it always does—the home screen with Vera's laughing face, and under it the seldom-used buttons for e-mails, text messages, and browsers—only now does the fear penetrate down to her bones. The telephone suddenly feels hot in her hand. She leaps to her feet, calls the children, and runs with them over the lawn to the property's rear boundary, where a little brook is flowing, some very minor tributary of the Aller or the Oker, obliviously burbling along under the overhanging grass. There she shows the girls how to make little boats out of bits of wood and float them on the stream, just the way her parents had done with her. The girls run along the bank after the fleeing ships, and when Britta can be sure nobody's watching her, she drops her phone into the water. Even as the device is sinking, she realizes what she should have done instead. She should have shut it off, stored it in the refrigerator overnight, and brought it in to Babak as soon as possible, so that he could check to see whether it had been hacked, and if so, by whom. Getting into a panic and destroying the thing was simply stupid. It's not like her.

The brook carries the device along for a little way, but then it gets stuck on the bottom, glinting silver like a dead fish between the stones. Britta stands up and sneaks behind a raspberry bush to vomit.

Chapter 9

When Julietta comes back three days later, The Bridge looks like a medium-size business during an audit. On the couch, the chairs, and the reception counter, on every flat surface including the floor, are piles of paper, manila folders, and plastic folders, overtopped by towers of ring binders. Babak and Britta examine, read, compare, hand individual pages back and forth, ponder résumés and personality profiles. Lassie's droning has become mere white noise. The algorithm tirelessly fishes names out of suicide forums, analyzes writing styles and word choices, links the results to shopping lists, travel data, music and film libraries, e-book evaluations, surf biographies, and so on, and then lays her catch in stacks before her masters' feet. When Babak pointed out that they already had four candidates under evaluation and that the large-scale searches they were conducting risked exceeding their capacities, Britta nodded and said, "Keep going."

Babak had no comment when Britta told him how she'd got rid of her smartphone.

In passing, he's assembled a few examples of mentally unstable, solo perpetrators who planned and carried out their attacks on their own, which didn't prevent ISIS from claiming responsibility for them afterward. Nice, Würzburg, Bratislava. The selfie video of a young Afghan, waving a kitchen knife around and speaking to the camera: "I am a soldier of the Caliphate."

Britta is, of course, familiar with these cases; she's familiar with all such cases. But ever since the jihad lost its attractive force and The Bridge started fishing potential lone wolves out of the market, such berserker-like operations no longer take place. And there are further reasons why Babak's broad suggestion comes to nothing.

"The perps in Leipzig weren't solo actors," says Britta. "There were two of them. Besides, solo suicide bombers target street intersections or regional trains or cafés or concerts, but certainly not airports. A terrorist who wants to get into an airport needs logistical support."

But neither Britta nor Babak can disregard a basic contradiction: an institution, not individuals, was responsible for the action in Leipzig, but the work was so disastrously shoddy that any lone actor on psychotropic drugs could have done better. This contradiction is putting reams of paper on the furniture, bending their backs, making their heads spin. They've limited Lassie's selection to around one hundred twenty very promising names, which careful vetting will reduce to forty. As for Julietta, they've already forgotten her.

"What's going on here?"

Before anyone has seen her coming, she's standing in the room. She looks to be in a good mood; there's even something triumphant in her manner. With deliberate slowness, Britta looks up from her stack of documents and moves her lower jaw as though chewing gum. "Inventory," she says. She rises to her feet in one quick movement, avoids Babak's eyes, and picks up her jacket from the back of the chair. "Come."

After a couple of summery days, the weather has turned cool again, and a surly wind is yanking on anything that's hanging loose. Britta and Julietta wrap themselves in their jackets and put up with the light drizzle blowing in their faces. In spite of the weather, the city park is full of the usual activity. "Sport Is Public" groups, grandmas with little dogs. Young men using their unconditional basic income to sit on benches. Early retirees tending their tomatoes in the public planting areas. Mothers pushing baby carriages so thoroughly covered with plastic netting and cloth blankets that no one knows whether there's anything inside.

By the time they reach the Babylon, they're very wet and very chilly. They keep their jackets on as they sit on two of the folding chairs that the kebab shop, one of the last Arab bistros in the city center, is furnished with. Although they have yet to order, Sahid brings them green tea, asks if they want anything to eat, and withdraws behind the beaded curtain, sure that no more customers will be turning up at this hour.

Jittery, Julietta wiggles around on her chair, looks over at the door, smiles at Britta, rubs her thighs and forearms, looks over at the door again. Maybe she's medicated. Or maybe it's the fact that she's understood something. Britta waits. The candidate must begin the conversation. This too is one of The Bridge's rules: they want something from us, not we from them.

"Took me a while to figure it out," says Julietta.

"What?"

"You send people away to see if they come back."

She smiles and raises her eyebrows in a request for confirmation that goes unanswered. Britta has emptied her face of all expression.

"So here I am," says Julietta. "Have I passed the test?"

"Yes."

"And now?"

Now Julietta has reached Step 2. Small fanfare. Inaudible. Britta's reluctance makes her clench her teeth while she stands up to ask Sahid for some writing materials. Julietta's young and gorgeous; the media will love her. You can sense her determination, and underneath it something else, hardness, yes, even cruelty, not only toward herself but also toward all mankind. At first glance, the perfect candidate, and The Bridge needs perfect candidates, especially at the moment. But Britta doesn't want that. She wants Julietta to disappear. The problem is, it would be against the rules to place her personal feelings above the results of the evaluation.

Sahid sits at his camping table, working on a crossword puzzle. Next to him is a tablet with a television series running soundlessly on its screen, and also a radio, softly babbling to the mute pictures. He's happy to lend Britta pencil and paper, and she goes back to Julietta. Her handwriting is so bad that she doesn't have to hide what she writes.

"Why do you want to kill yourself?"

"Why not?"

Good answer. Britta has never received a better one. However, she must insist on further explanation. "I'll ask the question differently. Why do you want to be dead?"

"Always wanted to. Just like other girls wanted a horse." Julietta shrugs. "Humanity's repulsive. Everyone should do the same as me and arrange to disappear quick."

"Sounds pretty decadent." Britta makes a note. She's writing down points she'll want to go into more deeply later; the first conversation chiefly serves for taking stock. "In other places, girls are literally fighting for their lives, and you're sitting here and suffering."

"You don't get it." Julietta sips at her tea. "*I'm* not suffering. We all are. That's the problem. In a world where the people doing the best feel the shittiest, something's completely wrong."

"Complicated sentence."

Julietta shrugs again. "I don't care what you think."

"So there's nothing holding you back?"

"My cat will miss me."

"And your parents?"

"Why are you asking me about my parents?"

"I always ask about the parents."

Julietta shakes her hair and runs her fingers through it. It's starting to dry, there's a damp smell in the room, the hot tea's doing her good. Outside the rain has stopped; for a moment, the sky opens up and lets some freshly washed light get through, but then fast-moving clouds shove it down under the street. Paper scraps and empty bags blow through the light-and-shadow theater. Even in a tidy city like Braunschweig, the wind can always rummage in the remotest corners and find some trash to play with.

"The question sounds like psychotherapy."

"This *is* psychotherapy."

"Spare me."

"The confrontation method—"

"No, no, anything but that!" cries Julietta. "Can't we do without psychobabble?"

Britta sucks on her pencil until she realizes that a slight flavor of cooking fat is clinging to it. Suppressing her need to dash to the restroom and rinse her mouth, she considers whether she should go back to Step 1 and send Julietta away. The girl's staring at her as though she's already thinking about getting out of here. Nevertheless, Britta opts for a different way. Julietta's young and shrewd, and she's also a woman. With her, there won't be any need to break down dominance behavior; the young thing's primarily afraid of not being taken seriously.

"Now I'm going to explain to you what The Bridge does," says Britta. "What we can do for you." She drains her teacup. "We guide you through a twelve-step process that enables us to discover whether you really want to end your life."

"I already know the answer to that."

Britta leans forward and looks straight into Julietta's eyes. "It's absolutely crucial for us to assess your decision from all sides. *That* is what we do. We break down suicidal thoughts."

Julietta's rage changes into pensiveness. "Do a few of them remain intact?"

"A few."

"What really happens if I pass all twelve exams?"

Britta keeps quiet.

"You place me with an organization that can use my death."

Britta keeps quiet and puts on her impassive mask once again. Julietta starts nodding slowly. "Okay," she says.

Britta spins her page of notes around and pushes it across the table. "Write your name and date of birth."

Julietta takes the pencil. "I can e-mail you my résumé, if that would help."

"Not necessary."

The girl laughs. "By tomorrow morning at the latest, you'll know more about me than I do, right? You've got an algorithm. That's why that den of yours buzzes so much."

To this observation, Britta makes no response. Julietta leans back, pushes her hair away from her face, stretches her shoulders. Her whole body relaxes. For the first time, she looks frankly into Britta's eyes. Her beauty is shocking. Smooth skin, straight nose, arched eyebrows, long dark eyelashes. Julietta's lips are a little pale and look bitten, because when she's thinking hard, she sucks them in between her teeth; but this blemish, rather than spoiling her perfection, completes it.

"There's nothing I can do about it," says Julietta, reading Britta's thoughts.

"I know."

"My looks have never done me any good."

"Doesn't surprise me. Tell me about your parents."

In the course of her work for The Bridge, Britta has heard countless life stories. She's spoken with people who regretted committing a crime. With fathers who had lost a child. With men abandoned by the women in their lives or tormented by desires they themselves found repellent. Britta has looked into all the possible human abysses, and in doing so has learned that when it comes to tragedy, there's no sort of fixed scale. Many people suffer more because their parents have bought them the wrong gym shoes than others do because they receive three beatings every day. If there's a difference to Britta, it tends to lie in entertainment value. In this instance, it quickly becomes clear that Julietta's story is one of the boring ones.

Only child, academic household. Terrifying perfectionism, compelled happiness. Father would come home for dinner, kiss his idiosyncratically dressed wife and silent daughter, sit at the table, and talk politics. Efficiency, renationalization, popular hygiene. Both parents were CCC voters from the very beginning. Julietta would clean her plate, no matter what was on it. She'd always go to bed at the same time, no matter whether she could sleep or not. Her father doted on her. She was such a good girl, strikingly pretty besides, and always cheerful.

"You spend much time at a computer?"

"I like the Darknet. And suicide forums."

If Julietta were a man, Lassie would probably have identified her years ago, and Julietta would have received mail from The

Bridge. But women are Lassie's lowest priority. Women talk a lot about suicide but rarely commit it. Moreover, the target of their aggression is chiefly themselves, which makes them useless as assassins. There's no rule preventing The Bridge from taking on female candidates. But no woman has ever scored very high on the indicators in Lassie's system. Britta prefers to work with men. Men are what she's used to.

"Do you live in Braunschweig?"

"I've rented a room."

"Please move into the Deutsches Haus hotel. We have a business agreement with them. We'll cover the costs."

"Suppose I disappear in two weeks?"

"That's a risk The Bridge is willing to take."

"How can you afford that?"

"People whose lives we save are happy to give us money."

"And the others?"

Britta smiles. "Them too."

Julietta grins broadly. "Does this mean I've been accepted?"

"Congratulations," says Britta, wondering what Babak will have to say about this.

"I still have a condition," Julietta adds.

Britta, who was already getting to her feet, slowly sits down again.

"It has to be for the animals."

"We've already discussed that," says Britta, controlling herself. "We evaluate your suicidal tendencies, nothing more."

"But in the end," Julietta insisted, "when I've gone through all twelve steps. Green Power would be super. Or something else to do with protecting animals."

"The Bridge's candidates don't impose conditions."

The fact is, The Bridge's candidates typically don't know what they want.

"But who makes the final arrangements? Don't the candidates have the right to participate in the decisions?"

As a rule, arrangements are made conjointly; The Bridge offers recommendations, the candidate selects one, and then the firm verifies the demand for the chosen service. Britta doesn't take the selection process lightly. The choice must be suitable. But none of that is material for discussion at Step 2.

"Don't muck this up," Britta says, pushing back her chair.

"There's one thing you have to know." Julietta points directly at Britta's face. "I'm going to do this, one way or another. With or without you. It's your decision."

"Finish your tea."

The rage that takes hold of Britta is both powerful and unprofessional. She leaves the table and locks herself in Sahid's tiny restroom, sits on the toilet lid, puts her hands on her knees, and tries to account for herself. But new waves of rage keep rising up in her; what Britta would really like to do is to destroy something, the mirror, say, or the paper towel dispenser. She's got a good mind to run Julietta off, not so that she'll come back, no, not this time, but so that she, Britta, can be rid of her forever. Why? Because she's not suitable. The Bridge's candidates have no goals; instead they suffer from the absence of goals. A person who has goals doesn't want to kill herself. In the end, the few who successfully make it through the evaluation are grateful to be provided with a purpose.

I sell convictions, Britta thinks, *and I can't sell this girl anything.*

Most of all, Britta is furious at Julietta's self-confidence. The passion in her voice when she said "I'm going to do this, one way or another" gave her—gives her—exceptional force. She's half a child, and she's sitting there like a boulder. Being next to Julietta fills Britta with a sense of her own weakness. Her own fluttering, her soft vacillation. There are things that Julietta hates. Britta hates nothing and no one. In order to hate, you first have to understand what matters.

After a couple of breathing exercises, Britta leaves the restroom and signals to Sahid that he should put the bill on her account, as usual. Julietta is sitting bent over in her chair. When she hears Britta, she doesn't raise her head but instead rolls her eyes up and gazes at her from below, like a lurking animal. Britta doesn't like that gaze. It says: *I win. Always.*

Chapter

"Hello, hello! Good news!"

The concrete cube's front door slams against the wall so hard that for a brief moment it's unclear whether the milky glass panel will fall out of the frame. Britta abandons stove and pot and runs to the entrance hall, where Richard, with rather more care, is just closing the fortunately undamaged door. He's smiling from ear to ear and brandishing a bottle of Dom Pérignon. All signs point to a Category 1 celebration. With lightning speed, Britta mentally scans all the possibilities she may have forgotten—birthday, passed test, some Vera success or other—and finds that nothing at all occurs to her. Something must have happened.

The smell of food wafts through the house. As a rule, Britta doesn't cook; what she's doing now is displacement activity. Instead of going back to her office after her meeting with Julietta, Britta picked up Vera from day care early. Then she spent the whole afternoon busying herself around the house, seeking out cobwebs, eliminating dust, polishing away all the smears that Henry notoriously overlooks. And all the while, her thoughts kept returning to Babak. Thanks to Lassie's special mission, he has hardly slept for days. To keep himself awake during the waiting periods, he works on his dot picture, which has grown mightily, regularly, from the corners in. Babak's strength is all but gone. He was against Lassie's mission; however, the idea of ignoring Britta's instructions would never occur to him. She loves him for his loyalty. She should have bought a couple of döner kebabs in the Babylon and gone back to her practice with them. The aroma would have filled the office spaces, and for a brief while things would have been the way they used to be, the ordinary Britta-Babak relationship: kebabs, dot picture, three or four candidates in the evaluation loop, in the evenings family for Britta and gay bars for Babak, a life of many calms and few storms, a life under the radar, a perfect life, an uncommon life.

The pervasive smell at the moment is not kebabs, however, it's curry. Britta didn't go back to her office because she had no desire to answer Babak's questions about Julietta. He'll explode from curiosity; leaving him hanging like this is cruel. But Britta doesn't want to discuss what's so great about Julietta right now, and she wants even less to discuss what's so disturbing.

She gives Richard a fleeting kiss on the cheek and then leaves him standing in the hall as she hastens back to the kitchen to prevent the onions she's sautéing from turning to charcoal. Next to the stove sit little bowls of chopped lemongrass, coriander, garlic, cumin, and oyster mushrooms. It's a recipe Britta downloaded from the Internet, although Richard usually prepares it for her; it's one of their favorites from the time when they were getting to know each other. Because the dish is too spicy for Vera, cooking it anyway always constitutes something of a small rebellion.

Richard comes into the kitchen, embraces her from the

side, and presses a kiss into the parting of her hair, whereupon she spreads her hands, making it clear that her fingers are hot with pepper juice.

"You're cooking for me? Do you already know?"

"A miracle of telepathy," Britta says, laughing. "Or a coincidence. Whichever you prefer."

"I pick telepathy."

"What's for dinner?" Vera shuffles into the kitchen, a Mega-Melanie doll in each hand. "Ugghh, I don't like that."

"You're having kids' pizza."

"I always have kids' pizza."

"You haven't had kids' pizza for days."

"Kids' pizza is boring."

"We've got something to celebrate!" Richard grabs his grumpy daughter by the arms and shoves her around the kitchen, swinging his hips a little, as though they were dancing to some inaudible music.

"Let go of me! What's wrong with you?"

"Good mood!"

In fact, it's been ages since Britta's seen him in such high spirits. Now he's holding Vera high above his head and turning around in a circle with her until she starts to laugh in spite of herself, and then they both sink down to the kitchen floor, giddy and whooping. Before she puts the bottle of Dom Pérignon in the freezer, Britta glances at the price tag.

"Do you want to propose to me?" she asks.

"We're already married."

"Do you want a divorce?"

"Actually, no."

"Have you won the lottery?"

"Without playing?"

"Why not?" Britta jauntily pours more sesame oil into the

frying pan. "As far as I know, the chances aren't substantially better for people who do play."

"Guess as much as you want, you'll never get it right."

"Set the table. We're eating on the terrace."

Britta pushes ingredients into the pan with the spine of her knife, lets them sizzle briefly, and adds coconut milk. The scent becomes so intense that she closes her eyes for a second. As part of the celebration, Richard has also brought Vera a present. He hands it to her, or rather tries to, but before his arm is fully extended, the little girl snatches the gift from him and tears the wrapping to shreds in the air. Two new members of the Mega-Family, Mega-Milan and Mega-Miró, emerge. Britta is familiar enough with Mega-World by now to know who these two are. He's a pianist from Zagreb, she's a painter from Paris; they're both successful, with penthouses in Brooklyn and Moscow, and famous for their extravagant wardrobes. On the weekends, they stroll arm in arm through the Mega-Mall, spending their artistically earned money. Occasionally, a concert or a vernissage also forms part of the program. Now that they've wound up with Vera, the two artists will probably be shot down in a Mega-SWAT operation before too long.

"How cool, how cool," Vera repeats countless times before disappearing into her room to brief the newcomers on their assignments before dinner.

The bad weather has passed; the evening is mild. The three of them sit out on the graveled area in front of the concrete cube, Vera bending over her pizza while Britta's still serving Richard and herself. The light breeze carries barbecue smells—grilled meat, charcoal, lighter fluid—from the neighbors' garden, along with the sounds of laughing children, clattering dishes, the dull thump of a soccer ball, and adult voices in muffled conversation. The curry tastes divine. If Britta breathes through her nose, her whole head fills with the smells of lemongrass and ginger. They bring her back to the party where she saw Richard for the first time, leaning in a doorway and chatting, a tall, broad-shouldered, and yet amazingly supple man with sun-bleached hair. He swayed his hips while recounting an anecdote, the words just gushed out of him, interrupted by laughter, a tale about some guy trying to approach a girl and repeatedly saying the wrong thing, maybe from a movie and not funny at all, but because Richard told the story so well and was so obviously enjoying himself, his listeners laughed with him, good cheer spread out from him in concentric circles, and Britta thought, *This is a person from another time, he's unscathed, I want him, I want to live with him,* and she dreaded the moment when he would turn around. And then he turned around because someone called his name, and Britta saw his face and wanted to say, more than anything, *Well, there you are, what took you so long?* Thai curry was served at this party, because the host had just returned from a long stay on Ko Samui; you scooped your helping out of a pot as big as a field kitchen and ate standing up, using plastic utensils and a plastic plate, and Britta placed herself next to Richard and told him she had just founded a healing practice and for the first time earned her own income, which she planned to use to leave Leipzig, and she asked him to pick a city for her to move to, its population mustn't exceed 300,000 and it couldn't be farther south than Koblenz, because the southern dialects, Swabian and Bavarian, made her sick. He could have said Kassel or Siegen, Bremerhaven or Paderborn, but he said Braunschweig right away, without stopping to think, even though he wasn't from there, he came from Hagen, which was a sad story in itself. They left the party together and soon moved to Braun-

schweig together, and in between only three or four months
had passed, and in those months they'd cooked a whole lot of
curry.

"You like it?"

"It's outstanding. I've always known that you just pretend
you can't cook."

"So are you finally going to explain yourself or what?"

Richard lays down his spoon and, with a flourish, extracts
the champagne from the freezer. "No more doorknob polishing," he says as he removes the foil from the neck of the bottle.
"No more ass kissing, no more sucking up to denim-shirted,
shaven-headed jerks," he says as he removes the wire net from
the cork.

"You said 'ass,' " Vera cries, her mouth full of pizza.

"You got fired," Britta says in amazement.

"I own a third of the company, remember? The only person
who could fire me is me." While Richard's restraining the cork,
keeping it from exiting the bottle too fast, his knuckles turn
white.

"You've taken a lifetime sabbatical."

"Better. This afternoon, out of the blue, this guy gets me on
the line. His name is Guido Hatz."

"Never heard of him."

"Google doesn't know him either."

"And therefore he's very insignificant. Or very important."

"Above all, very rich. He's a venture capitalist, and he wants
to get on board with Smart Swap. Comprehensively. A private investor, not a fund. The usual conditions—he gets a say,
he gives advice, he shares the take. Monthly confessions, total
transparency."

"How much?"

"I can't say. In any case, seed and early financing are covered, and probably a portion of the late-stage financing too. There'll be no problem getting Swappie market-ready."

Britta knows she's got to be happy for him; she can't have more than a few seconds left before the fact that she's not jumping with joy makes Richard cross.

"What does this guy look like?"

"No idea, love, it was a phone call."

"And you two made this ironclad deal, just like that?"

"Hatz knows what he wants. He immediately sent over the preliminary forms, so we've already got a rough framework in place."

"How did he know about you?"

"Sweetie, I don't go to work just to play darts! Customer acquisition! Advertising! Networking! It's not completely impossible to know what Swappie is." He leans forward, pours champagne, and seizes her hand. "Don't you understand what this means to me?"

"Of course I do. Congratulations."

"Everything will change now. Swappie will be up and running. Emil and Jonas will calm down. We can hire people, we can become a normal business, I'll get a workplace where I can actually work!"

"That's wonderful." They clink glasses; Britta rises halfway from her chair to kiss Richard across the table. "I'm awfully happy for you. You have so earned it."

His radiant smile is just as winning as it was twelve years ago. And in general, he's hardly changed. He still comes across as a person who lives in a world where everything's all right.

"I love you," says Britta.

"Bam!" yells Vera, because Mega-Miró has suddenly shot Mega-Milan.

After the meal, Richard carries the dishes into the kitchen,

Vera excuses herself to go and play with her dolls, and Britta remains seated for a while longer, savoring the mild air and her third glass of champagne.

She has just convinced herself that there's absolutely nothing peculiar about Richard's stroke of luck, and she's looking forward to putting Vera to bed and continuing the little celebration on the couch, when she hears the sound of an engine. Someone's driving down the street, slowly but not at a walking pace. She figures she'll see a police patrol car glide past, but what enters her field of vision is a white pickup. A Toyota Hilux.

This time she can make out the driver's face, for he's wearing neither sunglasses nor visor cap. Dark, not exactly newly trimmed hair; a man in his late forties or early fifties, a German teacher or car dealer, an average guy, utterly forgettable if it weren't for that mustache, also dark, badly trimmed, a bushy, disruptive element between his nose and his mouth. When their eyes meet, he steps on the gas. The pickup leaps forward and at the end of the street turns right, and Britta can hear the engine roar as the driver leaves the neighborhood, heading downtown.

"Hey, you still look totally frightened." Richard laughs, goes down on one knee next to her chair, and takes her hand. "Is it really so scary if something goes right for me too once in a while?"

Britta summons up a smile and a shake of the head; at this point, it's only speech that she's incapable of. Richard kisses her fingertips.

"You'll see," he says. "Everything will be fine."

Chapter **11**

"So, Jawad, how was it?"

"*Wallah,* Frau Britta, real good, I swear."

Although Jawad's twenty-three, Britta's always tempted to speak to him as though he were a child. "Were the aunts and uncles nice to you?"

"Yo, they gave me pills, real strong, I only take naps, day and night."

Jawad has spent the past ten days plus eight hours in Langenhagen, a psychiatric clinic near Hanover.

At Step 5 of the evaluation process, candidates check themselves into a clinic as suicide risks and complete a stay of at least ten days, including participation in the entire range of therapy offerings. Checking himself out on the morning after the end of the ten-day period is an indication that Jawad's stay in the clinic maybe wasn't so "real good."

"I am new person, Frau Britta, I swear."

He laughs and lights a cigarette. Britta and Babak don't like people smoking in the office, but Jawad notoriously violates prohibitions of every kind, not out of insubordination, but because there's an area of his brain dedicated to ensuring that prohibitions are immediately forgotten. Britta finds reprimanding him too tiresome.

"If you liked the clinic, why didn't you stay longer?"

"*Abu,* Frau Britta, nothing but sleep and yak, yak and sleep. So I wake up in the morning and I want my head back. Doctor comes, and I go like, '*Wallah,* brother, no more pills, for me full contact.'"

"Aha."

Britta leafs through the discharge papers, among which there's also the medical report. Ativan daily, along with citalopram in the morning and mirtazapine in the evening. No wonder Jawad wants his head back.

"Did you participate in the therapy sessions? Were you cooperative?"

"Normal, real coparative, or something."

"Can you imagine continuing with the therapy?"

"Eh, what?"

"Did you feel a desire to give up your suicide plans and lead a normal life one day?"

"You are kidding me, no?"

"I have to ask that question, Jawad. It's part of the process. All candidates get asked that after their stay in the clinic."

"Normal, eh." He stubs out his cigarette on the sole of his shoe and laughs again. "I thought you want to get rid of me."

His ingenuousness gives Britta a twinge. She accepted Jawad into the program in the secret hope that he'd heal as soon as possible, leave The Bridge, and return to life. Although Lassie plucked him out of the Net with a high value of 10.1, to this day Britta doesn't rightly understand why he wants to kill himself. Certainly, he doesn't have the most promising future ahead of him. He can barely read and write, which explains his terse weekly reports ("today rain, me movies"). Moreover, according to Babak, Jawad's Arabic is even worse than his German. He has no high school diploma and nothing resembling career aspirations. But other boys like him sell drugs, fight with doormen, dream of muscle cars, and fantasize about girls as obedient as Arab girls and as broad-minded as German ones. Such young men live lives of their own, on the margins of a society that doesn't want to have anything to do with them.

When Britta talks to Jawad about his death wish during their weekly sessions, he says, "I go Allah, Frau Britta, I swear." As for the rest of the fifty minutes, he tries to make them pass in arguments about his smoking or with a bit of innocuous jabbering. The fact that he hasn't fallen into ISIS's hands is definite proof that they're not recruiting anymore.

Even though he's such a pain in the neck, Britta has a soft spot for him. And in his own screwed-up way, Jawad absolutely wants to please her. Contrary to her expectations, he's sailed pretty effortlessly through the evaluation process so far. The external psychological test required in Step 4 identified, in his case, narcissistic personality disorder, a low intelligence quotient, and extremely strong suicidal tendencies. His stay in the clinic as prescribed in Step 5 has obviously left him entirely unimpressed. Britta sighs. One of The Bridge's basic rules forbids displaying friendly feelings toward candidates. She knows she must start looking at Jawad with different eyes. He's not an amusing big baby; he's a potential suicide. The waterboarding in Step 6 will show how well he copes with mortal fear. Next will come self-harm and breaking off contact with everyone close to him. After a few further steps, he'll get his final marching orders. Slowly but surely, the time for Britta to start worrying about Jawad's usability is approaching.

She ends the conversation, sends Jawad back to the hotel,

and gets to work on the other reports. On the top of the stack lie the outpourings of Mr. Marquardt, a stiff, prim gentleman who sits bolt upright on the edge of his chair and answers Britta's questions with formulations as recherché as they are long-winded. He usually fills several pages a day with his crystal-clear miniature handwriting, and Britta dreads slogging, once again, through a compulsive's interior life.

All the same, Marquardt has quickly and quietly managed to reach Step 8; when he was waterboarded, instead of wildly twitching and writhing the way most victims do, he simply went limp, and afterward he declared that he had seen a bright light. He is, at the moment, the most promising candidate. He'll probably reach Step 12 with little difficulty and soon thereafter carry out a surgically clean operation for whatever group employs him.

Britta pushes Marquardt's effusions to the edge of the coffee table, yields to curiosity, and reaches for Julietta's notes. On the day after their conversation in the Babylon, Britta came into the office to find Babak already sitting at his dot picture. He looked at her with tired eyes. He'd spent another night with Lassie.

"So?" he asked, and Britta nodded. Babak raised his eyebrows in acknowledgment and likewise nodded. That was it. No further questions. Britta loved him for that.

Julietta has been an official part of the program ever since. She has a dossier, a hotel room number, and a coefficient of 8.7. On a hunch, Babak carried out a second scanning, switching the sex indicator to "male." When Lassie spat out the results, he gave an admiring whistle: 11.3. The highest score ever given at the beginning of an evaluation.

The little sheaf of notes contains ten pages, which means that Julietta averaged a bit more than one page a day.

Instead of reading, Britta flips the pages back and forth. They're numbered and dated and obviously belong together. However, they exhibit three distinct handwritings, and Britta considers whether Julietta could have handed in material written by other people. Looking more closely, Britta sees that the writing changes in the middle of sentences, going from flowing cursive to ponderous printed capitals, succeeded, one page later, by a barely legible scrawl. The hair on Britta's arms stands on end. She's heard of this phenomenon but never before seen it with her own eyes.

The text presents an unusual picture in other ways too. It runs down each page in two columns, as if Julietta has put her thoughts on paper in the form of a long poem.

Always the same
again and again the devil's
merry-go-round
round and around
I extinguish thoughts

I do not
hate
the world
life
myself
it's not
worth it

indifference kills
There! That's how you are.
stupid and nasty

I extinguish feelings
I go out
my mask belongs to me
Reality and I
we don't fit together

I'll help you
out of there

scream
scream
scream

rehearse nothingness
spark
fire
night

. . .

"Hello, sorry, can we talk for a minute?"

When Babak comes in, Britta, relieved, puts the page aside. Normally she doesn't like to be disturbed while she's reading, but Julietta's lines dig into Britta's brain with barbed tips, *scream scream scream,* she runs both hands through her hair, scratches her scalp with her fingernails. They make a booming sound, unnaturally loud, as if the inside of her skull has turned into an empty space.

"Everything okay?"

She nods, releases her hair, and concentrates on Babak's face. It looks considerably better; it's not so gray as before, the rings under his eyes have disappeared, the youthful dimples in his cheeks have returned. Now that Lassie has fallen silent, Babak's spending his nights in bed again. All told, he and Britta have picked out a hundred possible candidates, enough to put together a small army. It would take months to prepare these people adequately, but Britta feels more secure with such a trump up her sleeve.

"You wanted to tell me something?"

"I've just come from the lawyer's office. My application's approved."

"You can't be serious."

"But I am. I'm going to talk with Markus Blattner, the perp who survived the Leipzig attack."

"How can you?"

"I am now Blattner's cousin. Torsten Mayer, twenty-six, resident of Bitterfeld. I've got special dispensation for one thirty-minute chat."

"You don't look like a Torsten."

"But I can prove it. Look, I have—"

"Stop!" Britta cries. "I don't want to know anything about that. Any conditions?"

"The magistrate ordered acoustic monitoring."

Britta shrugs. "What did you expect? This is a terrorism case. They're probably letting you in only so they can see if he'll sing to you."

"Shall I go on with those?" Babak asks, pointing to the weekly reports. "Then you can pick up Vera early from her school."

Britta feels a clump in her throat. For days now, Vera's been spending the afternoons at Janina and Knut's, because Britta's at the practice until evening and Richard's so busy with his new investor. Britta's secretly glad she's promised to provide financing for the country house because that way she doesn't have to feel guilty about asking so much of her friend. "You buy your friends," her mother—a specialist in such pronouncements—would say if she knew, "because you can't bear to be grateful." Britta fails to see what's so bad about the principle of buying and selling; after all, the entire world functions on it. Furthermore, there are indeed people she's actually grateful to. Babak, for example.

"You're a sweetheart," she says, jumping up, acting as though she wants to kiss him on the mouth.

Laughing, Babak wards her off. "Get out of here!"

Feeling the special bliss of skipping work, Britta walks to the door. She's almost outside when Babak calls her again. "Hey, Britta," he says. "When all this is over . . ." He gestures toward the piles of documents that Britta has shoved behind the reception counter. "When this is over," he says again, "then you're going to the doctor."

She herself hardly notices anymore that she constantly holds one hand pressed against her stomach.

Chapter **12**

When Richard comes home, she's already in bed, though still awake. It's been the same for days, she's dog-tired but can't fall asleep, and now she's beginning to get angry. Which doesn't make things better. She keeps telling herself that her private life is in perfect order, and that professionally there are at most a couple of small discrepancies. With a job like hers, she can't expect a lifetime of smooth sailing. Britta knows that. But her body doesn't. Instead of letting her sink down in exhaustion, it's sending electric shocks through her system. You can force yourself to do many things, but not to fall asleep.

She's relieved to register the beeps of the combination lock on the front door, pricks up her ears, and follows Richard's progress through the house, down the entrance hall to the kitchen, the refrigerator door opening, the hiss of a beer can, and then more footsteps, straight to the bedroom. The half-closed door is carefully pushed open; he peers inside, sees her sitting in bed, awake, and comes in. Big smile.

"Hello, sweetheart."

"How was it?"

"Sensational!"

He throws himself onto the bed and kisses her, spills a little beer on the blanket, laughs, and rolls around until he's lying stretched out next to her. When Britta came home with Vera, Richard's note was on the kitchen table, informing her that the new investor had, on the spur of the moment, invited the partners to a meeting, and so Richard and Emil and Jonas had gone to Berlin; they would take the last train back, the note said.

"Imagine a film from the last century. Black limousine at the train station; the driver probably has a PhD. We've hardly sat down in the car before the drive is over. We get out at an address on Unter den Linden. An elevator brings us to the roof—penthouse with terrace and view of the Reichstag."

"Private residence or office?"

"A combination, I think. Guido's a funny guy. I wouldn't be surprised if he lives mostly in hotels."

"You're already saying *Du* to each other?"

"Almost before we're over the threshold, the champagne is open, formal language has been banished, and a bit of paperwork taken care of. After that, he drags us out to the terrace, pours more champagne, and explains the view."

"He talked about Berlin? How old-fashioned."

"In his way. Guido Hatz's primary occupation is geomancy."

"He's a dowser? Divining rod and all?"

"More like a kind of geo-healer. He talks about how building projects harm the earth and how Berlin is basically a giant wound. We're faced with such vigorous catastrophes everywhere, he says, and they represent our next great task, namely reconciling mankind and the earth again. And he showed us where the city angel prefers to sit."

"I can't believe it."

"On the Quadriga above the Brandenburg Gate."

"Of course. I'd like to sit there too. If I were an angel, I mean."

"The whole time, Emil and Jonas are asking him eager questions, like the class geeks on Open Doors day. Arm in arm, best of friends, red cheeks."

"From the champagne?"

"From the money."

"And you?"

"No idea. The man is a lunatic, but also interesting somehow."

"He's a Hatz-shot."

"Exactly."

Britta picks up his can of beer, takes a few swallows—even though she's already brushed her teeth—and snuggles down into the pillows again. It's nice to listen to Richard and nice to look at him, positively glowing as he is with success and happiness and hope.

"And here comes the best part. While he's talking and explaining, he suddenly pushes a chair against the balustrade that goes around the roof terrace. Then he clambers up on the chair, talking the whole time about radionics and ley lines and earth chakras and so forth, puts his glass down, climbs onto the railing, and says look, this is where a something-or-other line runs, right here, I had this terrace specially built, I can shut my eyes, because I can feel it. He closes his eyes, spreads his arms wide, and walks along on the balustrade. On the other side, there's about a sixty- or seventy-foot drop to the ground, with tourists and cars and traffic lights and bicycles."

"Intense."

"I filmed it."

Richard takes his smartphone out of his pocket, fingers the

screen until he finds the right video, leans over to Britta; they put their heads together; this is all a lot of fun, they'll probably have sex later, as soon as the clip is over. Then the video begins. Sky over Berlin, rooftops, a balustrade, Emil and Jonas in semi-profile, appalled, giggling, with champagne glasses in their hands, effusive exclamations on the sound track, *Man, this is wild, what are you doing, this is insanity, lunacy, just look at this.* Completely unfazed by his companions, a man is on the balustrade, eyes shut, arms stretched out, obviously relaxed, smiling, confidently setting down one foot in front of the other, moving pretty briskly but without haste, a man who knows where to go. In the middle of his face, a conspicuous mustache, chestnut brown like his hair.

Chapter **13**

Hey Mom, hey Pops,

When you read this letter, I'll already be gone. The news of my death surely fills you with horror, and you're asking yourselves a bunch of questions. Why did she do that? Was she unhappy? What did we do wrong?

Let me start off by saying that you'll remain alone with those questions forever.

The healing practice that helped me find the right path offers its candidates sample texts for their suicide notes. The samples contain boilerplate like "You bear no guilt for any of this," "My decision has nothing to do with either of you," or "My share of the distribution is to go to you, dear Mama, so that you can finally buy yourself XYZ. And every time you use XYZ, you must think of me and how much I love you."

As far as I'm concerned, none of the samples was appropriate. I'm donating my fee to the animal shelter.

Dear Mom, dear Pops, if you're totally devastated right now, you should simply think it's because of your feeling that you failed as

parents, and not because you miss me. You've reduced the universe
to the outline of your persons, and you're empty inside. Don't delude
yourselves by thinking you're capable of genuine feelings. Imagine
that I'm studying abroad, and then that I get a job, a husband, and
children. In London, say. Or Boston. I wouldn't have gotten in touch
with you anyway, so it really doesn't make any difference.

Best of luck with everything else,
Julietta

Britta has read the letter ten times. Reading it an eleventh time
is not a requirement of her work, certainly not in this situation,
sitting uncomfortably at the wheel of her parked multivan
with a briefcase full of weekly reports on her lap. Nevertheless,
that's exactly what she does: she reads the lines one more time.
The words trigger a strange feeling in her, like a scab that must
be scratched and scratched until the blood comes.

An amazing number of candidates fail at writing their suicide note. When it comes to addressing their loved ones in concrete words, their death wish slams into reality. The Bridge's
statistics show that a third of its candidates leave the program
at this point and return to their lives, so Britta has moved the
letter-writing requirement up to Step 3. Many aspirants spend
weeks toiling over this task, trying out every one of the sample texts, tossing away one attempt after the other, until they
realize that when the chips are down, they don't really want to
kill themselves at all.

Julietta didn't toil. She put her words on paper in a flowing,
coherent script that shows how much joy she took in what she
was writing. Britta feels as though she's come in contact with
something great. Julietta's words express hardness, cruelty,
and hatred, and with them the capacity to accomplish amazing things. Britta feels a sudden urge to write her own parents

a suicide note. She stares through the windshield at the desolate parking lot of the Leipzig prison, mentally testing possible formulations, considering what her opening might be: *Dear Mama, dear Daddy, when you read this letter* . . . She jumps, startled, when she recognizes that the sentences she wants to write are Julietta's, word for word.

She straightens up with a jerk and puts the letter aside. The Bridge's rules forbid identification with candidates. Mind games of this kind are unprofessional. And anyway, Britta shouldn't be here at all, she should be at work, sitting in her office, not in a vehicle parked outside Leipzig prison. Against all reason, she'd insisted on accompanying Babak to Leipzig. They'd left Braunschweig shortly after dawn in order to be at their destination by eight o'clock. During the whole drive, she tried to tell Babak about Guido Hatz. But every time she was about to open her mouth, her head would empty out. *He has a mustache* was all she could think of.

Now she lets down her window and takes a deep breath; her problem is simply that she hasn't been sleeping much. She sticks Julietta's letter back in the briefcase and is just about to take out a few more documents when the outer door of the prison's main building opens and Babak appears. It's too soon. Counting the half-hour visit he was granted and the attendant formalities, he shouldn't be leaving the prison before nine. Britta's dashboard clock reads a quarter past eight.

Babak takes a few steps in the direction of the parking area, strays over to the empty bike racks, and stares at the curved metal tubes as though wondering what they're good for. Then he slowly raises his head, looks around, and begins what looks like an unhurried return to reality. When he spies the VW bus, he takes off, moving quickly, almost running. Britta leans out the open window.

"What's wrong?" she calls softly. "Did they spot you?"

"Markus is dead."

They sit in silence on the way back, Britta behind the wheel, Babak in the passenger seat, both gazing straight ahead as the multivan's blunt muzzle swallows up the road, meter by meter. They have an urgent need to talk, but it's not happening. Britta is sure Babak's mulling over the same thoughts she is. Two-point-five. That was the score Lassie gave Markus in relation to his suicidality: 2.5 points out of a possible 12. A score of 2.5 corresponds to a superficial death wish, like someone ogling the emergency exit; nothing more. And yet Markus is supposed to have hanged himself in his cell.

Britta can't shake the feeling that she's part of a puzzle that absolutely refuses to make sense. The attack in Leipzig, the Hilux in front of her house, Julietta, Richard's very opportune investor with the stalker mustache. Markus Blattner's death. She must get something to eat soon, her stomach's aching; it's as if somebody were in there, poking in all directions.

Would Markus still be alive if Babak hadn't tried to visit him?

It's only ten thirty when they pull into the Kurt Schumacher Apartment Blocks' parking area. An absurdly early time of day, considering the distance they've traveled so far. Britta massages her wrists, stiff from clenching the steering wheel. Babak gets out of the car immediately and disappears down the Passage without waiting for her. When Britta reaches the office, she hears bumping and banging sounds coming from the lower floor. She slowly descends the spiral staircase and leans in the doorway of the server room. It pains her to watch Babak as he yanks cables out of the walls, disconnects everything, pulls components apart. Cutting The Bridge's heart out of its body.

Britta doesn't help him; she sits on the couch upstairs with a cup of coffee that she neglects to drink. Now and again, Babak hustles past her, carrying boxes or bins, cable spools, monitors, bags full of small parts. A shrill screech from downstairs fills the air, a howl repeated whenever Babak shoves the next load of paper into the shredder. Britta doesn't have to look closely to know that the documents being destroyed are the results of the most recent large-scale searches.

A good hour later, Babak surfaces for the last time, panting, heaving up his Blade System enclosure, stair by stair. The shredder has fallen silent; the silence weighs heavy.

"See you later," Babak says, smiles weakly, and disappears out the front door.

Britta reassures herself that Lassie is going to be put back together somewhere else. In a place that not even she knows about. She tells herself it's only a relocation, a security measure. Nevertheless, it feels like something is coming to an end.

"Oh, are you closing up already?"

Guido Hatz is leaning on the hood of his white pickup. It's the same model the ISIS lunatics used to drive through the deserts. His arms are folded as he smiles down on Britta, who's at least a head shorter.

"What is it you want?"

"Information about the services you offer."

They look at each other with such different expressions—Hatz friendly and expectant, Britta torn between fear and anger—that it's a miracle that they can see each other at all.

"Maybe we can go inside?" asks Guido Hatz. "I'd like a brief chat with you."

For a moment, Britta toys with the thought of leaving him standing there and driving home. She's so tired. Reluctantly, she unlocks the door again, steps in, and plants herself in the middle of the lobby. When Hatz grasps that she's not going to offer him a seat, he sets out on a little tour of the practice, gawking at the reception, the sitting area, the dot picture.

"How interesting," he says, leaning over Babak's work. "I

can recognize energy centers. Here, for example." His finger circles over the portion that Babak last worked on. "A region of immense compression. Something that cries out for resolution. Is this about a method for detecting energy nodes? Did you develop this yourself?"

He's good. Britta is actually unable to say whether he's being serious or playing with her. She can feel fear begin to flicker behind her thoughts, and she fakes a yawn to relax herself, a ploy that Guido Hatz surely sees through.

"Let's get to the point," she says. "What's this about?"

"Maybe your husband's already told you that I'm interested in geomancy."

Britta raises her eyebrows in surprise. So he's making no secret of his connection with Richard. Nor has he introduced himself or asked her name. Obviously he's taking for granted that each of them knows who the other is. A wise old saying holds that the right solution is usually the simplest one; according to this wisdom, Hatz is probably nothing more than an eccentric millionaire who enjoys investigating the contexts of his investments. Britt pulls herself together and sets her dispositional dial to "normal conversation."

"Richard showed me the video," says she. "The one where you're balancing on a railing."

"Child's play," says Hatz, dismissing the feat with a wave of his hand. "Anyone who concentrates a little can do it. But this here"—he points again at Babak's picture—"requires significantly deeper insight into the energetic constellation. Perhaps you could give me a brief explanation of your method? I am, to a certain extent, a professional in these matters."

"The Bridge has nothing to do with the esoteric arts. I'm a healing practitioner in psychotherapy."

"Esotericism is a meaningless term." Guido Hatz strokes his

mustache. "Anyone who wants to heal people has to deal with energy."

"That's true." Britta nods slowly to gain the time she needs to trawl her memory for techniques from her schooling. "The Bridge's offerings include breathing therapy, autogenic training, and hypnosis, along with brainspotting, CRM, and EMDR."

Hatz looks like someone making an effort to repress a grin.

"Recently, however, we've been specializing, even though you might say that specialization contradicts the basic principles of alternative medicine. In many cases, contradictions are precisely the means of releasing the greatest energy."

He acknowledges this rhetorical chess move with a smile. "Self-managing, life coaching, ego polishing," he says. His voice betrays no hint of irony as he quotes the sign on the door of the practice.

"A simple truth is hidden behind those concepts," Britta explains. "The Bridge cures suicidal tendencies."

"Do your patients get initiated?"

"We use a twelve-step method."

"To the fourth degree?"

"In particular cases. Even though we have a different name for it."

"The others are eliminated beforehand?"

"The vast majority leave us in one of the earlier steps."

"Cured?"

"In a manner of speaking."

"Not everyone is fit to be a master."

"As it were."

"Do you have a statistical report?"

Britta gives him an appraising look. His facial expression hasn't changed; he still looks friendly and interested.

"Does the question surprise you?" he asks. "I'm a money person. Figures interest me."

"The Bridge keeps statistics on everything. But the data is confidential."

"Please give me a vague idea. How many clients reach the final step?"

"Fewer than ten percent."

"That *is* extremely vague." He laughs.

"Let's leave it at that."

"May I hold your hands for a moment?"

Britta's irritation lasts for only a fleeting second. Her work at The Bridge continually brings her into contact with the New Age milieu. On their desperate search for meaning, adherents hang semiprecious stones on themselves, wear magnetic armbands, and refuse to shower after their prana yoga class so as not to wash off the energy. Until one day it occurs to them that a clean ending would be the best solution after all. Esoterics talk a lot and can't listen. In that regard, Hatz isn't a typical specimen. Furthermore, he's not wearing any healing stones. Hoping to end the surprise visit, Britta stretches out both hands, palms up, and Hatz carefully places his own on them, a very light touch, so light that Britta can't be sure it took place. After only a few seconds, Hatz begins to nod appreciatively. "No wonder you're so successful," says he. "This is extraordinary."

Britta withdraws her hands and thrusts them into her jacket pockets. She feels a sudden need to wash herself with a great deal of soap and hot water, preferably under a large, high-pressure showerhead. But instead of leaving at last, Hatz points to one of the chairs.

"Mind if I sit down?"

Britta would love to invent an appointment as a pretext for getting rid of him. But her reason tells her she must take advantage of this opportunity to get him to talk. Whatever he may turn out to be—a harmless crackpot, say, or the emissary of some enemy power—she wants to know where she stands.

She offers him a chair and seats herself on the couch. Hatz makes himself comfortable and seems to be waiting to see if she'll produce some coffee. When it's clear that she won't, he leans back, puts a smile on his face, and waits. Britta's feeling too weak today for a war of nerves, and so she prefers to start the conversation herself, right away.

"Why are you investing in Smart Swap?"

"Ah." Guido Hatz's smile broadens. Apparently, he wasn't expecting this question. "Does that scare you? Are you concerned because I'm buying something that belongs to you?"

You buy your friends, says Britta's mother's voice. *You enjoy having Richard dependent on you, because then you can be sure he won't leave you.* Britta concentrates on making sure that none of these submerged thoughts reaches the surface. Her expression remains unchanged as she holds Guido Hatz's gaze.

"I invest because I'm rich."

"That's no reason."

"Because I want to get even richer."

"With Swappie?"

"The idea has potential. Your husband's good. Even though you consider him a failure."

A full broadside. He obviously wants to provoke her, but Britta's determined not to be lured out of her reserve. In the ensuing silence, she notices how much she misses Lassie's busy humming.

"You know, my chief reason for coming here was to tell you you're doing the right thing." Hatz raises an index finger, signaling that he finally wants to get to the point.

"In what respect?"

"You're getting ready for some downtime. Throwing your cell phone away, unplugging the computers."

Before she can say anything, he waves his finger back and

forth near his ear, which seems to mean that he hears what she hears, namely nothing.

"The servers are being serviced."

Hatz doesn't consider it necessary to respond to this absurd excuse, and Britta can't blame him.

"Maybe I can't read thoughts," he says, "but energy fields are clear to me. You've reached a boundary. What's waiting beyond it is the abyss."

Britta bolts internal doors and windows to keep Hatz's words from getting to her. She wants him to shut up but doesn't try to stop him. She must hear what he has to say.

"Viewed from outside, it's all totally obvious. You're going through a paranoid phase, you feel persecuted, and whatever happens, you take it personally. Confusion, obsessive thoughts, sleeplessness, panic attacks. The feeling that something terrible is just around the corner. And then, of course, there's the nausea. The constant nausea."

He leans forward, raising his hands slightly, radiating compassion and tenderness.

"Diagnose yourself for a change, Britta. This is burnout. You're on the verge of a nervous breakdown."

She knows that she shouldn't just let this impertinence go, but she keeps staring at him, frozen in place like a rabbit faced with a snake. How can it be that he knows so much about her? With all her strength, she maintains her facial expression, which must remain as it is, unwavering. *Breathe: in, out. Don't try to smile, don't move a finger, don't look away, don't blink, simply breathe. In, out.*

"You're a strong woman, Britta. But your guardian angel's worried."

"My guardian angel?"

"That's me."

Hatz gets up and smooths his trouser legs. "Simply imagine that I'm a friend of your family. Someone who's been watching you from a distance for a long time and who occasionally steps in without advertising his intervention."

Now it's definite, Britta thinks. *He's crazy.* Her thought turns into interior rejoicing, *crazy, crazy, crazy;* her head sings it to the skies. Relief lifts her up, as if it would carry her from the sofa to the ceiling. A rich crackpot who thinks he's a guardian angel, a millionaire stalker who for some reason has decided to do good things for her and Richard. Weird but harmless.

"You've been successful, you've earned a break," says Hatz. "Let your husband take the wheel. I want to see Swappie worth a lot of money on the stock market in a few years. Until then, Richard can use all the support he can get. It's important for you to have his back." Hatz strokes his mustache and looks around the office once again. Then he nods, as though he's convinced himself of the accuracy of his pronouncement.

"Give yourself some time off. Things will fall in line."

Britta remains seated as he moves toward the door.

"Suppose I don't?" she asks, just as he's pushing the door open. A light drizzle is falling outside, as fine as sheer fabric; maybe it's even fog, slowly sinking to the ground. Hatz lets go of the door, which reattaches itself to the padded frame with a dull thud. "Suppose I don't follow your advice?" she goes on. "What then?"

He gives her a piercing look. "To be honest, Britta," he says, "I don't know."

Without another word, Guido Hatz has left Britta's office and climbed back into his Hilux. Now she's standing in his empty parking spot, as if she must make sure nothing's there anymore. She raises her head and lets the fine rain tickle her face. She has an urge to spread out her arms and spin around and around on her own axis under the low-hanging sky. It's glorious to stand out on the street and be a normal person with a normal life. No obsessive thoughts, no pointless questions doing loops inside her head. A boring passerby who stops for a moment and gazes at the sky while the drizzling rain gradually soaks through the layers of her clothing.

Guido Hatz is crazy; therefore, Britta isn't.

For a while she considers it possible that recent events have absolutely nothing to do with her. A failed terrorist attack, carried out by two idiots who turned a really bad idea into even worse action. A multimillionaire crackpot who drives around in a pickup truck playing the angel. A dead would-be terrorist who takes his own life while behind bars, probably with the help of belt or shoelaces, which, *pace* Hollywood movies, prisoners in detention are definitely allowed to wear.

When someone once asked Janina how she always managed to be cheerful in these troubled times, she replied, "I just relish the thought that the great majority of things have nothing to do with me."

Britta peers at her face in the VW bus's tinted side window. To her surprise, she looks the same as always. The events have left no visible imprint. She likes what she sees. The face is pretty in a way that doesn't remain in the memory. The clothes expensive, but sending no signal. The blond hair too short to wish to please. Middling tall, middling slim, a woman without burdens or passions, a woman who eats in moderation, loves in moderation, exercises in moderation. A living average, she is, and things will go on that way, a life lived in a straight line, right to the end. While she watches herself, Britta feels her consciousness rise to the surface again after days of lying buried deep inside her, where there's nothing to be found. Health and happiness lie on the surface, not underground. The deeper a person sinks into herself, the more despair she feels. Britta knows that from her work. Now all she wants to do is to go home and stand under a hot shower, which will cleanse her outwardly and inwardly, will wash off everything that's been stuck to her since the Leipzig attack. After that—she knows this with certainty—she'll be free.

When Vera's asleep, Britta talks to Richard about Hatz. They're sitting in the living room, each of them holding a glass of wine, and looking out through the picture window. Although there are still some two hours remaining before sundown, it's almost dark; the drizzle has grown into a heavy downpour. The water plunges down out of a black sky, plants and trees bow under the torrents, and cars drive slowly, pushing little halos before them.

"He came to the practice today. Guido Hatz."

"Is that so? What did he want?"

"Basically, he said I have a terrible aura and he's my guardian angel."

"Typical Guido!"

While Richard laughs, Britta gets annoyed because he calls Hatz by his first name. It sounds affected.

"Furthermore, he thinks I should take a break from work so you can concentrate on busting your butt for Swappie."

Richard suddenly switches to a serious pose and says, "The next months will be pretty hard, it's true."

"Tell me I didn't really hear that," says Britta, stunned.

"Wait a second, darling. You've worked so hard for several years now, you've fed the family and financed the house. Why shouldn't you take it easy for a change? It would be only right."

"Come on, don't you get it?" Britta sounds more aggressive than she means to. "How much I work has absolutely nothing to do with you and Smart Swap." She gazes at him, appraising him. "Or do you think like him? You think I'm suffering from burnout?"

His hesitation wounds her. He's supposed to believe she can deal with anything. Always. That's what he's there for.

"No," he says. "I think we have to get a handle on your stomach pains. You must let a doctor examine you. No more putting it off."

"Have I ever complained?"

"That's beside the point. You haven't been yourself for the last few weeks. And you're gone a lot. Vera constantly has to stay at Janina's."

"Did you and Hatz talk about me?"

"No."

"You really didn't?"

"No! This has nothing at all to do with Hatz!"

"Have you ever wondered whether he might be crazy?"

Richard looks at her queerly. "You mean you think someone has to be crazy to invest in my ideas?"

Now a quarrel's in the air, a spat Britta didn't want. The conversation has taken a completely wrong turn. She gives irony a try: "Right! Only psychopaths believe in Swappie!" She kisses him, which costs a bit of effort. "Anyway, you've got to admit, Hatz is a strange bird. Why is he following me? Why is he so concerned about my health?"

"Following you? I thought he was in your office today."

"Do you know what kind of car Guido Hatz has?"

"Probably lots of cars."

"A Toyota Hilux."

"So what?"

"It's a white pickup."

"I don't understand what you're getting at."

"Remember our trip to Wiebüttel? The pickup that kept running up behind us."

"Britta." Richard puts down his glass so he can take her hands. "That's just ridiculous."

"A few days later, he drove past the house. I saw him."

"Stop it, please!"

"I'm dead certain. You'll have to cope with the fact that your golden goose is a nutcase. At the very least."

"Darling, what you're saying is absurd, can't you see that?"

"You think it's normal for him to come and see me in my office?"

"He wanted to meet you. He's something of an oddball, that's all."

"So you think I'm the one who's nuts, not him?"

"Nobody's nuts." Richard tries to stroke her hair, but she evades his hand.

The next morning, she takes her bicycle to work. Despite the argument with Richard, she slept for a few hours during the night and feels rested. She's still pretty furious with him, however; at the breakfast table, the two of them barely spoke.

In the dental lab, the blond receptionist in the white coat is already at her station. When Britta greets the girl, she merely stares through her. Britta wonders whether she's sat there the whole night, and whether she's a human person or a surveillance robot installed by Guido Hatz.

She can tell at a glance that Babak's not in. The ceiling lights are off, the dot picture lies untouched. She doesn't bother to get off her bicycle and unlock the door; instead she resumes pedaling at once, past the shops in the Passage—the great majority of them standing empty—and back to Kurt Schumacher Street, where she heads farther downtown. John F. Kennedy Square is a work site yet again, traffic's been rerouted, and everywhere there are yellow plastic barriers, clattering jackhammers, bellowing workers. As far as Britta knows, a "Sport Is Public" venue will be built in the middle of the intersection, with yoga areas, Nordic walking parcours, and trampolines, but who knows if that's still the plan. When the CCC took over the city administration too, she stopped following the local news. The monitors on the traffic lights announce the start of a culture festival, "Folks, Rock," with concerts, panel discussions, and programs for children.

As she passes the Babylon, she casts a quick glance through the window. It's not Sahid who's sitting at the counter, but a woman with ash-blond hair. *So what,* thinks Britta. *It's got nothing to do with me.*

Babak's apartment is on "the Top," a narrow street that ends at the pedestrian zone. According to Babak, he bought the apartment mostly on account of its address, because he gets a kick out of coming home and thinking, *This is the Top*. A few years previously, Babak had his apartment painted, and now it's aglow with freshness and cleanliness, the windows spotless, the plants on the balcony carefully arranged, the awnings colorful and decorative. Under one of them, however, the flower boxes hold only a few withered stalks. Babak doesn't really know what to do with a balcony.

Britta locks her bike to a lamppost and rings the doorbell. Nothing happens. As she figured. Once Babak decides to sleep, he sleeps: twelve to fourteen hours at a stretch. When Britta rings the third time, she holds her finger on the button until the door buzzer sounds. She hurries to the stairs—the stairwell smells like roasted vegetables—and goes up them two at a time to the fourth floor. Babak's door is ajar, and just as she's about to push it, it's opened from inside.

Incredulous, Britta scrutinizes the half-asleep figure standing in front of her. It's not Babak, it's Julietta. She's wearing gray sweatpants, cut off at the knee, revealing her matchstick-thin legs. Her top is an extra-large black T-shirt that probably once belonged to a man. Britta shuts her eyes, fervently hoping that when she opens them again, Julietta will have disappeared. It doesn't work. Britta pushes the girl aside and dashes through the entrance hall to the living room, which is more like a huge storeroom. Little has changed since Britta's last visit, except that the quantity of waste glass, the piles of old newspapers, and the heaps of electronic junk have grown even larger. The mattress in the living room, covered with churned-up bedclothes, is new, as is the little pile next to it: books, writing materials, a cell phone with plugged-in earphones, a few articles of black clothing, and a studded belt that Britta has seen Julietta wearing before. There's also an ashtray filled with cigarette butts and marijuana roaches, as well as several boxes of pills, which Britta identifies as Ativan. She rushes to the window and flings both casements open, like a mother who comes home from a trip and must confront what her unsupervised daughter's been up to. Fresh air surges in from outside, surprisingly cool, and bringing a slight scent of autumn.

Julietta has followed her and is leaning in the doorway. "It's not what you think," she says.

Britta could have laughed out loud, except she's too furious to laugh. "Babak's gay, you silly cow," she hisses. "Where is he?"

"Sleeping."

"Not for much longer."

"Okay," says Julietta. "I'd better scram."

She walks over to her mattress, extracts a pair of black jeans from the tangled mass, and pulls them on without removing her cutoffs. Britta gazes at her for a moment and realizes, with some relief, that she's taking her cigarettes but not her pillboxes. The door of the apartment slams shut so hard that only seconds later, the bedroom door opens and Babak looks out sleepily into the hall. He looks overdressed in his checkered silk pajamas. The room behind him is pitch-dark.

"Coffee?" Without waiting for an answer, Babak shuffles off in the direction of the kitchen.

Britta's so perplexed that she remains motionless, fists clenched, while two cups are produced from somewhere in the kitchen and quickly rinsed, and shortly thereafter, the espresso machine starts to make noise. Babak reappears and hands her a cup of coffee with a lot of milk and sugar, the way she likes it. He's thrown on a bathrobe with differently colored checks that suits him as little as the pajamas do. He holds his cup in both hands and leans into the open window. Since there's no chair to be found anywhere in the room, and since Britta feels no inclination to sit on a cardboard moving box, she simply stays where she is.

"Are you mad?"

Given the situation, the question is a joke. Even though The Bridge has no hard-and-fast rules about where candidates should reside for the duration of the program, it's obvious that private accommodations at Babak's or Britta's would completely contradict the spirit of their method—which requires them to keep their distance, to avoid identification with clients, and most particularly to avoid befriending them. What stuns Britta most is that Babak has told her nothing about his new domestic arrangement. Then again, she's told him nothing about Guido Hatz, at least not so far, because Hatz is the reason she's come here in the first place. The harmony between Britta and Babak is so perfect that they even keep secrets from each other simultaneously.

"She was being harassed in the Deutsches Haus," says Babak.

"By the other candidates?"

"By the other guests."

"Did she follow instructions and have breakfast in her room?"

"Of course. She didn't go to the hotel restaurant, she didn't go to the bar, and she stayed in her room as much as possible. Nevertheless, people were always accosting her, in the elevator, on the stairs, at the reception desk. Once a guy knocked on her door and asked her if she'd like to go out for coffee with him."

"Shit." Britta sits on the floor and starts drinking her coffee in tiny sips. It tastes rich, much better than her office coffee.

"We didn't consider that," she says.

Any woman who stays alone in a hotel for weeks draws attention, to say nothing of a woman like Julietta. They put her in the Deutsches Haus because that's where they put all their candidates, the "participants in Bridge Coaching, Self-Discovery, and New Beginnings," corporate rates applicable, the hotel staff friendly and discreet; there have never been any complaints. But Julietta is the first woman in the program, and Britta has had no experience in that regard.

"One evening, there she was, standing at my door. Sure, I know all the reasons why I shouldn't have let her in, but she would have had the same problems in any other hotel."

"And when were you going to tell me about this?"

"Uh, never." Babak grins. "If you hadn't barged in here, you would never have found out." After a pause, he adds, "As a matter of fact, why are you here? What do you want?"

Britta clears her throat. She finishes her coffee. A fluttering in her stomach calls attention to itself. Now it's her turn to make a confession.

"Shall we go and have breakfast somewhere?"

Minutes later, they're sitting outside the corner delicatessen, wrapped in fleece blankets and ordering croissants, strawberries, and yet more caffè latte for Britta. She waits until Babak has shoved half a croissant into his mouth and then begins to tell her tale. About the trip to Wiebüttel and the white pickup that kept crowding them. About how the same vehicle drove by their house not long afterward. About the magical, out-of-the-blue investment in Smart Swap, the investor's mustache, and his appearance in the practice the previous day. About burnout, guardian angels, and the idea of taking some time off.

Babak chews his croissant while Britta speaks, and after she's finished he swallows it, washes it down with coffee, and remains silent for a while. The expressions on his face range from perplexity to amusement to horror. When he's reached a consensus with himself regarding a response, he raises his head, looks her straight in the eyes, and says, "And you accuse me of not telling you about Julietta?"

"I wasn't sure if I was imagining things or not."

"Since when have we stopped telling each other about things we imagine?"

"You're right. I'm sorry."

They look at each other, at first appraisingly, and then affectionately, and it's as if they have, in this moment, renewed a vow. To tell each other everything, and always to listen to the other's opinion. Britta puts her hand on Babak's; he smiles and tolerates the touch for a few seconds before pulling his hand back and hiding it under the table.

"Let's consider," he says. "Actually, there's only one possible explanation."

"And that would be . . . ?"

"I don't like saying this, but you were probably right from the start."

For the first time in her life, Britta's not happy to have been right. Just the opposite. Babak ignores her scowl and continues unmoved: "Guido Hatz has invested a great deal of money."

"We already know that."

"Not only in Swappie. He's put a lot of cash into an outfit that's in competition with The Bridge. And now they're doing their utmost to eliminate us."

"That's why he shows up at the office, talks about burnout, and recommends that I close up shop for a while?"

Babak dabs at croissant crumbs with a finger and sticks them into his mouth. "Well, it would be a plausible strategy," he says. "With the money for Swappie, he drives The Bridge out of the market—and that's it."

Now Britta too starts playing with her croissant, which she has yet to bite into. What Babak says sounds logical, but she doesn't like it, all the same. She much prefers the idea that Hatz is crazy, because in that case, she could simply go on as before.

"Next he'll threaten you with letting Richard's company go

bust if you insist on keeping The Bridge in business. And if Swappie does well, he hasn't even lost money. Two birds with one stone."

"How does he even know what we do?"

Britta is better aware than anyone that this is a stupid question. Any determined person could find out what The Bridge does. They've never tried to hide. Legally, The Bridge conducts its activities in a gray area. Assisting suicide is not a crime. The Bridge is not a terrorist organization. Operations are planned and carried out by the implementing entities. Britta and Babak take the laws of reason into account, maintain a low profile, emphasize digital hygiene, limit contact with end clients to a minimum, avoid developing behavior patterns that could make a profiler nervous. Remain inconspicuous, don't expand. In fact, their contacts with the authorities are limited to tickets for running red lights, as Britta occasionally does on her bicycle, and to their annual tax filing, in which they declare, as prescribed by law, a portion of their revenue as profit, while the rest is reinvested faster than the Revenue Service can say "cash accounting method."

"The question is, what do we do next?"

Babak is apparently taking pleasure in the role of strategist after spending a week protesting against every move Britta made. She sighs. At the neighboring table, a young woman is staring with bared teeth into her smartphone's selfie function and using her long fingernails to tidy up her interdental spaces. Diagonally across the street, the cashier in a health food store steps outside and lights herself a cigarette. A group of punks, every one of them over fifty, sporting graying mohawks and accompanied by old dogs, move past and then sit on the ground in front of a coffeehouse. Farther down the street, the bright yellow T-shirts of the Amnesty activists stand out; they've built a large booth, where they wait to accost passersby. Britta feels like a visitor to an open-air museum. There are actually still people who act as though you could face this haywire world and retain your composure. As though punk, cigarettes, and Amnesty still meant something.

Babak hasn't stopped talking: ". . . something really big," he's just said. "Something that will establish our position in the market once and for all."

"Are you suggesting what I've been preaching for days?" asks Britta.

"Hatz has caused a fundamental change in the situation." Babak raises the empty espresso cup to his lips and tries to slurp up the dregs.

"Well, there's no question about the right person to carry out a major operation," says Britta.

"I feel the same way," says Babak.

"Then we should start discussing possible buyers soon."

"Maybe it would be good to bring Julietta into the discussions as early as possible."

"Julietta?" Britta places her glass on the table, as carefully as if it could shatter into pieces at the slightest touch. "I was thinking about Marquardt."

"You can't be serious."

"Julietta's only on Step Three."

"She's the best candidate we've ever had."

"We can't know that yet. Marquardt is as good as finished with the program. He's reliable, conscientious, free of empathy. He's our man."

"What's wrong with you?" Babak asks her. When she looks down, he grabs her arm. "You took Julietta into the program for exactly this moment. Why are you backing away now?"

Britta mutely shakes her head. She could, if she wished to,

utter a series of vague sentences. She could say that she has a bad feeling. That Julietta's presence makes her uneasy. That the girl smells like trouble. Babak would sweep away such explanations with a simple wave of his hand. And he'd be right.

The truth is that Julietta scares her. But she would never admit that. Not even to herself.

"She's a woman," Britta finally says. "We don't have any experience with women. Women make people nervous."

"*She* makes *you* nervous."

"She attracts attention wherever she goes."

"Precisely!" cries Babak. "The media will run her story night and day. Her photograph will spread around the web like an epidemic. With the right planning, she has the stuff to be a superstar. Then it'll be clear that if The Bridge has such cracker-jacks in its program, Hatz or whoever else can take their amateur start-up and pack it in."

There's something contagious about Babak's zeal. It's great that he can at last feel enthusiasm for the big plan; it's great that they're both pulling in the same direction again. Besides, Britta of course knows that he's right. He leans forward and increases the pressure of his fingers on her arm.

"Marquardt's a safe bet," he says. "But Julietta's the bomb."

Chapter **16**

One hour later, Britta's alone in Babak's apartment, wandering through the squalid rooms. When she made the offer to wait for Julietta here while Babak traveled to Bochum, she didn't think about the mess. She can't sit down; she can't even bear to stand still for longer than a few seconds. It's as though the disorder will infect her if she doesn't remain in motion. For Britta, filth is an existential problem. Only from order can sense arise. But no matter what people do, in the end everything always sinks into disorder and dirt. Britta looks at Julietta's jumbled bed and, next to it, the unsightly pile of clothes and other stuff. The young woman seems to feel comfortable here. She fits in seamlessly with Babak's chaos, as though she's always lived with him. What do those two carry inside themselves that makes them indifferent to external clutter?

Britta starts by gathering together some scattered articles of clothing and stuffing them into the washing machine. Then she puts clean sheets on Babak's bed, sorts magazines, and puts them into folding storage crates, with which she builds a little set of shelves. In the dining room, she finds a stack of moving boxes, flat and unused, which she assembles and arranges as another set of shelves. In these she sorts whatever she finds lying around; one box holds Julietta's meager possessions, a second is for electronics, another for shoes, yet another for everything else. Britta opens the windows, fills and starts the dishwasher, aggressively vacuums all the rooms.

She's running hot water into a bucket and—in the absence of a floor-cleaning product—adding dish soap, when she hears a key turning in the lock of the apartment door. Barefoot, with rubber gloves on her hands, Britta walks to the entrance hall, where Julietta has remained standing, her eyes focused on the floor, her long dark hair in her face. How cynical of Mother Nature, to stick such a black soul behind such an angelic appearance! There's no doubt that Babak's right when he advocates so hard for her. If you wash and comb Julietta and get the right clothes on her, you can smuggle her in anywhere. As a volunteer at a television station, as an airline passenger in first class, as an intern in the Reichstag. She's the perfect terror doll.

"Are you all right?" Britta asks.

Julietta doesn't answer, doesn't look at her, doesn't speak.

"Babak and I have cleared things up," says Britta, pressing the cleaning bucket into her hand. "You can stay."

Julietta's unchanged expression fails to hide her relief completely. "My first mission?" she says, looking at the cleaning bucket. They both have to smile.

For the next two hours, they work their way through Babak's apartment. Britta forgets that she started housecleaning only to pass the time while waiting for Julietta. The project becomes a campaign they conduct side by side, soldier and commander. After the floors are clean, they tackle the kitchen. In the oven, a half-inch-thick layer of charred pizza crumbs has formed. In the refrigerator, shrink-wrapped food packages compete to display the oldest sell-by date. In the microwave, a glass of milk must have boiled over a long time ago. At some point, Julietta begins to talk. She tells Britta about her cat, which is named Jessie after a character in a novel, and which lays a dead mouse in front of her bed every night. About her parents, who have joined an organization dedicated to maintaining the purity of German culture. About their spacious villa, with a sauna no one uses, a fitness room nobody enters, and a music system that's never turned on. Britta and Julietta work together, always occupied with the same task: they bend side by side over the edge of the bathtub, jointly climb a folding ladder to dust the kitchen cabinets, polish the same window. Julietta moves about with great concentration, mixes cleaning products and water in proportions so precise she might be fabricating explosives, shows no sign of fatigue or disgust. How wonderful it must be, to serve an alien will! Julietta follows Britta's movements, anticipates her every thought, preempts her every instruction, and all the while seems completely calm and totally within herself. Almost happy.

To conclude, they clean all the wall tiles and hang the freshly spun wash on a collapsible drying rack.

Britta pulls off her rubber gloves and dries her face with a paper towel. The apartment smells like vinegar and lemon. Britta wonders whether Babak's going to get angry when he sees what they've done and smiles at the thought.

Julietta follows her into the entrance hall. Something that can't be put into words has happened. They calmly gaze into each other's eyes.

"See you tomorrow," says Britta.

Around seven o'clock in the evening, Britta's phone rings. Richard, carrying a bowl of creamed potatoes into the dining room, glances at the display screen and calls, "It's Babak!"

When Richard hands her the device, Britta takes it uneasily. She and Babak had agreed to discuss the results of his trip tomorrow, in the practice. But a minute later she's got her jacket on and is hurrying to the door. "Have to go out again! Office emergency!"

She drives through the residential district in the evening stillness and turns onto Saarbrückener Street. She passes the playground and continues in a northerly direction until she reaches the parking lot of the Waldhaus Ölper restaurant, where Babak's already waiting for her. With his Gore-Tex shoes and functional jacket, he looks like he's ready for a hike. They exchange a brief hug and walk the last several meters to the end of the paved street. A beaten path goes around the obstacle and meanders in a wavy line between tall trees before disappearing into the undergrowth.

The Ölper wood isn't big, but its growth is abundant and luxuriant, a fortuitously preserved patch of forest between the city and the autobahn, ideal for dog walking, drug dealing, and first kisses. Around dinnertime, there's no one to be seen there. An odor of mushrooms mingles with a fresh fragrance, so that the place smells simultaneously of the beginning and the end. The noise from the autobahn provides a soothing background music. A few weary birds chirrup in the bushes. The soft ground feels good under her feet, so good that Britta forgets for a moment her aversion to the chaotic character of Nature.

They go along side by side, and Babak has already begun to speak. He describes how he parked his rented car in a row house development in Bochum, among workers' accommodations from the days of lignite and smelting furnaces, today transformed into the lattice-fence, telescopic-clothesline world of the lower middle class. The Blattner residence differs in no way from any of the neighboring houses. Net curtains on the windows, birdhouse on the tree. The tiny patch of front lawn was freshly mowed, causing Babak to wonder whether he'd mistaken the address. But when Mrs. Blattner opened the door, he knew at once that he was in the right place. Her face looked like an old piece of paper, a page so yellowed that you couldn't read it anymore. She explained that her husband had gone to work, to his job with the sanitation department—in the office, not on a garbage truck—because work was his way of dealing with what happened. Mrs. Blattner led Babak to a room, obviously "the good room," with a small crochet cloth on the coffee table and a picture over the sofa of women gathering wheat straw. Babak declined her offer of coffee and, when he sat down, used only the front edge of the chair. Mrs. Blattner squeezed her hands between her knees and cautiously asked him how he'd known Markus. Before he could answer, she blurted out that she hoped he was not "one of them." Babak understood that he'd been "one of them" his whole life long, but he couldn't determine whether his being a Muslim or his being gay was in question here. He assured the lady that he came from a family of Iraqi Christians, and that he'd never visited a mosque in his life. Mrs. Blattner relaxed a little. He and Markus, Babak said, lying some more, had met while playing computer games on the Internet; he'd seen her son in person only a few times.

From the way Mrs. Blattner listened to him, seemingly unmoved but in reality barely suppressing her craving to know, Babak recognized that she was suffering not only from the loss of her son, but also, and at least as much, from the fear that Markus could have led a double life. Babak decided to help the woman, and besides, what he was going to say to her would be in line with what he had wanted to say to her anyway.

"I can assure you, Mrs. Blattner, Markus was no Islamist."

It took a while for this information to get through to her. It almost seemed as though the news media had already shaped an immovable reality in her head: ISIS's claim of responsibility, the headlines about the convert from Leipzig, the roaring of Interior Minister Wagenknecht.

But when she understood, her features softened, showing first confusion and then slight signs of hope, which were quickly clouded over again with mistrust. "How can you possibly know that?"

Babak told her that he and Markus had had long conversations on TeamSpeak, sometimes just the two of them, sometimes together with other players. They talked about God and the world, he said, or rather, about the loss of God and weltschmerz, and also sometimes about very private matters and opinions. To increase the credibility of his story, Babak wove in some small details he knew from Lassie: that Markus had liked to read romantic novels written for women; that he spent his free time in front of his computer, snacking on pistachios; that he loved martial arts movies from the last century; that he was scared of snakes and allergic to strawberries. Mrs. Blattner, spellbound, soaked up these descriptions, occasionally smiling when she recognized her boy with particular clarity.

"We played and chatted almost to the very end," said Babak. "If Markus had decided to convert to Islam, I would have known it."

Mrs. Blattner began to cry. She clapped her hands to her face like a child, sobbing "I knew it, I knew it," and in the end tried to kneel on the rug in front of Babak, which he forestalled as well as he could.

Then Babak came out with his request. Markus's death would give him no rest, he said, he didn't believe Markus had killed himself, he absolutely wanted the circumstances to be clarified. He fervently implored Mrs. Blattner to have an autopsy performed.

"If they tell you you're talking about incurring considerable costs, I hereby offer to cover them for you. Markus was my friend."

"Too late," said Mrs. Blattner harshly. "He was cremated this morning."

Britta and Babak have reached the end of the Ölper wood. The wire mesh fence separating the forest's edge from the autobahn has been trodden down in many places, so that deer or wild boar with the urge to run amok have no problem reaching the roadway. Trucks and cars thunder past in dense succession. Babak and Britta turn left, where the beaten path runs parallel to the autobahn for a few meters before retreating back into the wood and winding its way toward the fields. The sky, having freed itself from clouds for the last hours of the day, is a refulgent, saturated blue. The sunlight shines warm among the trees and sets midges dancing.

"The cremation has already taken place?" Britta asks.

"Someone called up the parents and persuaded them that it was the best thing to do. The state would undertake to pay all expenses, and in any case the cause of death wasn't in dispute. The father was on the phone and consented immediately. Incinerate the son of a bitch."

"And of course they don't know exactly who it was that called."

"Mrs. Blattner thinks it was someone from the prison administration, but she didn't understand the name. Around noon on the same day, an e-mail from the funeral home informed them that the urn would be transferred to Bochum. I had her show me the message. The designated clients are the Blattners themselves, and a brief annotation says, 'Invoice paid in full.'"

"Well, that stinks to high heaven," says Britta.

"The best is yet to come."

At the conclusion of his visit, Babak asked for a photograph of Markus as a souvenir of his friend. Mrs. Blattner led him from the living room to the staircase and then up to the attic, which served as a storeroom. It smelled like the cheap detergent that Babak's mother also used, a sweetish smell that nearly brought him to his knees. On the floor lay large squares of shabby carpet; light entered through a little skylight that dust and spiderwebs had rendered almost opaque. They bent over to make their way through hanging laundry, passed suitcases waiting to go on long-planned trips and baskets filled with toys longing in vain for a grandchild. In the remotest corner, something was glowing, and Babak recognized two artificial candles. On an overturned chest, Mrs. Blattner had erected a secret altar to her son: a framed photograph; a laptop computer, open but not turned on; a bowl of pistachios; a well-worn teddy bear. At this sight, Babak couldn't stop the tears that sprang from his eyes.

"If my husband finds this," Mrs. Blattner said, "he'll smash it all to smithereens. As far as he's concerned, Markus is an enemy of the state."

Babak cried. For Markus, for his mother. Because he was lying to her. Because she took his tears as a further sign of the genuineness of his feelings. She put an arm around his shoulders, as if she wanted to comfort him, and reached for the framed photo with her free hand. "It's quite new, not even four weeks old," she said.

Suddenly, there's a thumping sound in the distance, a hissing and rattling like a machine gun, and then some deep thuds that make the foliage in the Ölper wood tremble. The CCC's culture festival in the city park is getting under way. The forest falls silent; birds and insects seem to be holding their breath. Britta doesn't like fireworks. When she hears the detonations, she feels an urgent need to throw herself on the ground.

"Do you have the photo with you?"

Babak hands her his cell phone. In spite of the bad light, he succeeded in taking a decent snapshot. The picture shows a man in his middle twenties, his hair cut short and an insecure look in his eyes.

"What's that on his neck?" Britta asks.

The neckline of Markus's T-shirt reveals part of a tattoo, several letters—TYHEA—belonging to a longer inscription; the rest is hidden under the black fabric. Britta flinches at the next fireworks explosion.

"I asked his mother," says Babak. "The tattoo is new."

"What does it say?"

"'EMPTY HEARTS.'"

"A Molly Richter fan?"

"The song will make it hard for Lassie to come up with anything useful."

They stand still, looking at Babak's phone like two hikers bending over a map.

"Do you notice anything else?" Babak asks.

Britta looks again, more closely this time. Insecure eyes, high forehead, nose a bit too small, square jaw, and a disagreeable facial expression somewhere between weakness and insolence. Something seems to be missing. Britta concentrates so hard that it almost hurts. She's barely aware of the exploding fireworks.

"Did he normally wear glasses?" she asks slowly.

"He used to, but then he opted for contact lenses."

Britta mentally puts a pair of eyeglasses on the tattooed man. Then she's got it. She stares at Babak in astonishment. The detonations reach their high point, accompanied by intense crackling, until a final bang rings out, resonates, and subsides in waves, as though a high-rise building has been blown up somewhere.

"He was in the program with us," she says.

"More than five years ago," Babak replies. "He dropped out because of misconduct."

Chapter **17**

The next evening, she and Richard have another quarrel. Britta briefly swings by the house, helps Vera with her homework, and tells Richard she has to leave again for a business appointment.

"Does that mean you're going to miss dinner again?"

"Only today."

"Yesterday too."

"Yesterday was an emergency."

"Suppose you cook dinner again soon? Like you did a few days ago? That was really nice."

Recently, he's been weaving hints into their conversations. Might she be able to take Vera to school tomorrow? Wouldn't it be possible for her to help look after the garden now and again? Or he asks her how she's feeling. Wonders if she's having more stomach problems. Says she looks tired.

All of which annoys Britta. She's been providing for the family for years, and now, only because this Hatz person has suddenly appeared, she's supposed to retire, without further ado. As if her work has always been nothing but a temporary solution, a stopgap measure until the day when Richard would finally start earning money! As if The Bridge could be switched on and off like a lamp!

"But you don't have to stop," says Richard. "What we're talking about is only a sabbatical."

She wants to retort that Swappie, no matter whether it brings in money someday or not, is still just another toy for the stock market assholes. A tool for making the world a slightly worse place. Whereas her work makes the world better. Nowadays, whoever's in need of an assassin no longer has to fall back on purblind jihadis with narcissistic personality disorder or half-children with weapons fetishes or psychopaths who hate foreigners and women. Instead, such employers can receive a professionally trained, thoroughly tested martyr who wants to die for a higher cause. The Bridge has put an end to terror anarchy. Now there are binding agreements and controlled victim counts. Slowly but surely, the industry players have adopted this business model. The practiced media report successful attacks, show pictures of uniformed security forces, and interview politicians, who stress that the threat level has been and continues to be high, but is no cause for panic, while their staff gets to work on the next security package. The level of hysteria has considerably decreased. It's not very easy to put into words, and yet it's rather obvious: since The Bridge has been around, suicide attacks have become less chic. Free-floating copycat attackers have practically disappeared. On the other hand, "crash driving" has become much more common, and the number of its victims has exceeded the terrorist victim tally for a long time now. Britta and Babak have often discussed this: every industrialized society seems to need a certain number of berserkers running amok, while the outward form the murderous frenzy takes is only a question of prevailing fashion.

Sixteen-year-olds who run through their schools with pump guns. Twenty-year-olds who blow themselves up with bomb belts. Eighteen-year-olds who blindfold themselves on the autobahn and mash the gas pedal to the floor. Mounting a charge against the walls of a monolithic order. The blind spot in the system. The itchy patch that every society needs in order to give itself a thorough scratching from time to time. The Bridge is part of a natural cycle that moves from war through pacification and then back to war. For Britta, this knowledge is sufficient to convince her that her work makes sense. It's always a question of a balance of power, of establishing an equilibrium between chaos and order, cleanliness and filth. It's enough for her to know that she's on the clean side.

Naturally, she can't explain this to Richard. Nevertheless, it's imperative that he know how important her work is.

She just leaves him standing there, slams the front door, and rides her bicycle into the city. She won't simply abandon the field. She won't cede her lucrative operation to an obscenely rich water diviner and his badly organized outfit. Let Hatz blather on about burnout and make threats and buy Richard and pressure her as much as he wants.

The whole business is going to blow up in your face, Britta thinks as she locks up her bicycle in front of the Good Times restaurant. *Literally, if need be. "Empty Hearts," really, what an adolescent name.*

Before she steps into the restaurant, she takes a few deep breaths and concentrates on being aware of the weather. It hasn't rained today, the air is warm, it smells of lilacs and asphalt. Slowly, she comes out of her trance.

Babak and Julietta are already there. They're sitting at a window table, their heads close together; Britta hears Julietta laugh. They look like a couple in love, those two. Or at least like old friends. While Britta is approaching the table, she looks at Babak and gently shakes her head. She's here for a business meeting, not a bar date among friends. Babak and Julietta apparently don't share this view. Babak's in a good mood, and Julietta has even done a little work on her appearance. She's woven her hair into small plaits and tied them into a loose knot; she looks like a jungle princess. In general, her affect is more upright than usual, her facial complexion is healthy, her cheeks and eyes radiant. Britta glances fleetingly at the window to see if this change is due to the lighting inside.

"Are you all right?" asks Babak.

He too looks quite rested, which can only come as a surprise to Britta. They've spent the day analyzing the latest findings and in so doing have once again let the weekly reports languish. It cost an enormous effort to uncover a worthwhile photograph of the second suicide bomber, Andreas Muradow, who died at the Leipzig airport. When Babak finally found a photo that could be adequately enlarged, it became clear that not only had Andreas, like Markus, sported an "Empty Hearts" tattoo, but also that he, exactly like his accomplice, was an old acquaintance from The Bridge's earlier days. Britta thinks she remembers that Andreas also participated in the program for no longer than two weeks, but she isn't completely sure. Since all data concerning processed candidates is destroyed, it's not possible to reconstruct details.

The conclusion—namely that former clients of The Bridge have joined together to compete with it—in no way represents an improvement in the situation. Even though the two perpetrators were in the program only briefly, they had inside knowledge of the enterprise. Britta peers into Babak's and Julietta's jovial faces. Apparently, she's the only one worried about the future of the practice.

Their food arrives, and they lean over it. Babak praises the lasagna and has Britta try a bite. A bloody steak seasoned with herb butter and accompanied by potatoes is lying on Julietta's plate.

"But you don't even eat meat," says Britta, dipping her spoon in her spinach soup.

"I'm not sure how, but I thought steak would be good for my project."

Now Britta understands the hairdo too: Julietta's not a jungle princess, she's a warrior. As arranged, Babak has informed Julietta that she might possibly be employed on a special mission in the near future. And Julietta has immediately begun to prepare herself for the assignment, even though she has no idea what its nature will be. This touches Britta so deeply that she forgets her bad mood.

"She's stopped smoking," says Babak. "No pills, no joints."

"And tomorrow I start with stamina training." Julietta begins to eat, grimacing only slightly as she does.

"You mustn't be scared," says Britta. "It's all part of the usual routine."

"I'm not scared," says Julietta. Her knife, fork, and masticatory organs work together in focused concentration. It's plain that she doesn't know if the food tastes good or not. She's eating because she has decided to eat.

"Normally, we don't discuss practical application until the end of the program," Britta points out, opening the business segment of their meeting. "But special circumstances have arisen that make a somewhat different approach necessary."

Julietta nods and chews. Babak has already told her the same thing.

"Regardless, we absolutely cannot propose a candidate who will then have a change of heart."

"I'm not going to have a change of heart."

Britta executes a hand movement intended to mean that Julietta has said all that's needed. "In your case," Britta goes on, "we'll speed up the process. The main thing is to find out quickly what you can be employed to do."

"I can do anything. You train me for whatever you want, and then I'll get it done."

Babak and Britta smile at her eagerness.

"We don't train you. We prepare you mentally."

"I'd really like to learn to shoot."

"Julietta, look at me."

She interrupts her chewing and lifts her eyes obediently.

"This isn't a video game. This is real."

"Do you think I'm stupid?"

"People will die."

"Me, among others." She laughs and sticks the next piece of meat in her mouth. Britta pensively watches her eat for a while. Julietta is almost too perfect to be true. They can only hope she's more than a child who thinks she's Mega-Melanie. Never before has Britta struggled so hard to keep her distance. She often feels an urge to give Julietta a slap; at other times, she simply wants to take the girl in her arms. *Pull yourself together,* her inner voice admonishes her.

"Does it matter to you how many victims there will be?" Babak asks.

"Is that some kind of joke?" There's genuine surprise in Julietta's eyes. "Just look around. If it was up to me, I'd say let's do something with ricin and the Berlin Waterworks."

"Okay." Babak nods. "Message understood."

"*We* are doing nothing at all," Britta says sharply. "We're a healing practice. Our business is psychotherapy. And The Bridge has clear rules concerning the maximum victim count."

Julietta and Babak remain silent.

"We'll give some thought to potential contractors later today," Britta adds, somewhat more calmly.

In principle, The Bridge doesn't differentiate between clients. Especially since they—when considered in the clear light of day—are all pretty tiresome. Focused on petroleum and geostrategy, ISIS is a by-product of American foreign policy and neither more nor less repulsive than it is. The tree huggers have achieved a level of blindness one could almost envy, and Separatists have a mind-numbing way of feeling they're always right. With Nationalists, you never know if you're going to find the stupid variety or the shrewd variety worse, and the Frexit, Spexit, and Swexit people are as insufferable as children who destroy a sand castle simply because they feel like wrecking something.

Fortunately, it's not Britta's task to adjudicate the legitimacy of human motives. The circumstances of an operation generally don't matter to her, as long as everything is done according to the rules. However, since—for the first time in its history—The Bridge is about to act in its own interest, an optimal reaction from the media is a top priority. For days, Britta's been mulling over the question of what could be done, and with whom. As she was lying beside Richard last night, sleepless again, the exciting idea came to her: they'll blow up a bridge, namely the Moltke Bridge in Berlin, directly behind the Chancellery. The Bridge sends the industry a powerfully symbolic message; the target is spectacular. All they need now is the suitable client. Maybe someone from what's left of Occupy. Or the Bavarian Separatists.

Ordinarily, the candidates are involved in the decision-making process; Britta thinks it important that people should be comfortable with their assignment. It's helpful when they have at least a rudimentary political consciousness, anti-Brussels or pro–climate protection or what have you. In most cases, however, the candidates are preoccupied not with politics but with their own personal misery, which is why part of Britta's job is to supply convictions. "You're so good at selling convictions because you yourself don't have any," Babak once said to her, meaning it as a joke. What's certain is that the more strongly candidates feel they're going to die a meaningful death for a good cause, the more happily they cross over the last bridge.

Julietta's busy cutting the second half of her steak into small pieces, adorning each with some dabs of herb butter and a slice of roasted potato, and shoving the resulting morsel into her mouth.

"What do you think about the government district in Berlin?" Britta asks her.

"Not much. That's where the CCC assholes are."

"Wonderful." Britta cleans her soup bowl with a piece of bread and gratefully accepts Babak's offer of the rest of his lasagna. "Then I have a lovely scenario for you."

Julietta nods. "The main thing is for it to be about animals."

"I was thinking about the Moltke Bridge."

"What does that have to do with animal protection?"

"Nothing."

"Then it's out of the question."

Suddenly, the lasagna doesn't taste so good, and Britta pushes the dish away. She'd somehow assumed that Julietta had forgotten about her animal protection hobbyhorse. Now Julietta's the only one who's still eating. She looks up from her plate. A fleeting glance.

"I'm doing this for animals. I said that from the beginning."

"And I said the decision wasn't up to you."

"That's not exactly how it went," Babak objects, but Britta cuts him short at once.

"You stay out of it." She points a finger at Julietta. Soldier and commander. "I give the orders, you obey them."

"Then why are we sitting here?" Julietta wipes her mouth with her napkin and gives Britta a challenging look.

"Maybe a compromise is doable," Babak says, trying again. "We'd like a large-scale operation, and Julietta's surely on board with that. Maybe we could combine the Moltke Bridge idea with a client like Green Power."

Now Britta directs her anger at him. "Since when do you work up the scenarios?" she hisses. "Are you going to be negotiating with clients from now on as well? Will you take care of establishing contacts? Doing all the paperwork? Maybe you think I should opt for early retirement too?"

"Whoa," says Babak, raising his hands, as if Britta were a galloping horse, coming right at him.

"And you," says Britta, pointing a finger at Julietta again. "The only reason you're so charged up about animal protection is that your best friend's a cat. What a load of crap! The Bridge isn't a petting zoo for bored daughters."

Now it's Julietta's turn to push her plate away. Two miniature towers of meat, potato, and herb butter are still on it. "Unlike you, I have principles," she says.

Britta's laugh sounds artificial. "Right, when they involve cute little animals! But think about people for a change. Go to the government quarter in Berlin and make a statement for democracy."

"Democracy? Wasn't that the system that put the CCC assholes in power?"

"Just because you don't like the results doesn't mean the process didn't work."

"It doesn't? Take a look at the so-called voters! Nothing but idiots and ignoramuses! Any monkey has more dignity and more compassion. More intelligence too, in most cases."

"People have simply forgotten what's at stake."

"Has this turned into a civics class?" asks Julietta, immune to Britta's arguments. "I thought you were totally apolitical. Neutral. Professional."

"She is," Babak says quickly, grabbing Britta's arm as though to keep her from jumping up. "This is just about the matter at hand. According to The Bridge's rules, the decision for or against a client is ultimately up to the candidate. Britta and I work only in an advisory capacity." He has spoken in Julietta's direction, but his words were meant for Britta. The fact that he's openly siding against her and is moreover in the right only increases her rage. She feels his grip tightening when her arm starts to tremble.

"Get out of here," Britta says between clenched teeth.

"Am I being sent away again so you can see whether I come back?"

"You're being sent away so the grown-ups can talk."

"Okay, okay." Julietta finishes her Coke and stands up. "I wanted to jog a few more laps anyway."

When she goes, Britta lets herself sink back in her chair and exhales for several seconds. Babak eyes her searchingly. "You really went to town on her, didn't you?" he asks.

"I told you we should take Marquardt."

"The young lady's showing some teeth. That can only serve our purpose."

"She's uncontrollable. A threat to our plans."

"Nonsense. You're just not used to being contradicted." Babak lays his hand on her arm again, very gently this time. "Nobody's against you. Julietta just has a clear goal. And that irritates you."

"Why should it?"

"Because it tells you something about yourself."

Britta yanks her arm away from him. "Please spare me the therapy speak."

"We're a healing practice for psychotherapy. Have you forgotten?"

Against her will, Britta smiles. When Babak sees that, he breathes a sigh of relief. "The Moltke Bridge is a magnificent idea," he says. "We can do that just as well with Green Power. As a sign of resistance against deleting animal protection from the Constitution."

"And suppose they're not willing?"

"We can ask."

Britta nods slowly. At least, that would mean working with G. Flossen, a man with whom she has a great deal of experience.

"Have you got the evaluation plan?" Babak asks. "Let's take a look at it together."

Britta produces a sheet of paper on which she's made some notes. Babak bends over it while Britta indicates the individual points with her pencil.

"Everything's either already completed or dispensable. That means"—she draws a ring around the remaining points—"that we can do Step Six next, and after that she'll start the final phase immediately."

Babak stares in silence at the paper for a while. Finally, he asks, "Can't we skip Step Six too?"

"You must be joking. Step Six is one of the most important in the whole program."

"But Julietta's a woman."

"The perfect candidate. As you said yourself."

"I know." Babak rubs his face. "I just don't feel good about it."

"You like her."

He takes his hands off his face. "Like a little sister. Maybe she reminds me of myself. When I was in the same situation."

"You weren't nearly so hard-boiled."

He has to laugh. "Well, there's a valid point," he says.

"Babak." Britta waits until he becomes serious again. "We have to determine whether she really wants to die. For her protection as well as ours."

"You're right."

"You can't be her friend. Suicides don't have friends."

"Ever since she started living at my place, she seems so . . . cheerful."

"That has nothing to do with you."

Babak knows as well as she does that in the course of the program, many candidates experience euphoric phases, especially toward the end, when the scenario is taking shape. Candidates focus on the task at hand and start to feel happy. But the delight of death is not the same as delight in life.

"Still, you absolutely want to use her for the big plan," says Britta.

"Because she's the right choice."

"We don't decide that."

"Step Six does. Among other things. I know."

They smile at each other and take deep breaths.

"Now beat it and go pick up some guy. Forget Julietta for a few hours. Go back to your own life. That's an order."

Chapter **18**

A second ago, the square lay silent in the light of the streetlamps, there was a silvery gleam of moisture on the stones, and the steel struts of a security fence glinted in the background. Now a man comes into the picture. He strides calmly across the paved surface, a tall, slender figure dressed in black, his face uncovered but hard to recognize in the half-light. His springy step is evidence of an exercise regimen; his upper body is broad, actually too broad, because of the explosive vest under his jacket. The man walks along the fence a short distance until he reaches the gate. Next to the locked entrance is a narrowly enclosed turnstile for pedestrian traffic. A flag is waving on the gatepost, and under it a brass plate is prominently displayed. Half-moon and star.

It wasn't easy to find the right assignment for Marquardt. In his meticulous way, he found arguments against every proposed situation and lapsed again and again into tedious monologues that nearly drove Britta mad. Until, in a moment of sudden inspiration, the PKK occurred to her. Marquardt has no real interest in Kurdish issues, but the AKP's slapdash ways disturb him. Britta's glad, because she doesn't often have anything to offer the PKK. The attention that a non-Kurd carrying out an anti-AKP operation will attract provides a forceful argument in price negotiations. In the early morning hours, the square in front of the consulate is deserted but under video surveillance, and before Marquardt ignites the bomb, he'll deliver a brief, prepared speech to the cameras.

Marquardt toes an imaginary line a few steps from the entrance; they've studied the area and divided it into grid squares, and the space where he's stopped marks the intersection of the axes of several cameras. In all probability, this is the moment when a watchman sitting in front of some monitor raises his weary head. The delivery of the message will take thirty-two seconds, after which Marquardt will move a little closer to the portal, in order to cause the greatest possible damage.

Just as he's turning his eyes toward one of the surveillance cameras, the van drives up: a silver Mercedes Vito, no license plates. It brakes right next to Marquardt; the side door slides open. Within fractions of a second, two masked men in black combat outfits have dragged him inside the vehicle. The Vito's tires squeal as it accelerates into a tight curve and speeds out of the picture.

"Mama!"

"Just wait a minute," Britta calls. Before she clicks the next video stream on her tablet, she puts the headphones over her ears and turns down the sound; things are likely to get a bit loud.

The perspective has changed, and now the frame displays a stark image detail from inside the van. Marquardt's brightly lit face fills the screen; Bernd is shining a Maglite in his eyes. His mouth is contorted, probably because Udo's pulling his head back by the hair.

"Now we've got you, you prick!" Bernd screams, close to the microphone. Britta turns the volume down to the minimum. "No more holy war for you!"

"I'm not a jihadi," Marquardt pants. There's the sound of a blow, and his face disappears from the screen. When he appears again, he's coughing and spitting. The sputum looks as though it contains some vomit.

"You speak only when you're asked a question," screams Bernd.

"Who sent you?" asks Udo, in a calm, friendly voice. The two men form a highly experienced team, they've been doing this for years, and they do it quite well.

"That's none of your business," Marquardt answers, as soon as his mouth is clear. After the following blow, it takes them a little longer to straighten him up again.

"We're letting you keep your tongue only so you can talk!" Bernd bellows.

"Do us all a favor and make it quick," Udo entreats.

It will go on like this for a while longer, so Britta fast-forwards a little.

"Mama! Maa-maa!!!"

"Wait a minute, both of you."

"We have a quesss-tion!"

"Ask me," says Janina, who's behind the steering wheel of the VW bus. "Your mama has to work a little longer."

"But you should both listen."

"I won't be much longer." Britta holds the tablet so that no one but her can see the display screen and looks for the place where the weapon comes into play.

Marquardt's kneeling on the floor, already just about done, even though barely a trace of violence is visible on his face. Udo and Bernd are pros. Apart from Step 12, Britta has nothing to do with them—she doesn't even know their real names. She suspects that they're former policemen who work for some security company and occasionally earn some extra income from The Bridge. They're reliable, tidy, discreet. Britta knows she can absolutely trust them. On the screen, Bernd is pressing a Glock against Marquardt's temple.

"You didn't acquire your boom-boom vest and all this other shit by yourself," Ugo says, off camera. "Who helped you? We want names."

"Fuck you," pants Marquardt, who has apparently lost his inclination to practice good manners.

Bernd, clenching his jaw, trembling with effort, presses the muzzle of the Glock against Marquardt's head. "Then your time's up," he gasps out.

"My colleague is right," says Udo's voice. "Sorry as I am to say so. If you have nothing to offer, you're worthless to us."

"Biowaste," Bernd adds. This is an expression he must be mighty proud of; in any case, he uses it every time.

"I'm going to count backward from five," Udo explains. "When I reach zero, my colleague pulls the trigger. If you have second thoughts, raise your hand."

Even before Udo starts counting, Marquardt begins to recite his PKK broadside. Kurdistan Freedom Hawks, revenge for the massacres committed by the AKP fascists. Britta is touched. Marquardt is using his last opportunity to carry out at least a part of his instructions. He speaks without faltering and stresses every word with the same meticulousness that characterizes his reports. He's been getting on Britta's nerves for weeks; now she's starting to admire him.

While Marquardt's speaking, Udo slowly counts from five to zero, Marquardt shuts his eyes, and Bernd squeezes the trigger. Nothing happens. A moment of shock ensues, and then

Marquardt begins to howl. He keeps on howling while Bernd and Udo talk to him, trying to soothe him. Now they're about to tell him that the evaluation comprises not twelve but thirteen steps, and that he's just completed the last one. That it was all just an act. That they'll take him back to the hotel, and that everything else he'll learn from Britta.

Britta turns the tablet off. She doesn't have to wait for Udo's appraisal to know that Marquardt has passed with flying colors. She has seen stronger men break down whimpering and beg for their lives. In such cases, the candidates leave the program shortly before its completion and return to their daily routines. For the most part, The Bridge profits from outcomes of this sort as well. Candidates converted late in the process tend to express their gratitude for their cure by paying exceptionally high fees.

"Can you finally listen?" shouts Vera from the back seat.

"Yes, sweetie, I'm finished." Britta stuffs the tablet into the knapsack between her feet and turns around in the passenger seat.

"What's a 'toff-tail'?" Cora asks quickly, while Vera resorts to angry grumbling. Apparently there was some kind of competition about who would ask the question.

"Not like that!" snaps Vera. "'Molo-tail'!" Both girls are aflame with eagerness because they're closing in on something they think is just for grown-ups.

"Molotov cocktail?" asks Britta.

"Exactly!" cries Vera. "What *is* that?"

"Something old-fashioned."

"How do you know such a word?" asks Janina.

"From Mr. Meyer." He's Vera's arithmetic teacher. "He said someone should go to Berlin and throw a Molotov cocktail at it."

"Your teachers talk like that?"

"Only the older ones."

"I see what he means." Janina laughs.

"Don't talk nonsense," Britta says sharply.

Janina takes her eyes off the road and looks at her friend in surprise. "Haven't you heard about the CCC's latest plan? Efficiency Package Number Six: the introduction of midterm examinations in elementary school. Underachievers to be separated out early. An absurd idea."

"Wha-a-a-at?" Vera and Cora yell, pleased with their own volume.

"There was a survey a few years ago," says Britta. "People were asked what they'd do if they had to choose between their right to vote and their washing machine."

"What was the result?"

"Sixty-seven percent chose the washing machine. Fifteen percent were undecided."

"So only eighteen percent wanted the vote."

"You're good at doing arithmetic in your head." Britta hears how caustic she sounds. "The CCC didn't just come out of nowhere. If people want to throw Molotov cocktails, then maybe they should throw them at other people."

"What's wrong with you?" Janina turns her head again and looks inquisitively at Britta. "Since when do you get worked up about politics?"

"Pull in there." She indicates the entrance to a filling station.

At the cash register, she asks for a card phone. Since there aren't any for sale—there never are—the attendant offers her his cell; so far, this ruse has worked every time.

She dials a number she knows by heart and leaves a brief voice mail message: the candidate is available and can be

booked starting next week. She gives the attendant a euro for
the call, buys four lollipops in different flavors, and goes back
to the car, where she shoos Janina out of the driver's seat.

While Britta sits in silence and drives, Janina goes on about
the sixth Efficiency Package, which includes the downsizing of
the school system, the so-called judicial reform, and the expan-
sion of governmental authority. All the same, Britta's pretty
sure Janina would have opted for the washing machine too. In
her friend's mouth, the CCC's plans sound like the side effects
of a creeping natural disaster that one watches with disgusted
fascination but can do nothing at all to stop. Britta would very
much like to tell her, once and for all, to keep her trap shut.
And all throughout Janina's chatter, Britta's mind is drawn
back to Julietta's words: "the CCC assholes," and "Unlike you,
I have principles."

On the day after the conversation at Good Times, Britta
made another trip to Leipzig. She walked around the city for
hours and then eventually rented a bicycle. She checked all the
parks, sought out all the trash bins, rode to shopping centers,
S-Bahn stations, and the university's various properties. Not
a trace of G. Flossen anywhere. It wasn't the first time she'd
been unable to track him down, but in this case the futility of
her search causes her great distress. She can't afford any delay.
And should Flossen remain impossible to find—because he's
on a journey around the world, because he's lying in a hospital bed, because he's resigned from Green Power—Britta and
Julietta are back at the beginning.

By the time they reach Wiebüttel, she's finished the lolli-
pop and gotten a grip on herself. Janina, for her part, is worn-
out from talking; the bored girls in the back droop in their
seats.

As they turn into the little village, Britta checks her rearview mirror for the umpteenth time. No white Hilux in sight. For a guardian angel, Hatz hasn't been particularly present lately.

With an elegant twirl of the steering wheel, Britta parks the VW bus in front of the old farmhouse, dozing as contentedly as a cat in the warm morning sunshine. The girls tumble out and disappear into the garden before Britta and Janina can issue the usual admonitions. The little party got an early start, and the morning is splendid. Sunlight shines in blinding beams through the foliage of the trees; the air smells fresh, as though the world has just been made. Janina finds the key under a flowerpot next to the front steps. There's no real estate agent this time; it's one last, private viewing before the buyers make a definitive offer. To "check the vibes," as Janina says, one more time.

The door swings open, Britta jumps, there's a hiss, and something flashes past them, *marten, polecat, weasel,* Britta thinks, and sees a gray mass disappear into the bushes. But then the apparition is followed, in a leisurely manner, by a fat, black-and-white-spotted cat. On its way past Britta, it looks her directly in the eyes, as if to say, *No matter what you think you're doing, we were here first.*

Once she's inside, it seems to Britta that the dust layer is even thicker and the dead fly count even higher than they were last time. With no men and no agent, the house is quiet inside. The twittering of birds ripples through all the rooms; a window must be open somewhere. In spite of the dirt, a certain dignity emanates from the house. Britta concludes that it's four times as old as she is. It has seen two world wars, births, deaths, every aspect of human fate. In the living room with its blond wood floors, an old rocking horse looks at them through amber eyes. Oddly, she didn't notice it last time.

They don't speak. They go through all the rooms once again and climb up the steep stairs. There's another bathroom on the upper floor, along with several bedrooms, one of which contains an old bed. They sit on it and look out through the window at the crowns of the old trees, in which extended families of sparrows are squabbling. Knut and Janina may have no talent for success, but it's possible they're just lucky. Britta can foresee how they'll live here, with little work and little money, with chickens, a vegetable garden, and another child crawling around on the wood floors. Model students of the unconditional basic income. Always kept busy by everyday concerns, but suffused with love for the place where they find themselves. All at once, Britta feels old-fashioned. Maybe the dream of country living is an anachronism, but so are long working days and the constant preoccupation with business. Britta has always looked down on mellow Janina and feckless Knut, with their old-fashioned, permanently aggrieved take on politics and society. But maybe Britta, with her nihilistic pride, is also a dinosaur, convinced of its superiority even as it's dying out.

As Janina lets herself sink backward onto the bed, Britta does the same. A grandmotherly smell rises from the mattress. They lie next to each other and look up at the ceiling, where an old light fixture is still attached, a sort of upside-down Mason jar with little cats painted on its milky glass. Was this once a child's bedroom? Did a little boy lie in the heavy wooden bed, and when he couldn't sleep at night, did he look at the cats on the ceiling light, some of them licking their paws, others curled up and purring?

Britta's whole body starts to tingle, and then, for the first time in days, relaxation overwhelms her. She feels as though she's on the verge of sleep. Maybe she *should* take some time off, after all. It surely doesn't have to be a full year, or half a year, but maybe three months or even a couple of weeks, an extended vacation during which she could help Janina fix up this house, and together they could pick cherries and bake cakes and prepare dinners for their families to eat under the trees on mild evenings. Britta hasn't taken a vacation in years; she doesn't know what life without The Bridge would feel like.

We can see Marquardt and Jawad through to the end and pull off the big thing with Julietta, she thinks, *and then I'll go on sabbatical for a while. What a sign of supreme confidence! Babak will hold down the fort, and the little boys from "Empty Hearts" will have learned that it's unwise to pee on a dinosaur's leg.*

When her diaphragm begins to flutter, Britta knows things won't happen that way. The thought of baking cakes unnerves her, and her relaxation slides into anxiety.

"Imagine you have a small box with a red button on it," she says. "If you press the button, all the grade-A nutcases in the world—Freyer, Trump, and all the others—will instantaneously die. What do you do?"

Janina turns her head and looks at Britta from the side. "The Molotov cocktails won't leave you in peace, huh?"

"Solve the dilemma. What do you do with the little box?"

"I pitch it out the window, high and far."

"What?" Britta sits up. "You agreed with the Molotov flinging."

"Ah, but that wasn't serious." Now Janina's lying on her side, propped up on an elbow. "We're in complete agreement, Britta. Violence is wrong. No matter what its purpose may be."

This answer rattles around in Britta's head; for a moment, she can no longer see, the result of having shut her eyes. Stomach acid surges up into her throat. Janina's voice comes from far away.

"Do you think we should keep this bed?"

But Britta has already leaped from the bed and run into the bathroom to throw up.

Chapter

"Are you comfortable?" Britta asks.

Julietta smiles. She looks more excited than scared. Britta knows what's going on inside her. Julietta is thinking that it has to be possible simply to hold your breath. She believes she can rely on her self-control. Besides, it's not a "real" situation. If something goes awry, Britta will stop. In a few minutes, everything will be over, Julietta will be given a towel to dry her hair, and they'll go out for coffee and talk about what happened. She won't be brought to a cell to be tortured some more with cold, heat, or noise. Julietta's almost looking forward to the experience; it's as though she were trying her hand at an extreme sport—free diving, perhaps, or parachute jumping.

Britta knows all that. She's been through it. Everything she expects of her candidates is something she's subjected herself to first, including the sojourn in the clinic, the spurious abduction, and the fake execution. None of that was nearly so bad as the waterboarding.

That first time, she and Babak had done Internet research and read CIA manuals and field reports for days until there was no more reason to put off the event any longer. While they were buying a plastic watering can in the garden department of the home improvement store, they kept bursting into laughter. They were surrounded by hoses, spades, fertilizers, and rubber gloves, and suddenly they could see torture instruments in the simplest things.

They were still living in Leipzig, and Britta's student apartment was their only choice for a venue. They laid a wide board over the bathtub so that the water would make as little mess as possible. A tossed coin decided that Britta's turn would come first. Babak tied her to the board with two cotton scarves, yanking and pulling at her for so long that Britta finally yelled at him to get on with it. Her lighthearted jitters had given way to genuine tension. Babak activated the timer on his cell phone. They'd agreed to a one-minute time limit. The decision to quit sooner than that was up to the active partner.

He placed a kitchen towel over her face. Britta thought she would take a deep breath, hold it, and keep her mouth tightly closed so no water could get in. Holding her breath for a minute was harder than she thought it would be, but it could be done. She'd been practicing.

Babak poured water onto her face.

Britta got through the first seconds with no problem. The towel became fully soaked, the cold water flowed over her face and neck and splashed on the ceramic bathtub. Nevertheless, she quickly realized that simply holding her breath wasn't an option, because the water entered through her nose. She thought she could take up thirty seconds by exhaling very, very slowly, and then time would be nearly up.

But the degree of counterpressure she could generate by slow exhalation wasn't enough. The water streamed into her sinuses, and so to get rid of it, she forcefully expelled the air in her lungs. After that, they were empty.

Britta tried to escape the water, jerking her head back and forth so she could breathe through her mouth, but the wet cloth already filled her oral cavity. She tried to blow out the water pouring into her pharynx, sinuses, windpipe, and gullet, but her lungs had already completely collapsed. She understood that she must not in any case lose control, and she lost control. Her form rigid as she braced herself against her restraints, she took deep breaths through her nose, drawing in more and more water; it ran everywhere, filling her eyes, her ears, her brain. Her body went wild. Britta knew she was going to die.

When the board tipped up and Babak dropped the watering can to catch her, not even forty seconds had passed. Britta needed ten minutes to come back to her senses. She crawled shivering under the bathroom sink and struck out at Babak if he attempted to get ahold of her. She was convinced he'd tried to kill her.

Babak didn't take his turn that day. Or the following day either. Britta was in no condition to perform waterboarding, on him or anyone else. She sought again and again to clarify what had happened to her. There was a threshold beyond which self-control and reason had no part to play. When she drew water into her respiratory tract, she had lost mastery over herself. Hell had swallowed her. She'd never felt a panic even remotely comparable to that. If she imagined having to repeat the experience, the panic returned at once. If she'd had the choice of letting her fingers get smashed by a sledgehammer or going through another waterboarding, she would have chosen, without hesitation, the sledgehammer. She would have sold her whole family. She would have said anything, done anything, given up anything.

Over the course of the following weeks, Babak insisted that she should subject him to the same treatment. They had to be on the same page. Britta knew he was right. She wouldn't be able to work with him anymore if he hadn't experienced the same thing she had. She improved the arrangement and found a way to secure the board. Babak's reaction was identical to hers. Britta cried the whole time. When she dropped the can, the stopwatch had reached forty-five seconds.

"Is that full?" asks Julietta, pointing to the green watering can. They're in The Bridge's basement. Julietta's lying on the treatment table, which Britta bought at a surgical supply store's closeout sale shortly after opening the practice. To avoid accidents, Babak bolted the feet of the table to the floor. The multipurpose room is tiled and has a floor drain, so they can simply let the water run where it will.

"To the brim," says Britta, lifting the can to show how heavy it is. It's still the same can they used the very first time.

"Then it looks like I won't get thirsty tonight."

Joking is also something they all try. Julietta's eyes are a little darker than usual. Britta attaches her to the table with straps and has her make a declaration of consent into the tablet's camera, just in case; nobody has ever complained afterward.

"Now I'm going to put a cloth over your face, and then we start," Brita says.

There was a time when she used to give a brief introduction at this point, explaining that this was a purely psychological procedure, that it entailed no danger to life or limb, that the straps were employed only for the candidate's safety, and that the whole experience would last less than a minute. When it became clear to her that she was speaking these words merely to reassure herself, she stopped giving the introduction.

Following an impulse, Britta smooths a strand of hair back from the girl's forehead. Julietta displays no emotion, but Britta nevertheless senses that she trusts her. She quickly covers Julietta's face with the checkered kitchen towel. Things are easier after that. Britta becomes a machine performing simple movement patterns. Lift the watering can, tip it forward slightly, let the water run out. Carefully at first, so that the cloth isn't dislodged, and then more liberally after the material is wet and heavy and clinging to the victim's face. Julietta's features show through the cloth, making it look like a death mask.

It's the same as when I water flowers, Britta tells herself. *Same container, same contents, identical movement.*

Julietta's degree of self-control must be a record. After twenty seconds, she continues to lie completely still. Britta finds this irritating. *Why make such an effort, you ambitious little twit, you're only human too, you work the same way we all do, there's no prize to be won here.* When another fifteen seconds have gone by, so has Julietta's resistance. She coughs, swallows water, jerks her head back and forth, braces herself against the lashing straps. Britta increases the amount of water pouring down on Julietta's face; the can gets lighter. The wriggling and writhing make Britta even more aggressive. *It's only water,* she thinks, *calm down, I thought you were a hard-ass, you're supposed to love tormenting yourself, where's your self-hatred now, super suicide girl?*

The anger does her good, it's the only way for her to cope with the situation. Finally the watering can is empty. Britta flings it across the room, clattering over the tiled floor. The stopwatch says fifty-five seconds. Britta takes the towel off Julietta's face and undoes the straps. Using both hands, she's careful to keep the girl from falling or slipping on the wet tiles, supporting her until they reach the low chair ready in the corner. Julietta looks a fright, her wet hair hangs in her face, she's bent in half, holding her belly, coughing and spitting like someone drowning. Britta's scorn for this broken fragment of humanity is so great that she must turn away. When Julietta finally grows calm and sinks into the chair like a corpse, Britta sits on the dry end of the treatment table, draws up her feet, and puts her arms around her knees. Julietta's chest rises and falls in regular breathing, almost as if she were asleep. Britta's about to ask her if she wants to continue in the program. She imagines that Julietta will curse her and then burst into tears and bawl, like a little girl something terrible has happened to. She'll just want to go back home to her mama. Britta will comfort her and rattle off a few formalities, to the effect that she won't be charged anything, that all her documents will be destroyed, that silence is to be expected as a matter of course on both sides. She'll tell her that a new stage of her life is now beginning, and that she'll understand one day why she was fortunate to work with The Bridge.

Babak will be sad when Julietta leaves the program. *Maybe the two of them will remain in contact and meet once a week to play darts. The sweet kid was just fooling us, big talk, nothing behind it, in the end only a little Mega-girl who lost her way.* Britta can't deny that she feels a certain relief. Marquardt will be happy when she tells him she has a special mission for him.

Britta lets herself slide off the table and goes to fetch a dry towel. She's wondering whether Richard will have enough time this evening to go out and do something nice, treat themselves, or whether they'll simply stay in and watch a movie in the cozy comfort of their own home, when Julietta says something Britta has never heard before. Not in this situation, not in this place, not after what happened just a few minutes ago.

Julietta says, "Again."

Chapter

Because Smart Swap's offices are in a pretty but rather cramped old building in the city center, Richard has reserved for the celebration a corner in the I-Vent, a restaurant-bar-lounge with a fine eighteenth-floor view over Braunschweig. Britta hates parties, and the fact that this one is being thrown by and in honor of Guido Hatz makes her attendance all the more absurd. She has come along only because Richard insisted she must. Official greeting of the new investor, a big moment for Swappie. If she weren't here, Emil and Jonas would ask where she was.

For the past half hour, she's been standing by the window with Lena and Charlotte, Emil's and Jonas's wives, holding a cocktail glass and listening to reports about their respective daughters' successes at painting, piano playing, computer programming, and equestrian vaulting. Then the topic shifts to the sixth Efficiency Package, which is just fine with Lena and Charlotte, particularly because of the extra levies imposed on foreigners doing business in Germany and the additional measures being taken to protect the German economy. After she hears the sentence "Sure, the CCC isn't very democratic, but many of their ideas are really quite good" for the third time, Britta carries her glass to the ladies' room, where she washes her hands and takes a long look at her face in the mirror. Ever since Janina gave her answer to the red button dilemma, nausea has become Britta's constant companion. She doesn't understand what's wrong with her; she hasn't had a very good grip on herself recently.

To calm down, she tells herself that everything is, in fact, going great. Julietta has successfully completed Step 6 and is still in the program. Since the waterboarding session, she's been wearing her hair loose again, she's resumed smoking, and she runs around in her customary black, baggy clothes. She has completed the next molt, the female warrior masquerade is over, she makes a relaxed, levelheaded impression. Tiredness makes her nose seem a little too large; maybe she's been sleeping badly since her experience with mortal fear, but sleep deprivation is good, it releases energy. Babak never leaves her side anymore. He accompanies her when she jogs in the city park, an activity for which, in order to be less conspicuous, she has even procured some red "Sport Is Public" T-shirts. He pays attention to her nutrition and joins her in yoga and meditation. Britta has decided to let him do as he likes; he's old enough to take care of himself, and he's been in the business long enough to know he's setting himself up for terrible suffering in the end. Julietta will not renounce suicide for his sake; Britta's convinced of that. Especially since Step 6.

Before long, she'll go to Leipzig again to look for Flossen, and if she doesn't find him, she'll establish contact with another environmental organization. She'll do this with a heavy heart, but so be it. As for Guido Hatz, she's heard nothing from him for days. This evening, apart from a brief greeting, he's paid no attention at all to her and spent all his time with Jonas and Emil. Britta wonders if he's forgotten his guardian angel shtick, and if he may in fact have nothing to do with Empty Hearts. One way or another, assuming everything goes well, in two weeks the whole business will be over, and after that there will be time for a bit of recuperation. There's nothing for her to get upset about, but her internal organs don't seem to be aware of that.

When two women, laughing and talking, come into the ladies' room, Britta turns away from the mirror and returns to the party. She sees at once that Guido Hatz has been waiting for her. His tall figure is easy to recognize, towering over the other guests. When he spots her, he raises an arm, beckons to her, and points to a window niche.

Britta gets another cocktail from the bar and ambles, with exaggerated slowness, over to Hatz, who's stroking his mustache and looking pensively down at the city. At least there's no precipice here that he can balance on, eyes closed.

With one finger, Hatz points over the main train station, indicating the Kurt Schumacher Apartment Blocks. "Look over there, behind the station."

Behind the station is where, among other things, The Bridge's offices are, but Hatz means something else. "Up there," he says, "on top of the apartment buildings. The spirits of the air, the sylphs, are meeting there. Can you see them?"

"I see nothing at all."

"This city is wounded. Something awful is going to happen if no healing takes place. But I'm saying that to a healing practitioner." He smiles at her, a smile totally free of irony. "It's great that you're here. Good training for your new wifely role."

Britta starts to turn away, but he lays a hand on her arm. "One more moment."

While they look at each other, Britta has the feeling that his gaze penetrates more deeply than hers. The discomfort grows. *This man isn't a lunatic, he's following a plan.* Maybe he's thrown this party so he could meet her here. To show her that he can compel her to appear.

"You shouldn't be afraid of me," says Hatz. "It channels your energy in a wrong direction."

Britta wants to say she's not afraid, but she knows it wouldn't sound convincing.

"Remember, I'm your guardian angel. I have your best interests at heart. I've watched over you all these years, and now I'm trying to save what can be saved."

"Saved from what?"

He bends down to her and speaks directly into her ear: "Say good-bye to Julietta, Marquardt, and the others. Close your practice, go home, and stay there. That's your chance. Your only chance, frankly."

He knows the names, naturally, that's no surprise. Nevertheless, Britta gets so dizzy that she totters. Hatz takes her glass from her hand and puts it on a table. He inconspicuously supports her by an elbow until her system stabilizes again. As Emil is tapping his glass to announce a speech, Britta's already on her way to the elevators. In his squeaky voice, which sounds as though it still hasn't changed, Emil searches for the first words, thanks the investor, praises the investor, and promises all present a splendid future. Guido Hatz is standing in the niche where Britta left him, nodding and smiling like a man celebrating his silver wedding anniversary.

It's dark outside. Britta gets on her bike and starts pedaling hard. She's annoyed at herself for reacting so strongly to Hatz's X-Files nonsense. To calm down, she goes as fast as she can. The airstream tugs at her hair. The wind is surprisingly cold for a summer evening; the weather this year has completely mixed up the seasons.

As she's passing under the tracks of the main train station and the Kurt Schumacher Blocks loom up before her, she decides to stop by her office and pick up a stack of weekly reports. Her current mood won't allow her to sleep in any case, so she may as well salvage what she can of the wasted evening by doing a little work.

Standing up to pedal, she climbs the ramp that leads from the thruway to the Schumacher Passage. Even from a distance, she can tell that something's not right. Admittedly, at first glance, it looks as it always does. No one's about; all the businesses are closed. The practice's display windows, the only clean windows in the whole Passage, reflect the light from the streetlamps. But a tiny detail is spoiling the picture. The door doesn't look like it's fully shut. There's a shadowy gap to the left of the knob, a black, perpendicular line that doesn't belong there. Britta's brain does what any other brain would: it seeks an explanation. Optical illusion? Not closed right? Or has Babak gone inside the practice and left the door ajar?

She brakes hard directly in front of the door and bends over the handlebars, balancing the bicycle between her legs. Traces left by some crude tool are readily apparent. Cat's-paw or crowbar. The aluminum profile was bent open until the latch and bolt slid out of the strike plate. The wrecked door was then jammed back into the frame. When Britta shakes the knob a little, the door swings open.

Theoretically, the intruder could still be on the premises, but Britta doesn't dwell on that thought. She crosses the consultation area, which looks untouched, and then hurries to the spiral staircase and down to the basement floor. There she switches on the light and stares into the empty tech room until she recalls that Babak, with what now proves to have been wise foresight, evacuated Lassie some days ago. Otherwise, everything looks the same as always; even the empty watering can is still lying on the tiles in the spot where Britta left it. She wonders what the burglars could have been looking for. The rooms seem too clean and tidy to have been ransacked by junkies who levered open an easy door on the off chance of finding something. Except for Lassie, The Bridge possesses no articles of any value; the equipment is scanty, the furniture cheap, the coffee machine now a good ten years old. Britta slowly climbs back up the stairs. In order to avoid attracting unnecessary attention, she doesn't turn on the lights—there's sufficient light coming in from the Passage. Back on the ground floor, she verifies that everything looks normal: the living room suite, the reception counter, the little table with the magazines no one ever reads. While she's inspecting the objects that for years have formed the backdrop of her life, an uncomfortable feeling comes over her, a stubborn ache between sorrow and dread, and perhaps this emotional state is the reason why it takes her so long to recognize the obvious.

The big worktable in the middle of the room is empty. Babak's dot picture is gone.

In its place on the tabletop, there's a quaintly glossy photograph with a white border, the kind you can still choose as a format option when ordering from an Internet retailer. Britta cautiously picks up the photo. She has to move it back and forth a little to find the proper distance from her eyes before she can make out anything in it. The picture is dark and washed-out, taken without a flash at night, orange-tinted from the light of the streetlamps, which look like the ones in Leipzig. A body lies on the ground, half-covered by an overturned bicycle whose saddlebags have spilled their contents. The lifeless figure is surrounded by plastic bottles, lots of them, conspicuously gleaming in the lamplight. It's a curious arrangement, as if something has fallen from a great height and splattered in the shape of a star over the grass and the gravel path. Even though Britta can't see a face, she knows that the person is G. Flossen, and that he's no longer alive.

She's paralyzed for a moment, but then she acts quickly. She thrusts the photo into her bag and runs downstairs again to fetch a folding ladder from the toolroom. Laboriously, she maneuvers the unwieldy thing up the curving stairs, places it in front of the entrance, and climbs up to the highest rung in order to remove the smart card from the little camera. Then she exits the practice, pulling the ruined door into the frame with all her strength so as not to leave it standing open.

During the ride through the city center, a mantra repeats itself in Britta's head: *Please let Babak and Julietta be home. Don't let anything have happened to them.*

After school one day recently, Vera asked her if the Good Lord was a character in *Star Wars,* and Britta felt somehow proud of her daughter's atheism. Now, however, Britta finds she's starting to pray. If there really is someone sitting up there, he's probably having a sizable laugh at her expense right now. The demonic way she's pedaling, her vexed breathing, her sweaty forehead. The way she's imploring a god who, in her personal opinion, doesn't exist. All at once she realizes that she quite liked G. Flossen, and she begins to cry.

That's how she reaches "the Top": out of breath, red-eyed from weeping. The entrance door is open. Britta runs up the stairs two at a time and then leans on Babak's doorbell with a finger while simultaneously beating on the door with the flat of her other hand, until finally he opens up and stands before her, unscathed and alive. She falls on her knees from sheer relief.

Babak puts an arm around her shoulders and brings her into the living room, where Julietta's lying on her mattress. With a look of surprise, she pulls the earphones out of her ears.

Britta cannot speak. She takes out the photo and throws it, for lack of a table, onto the floor, so that Babak must kneel down to look at it. He takes a few moments to get his bearings and then whispers, "Shit." When Britta pulls the little smart card out of her bag, he reacts immediately, gets a card reader and a tablet, and starts the film.

The three of them crouch around the display screen and put their heads together. They see The Bridge's consultation area, lying in semidarkness. The counter at the bottom of the image reads 2215 hours, 10:15 p.m.. Outside it's almost night; a little light is coming through the practice's big front windows. Two men step into the picture, one of them squat and stocky, the other tall and so thin that there doesn't seem to be anything in his oversize pants. They're both using small flashlights, and they aren't masked. Nor do they bother much about hiding their faces from the camera; sometimes they can be seen, obliquely from above, in profile, sometimes from behind, and sometimes head-on. They don't seem very interested in The Bridge's offices either; they don't look around, don't search for anything, don't even go over to the basement stairs. They've just dropped by briefly to pick up something.

When the burglars bend over the worktable and start rolling up the dot picture, Babak repeats, shouting this time, "Shit!" The thin fellow throws the photograph of Flossen's body onto the table. The squat one scratches his head, which makes his sleeve slide up his arm and offers a glimpse of a tattoo that can't be completely seen but is nevertheless easy to recognize.

They run the short film back five times, and then Babak

turns the tablet off. "Empty Hearts," he says. "So there are still more of them."

"Very observant," Britta hisses. "There are more of them, and they killed Flossen. But why did they steal your fucking picture?"

"Maybe we should all just calm down," Julietta objects, but she achieves just the opposite.

"Stay out of this," Britta snaps.

"It's a code," says Babak quickly.

"A what?"

"Are you deaf? It's a fucking code!"

"But for what?"

They're yelling at each other; that's no good. When two load-bearing pillars start to buckle, it means the whole building's in danger of collapsing. Britta tries to get a grip on herself, but she realizes that she has hardly any self-control left. Never before has she felt such alarm.

"Okay," says Babak, and then again: "Okay." He grasps that Britta is not furious but panic-stricken, and so he tries to exude calm. "Maybe I should have told you. But I thought it would be better for you to know nothing about it. I wanted a nonelectronic security system. Something that would work without being dependent on Lassie."

Britta stares at him. What he's talking about dawns on her slowly, but she can't find the right words for her thoughts. "You mean . . . you mean you've written something into the pictures?"

"They're data banks," says Babak. "They contain all the names that Lassie has ever spewed out, including the evaluation reference numbers and a note indicating whether the individual was admitted into the program and how far they got."

"Awesome," says Julietta, and then she laughs. "You're a genius, Babs."

Britta fleetingly registers the asinine nickname, but right now she doesn't have the heart to get worked up about it; she's entirely occupied with gauging the significance of what Babak is saying.

"So you've developed a secret code?"

For a moment, Babak's pride outshines the seriousness of the situation. He reaches for a pencil lying on the floor and also comes up with a death metal magazine that probably belongs to Julietta. On the magazine's back cover, he starts to draw a dense cluster of dots.

"All the letters and numbers have specific patterns; using different colors increases the combination possibilities." The pencil taps on the paper in a familiar rhythm, and Britta immediately feels nostalgia for the old, peaceful days. Babak pushes the magazine over to her. A small pattern no bigger than a penny fills a corner of the back cover.

"That's your name and date of birth," he says.

"How many data sets were in the picture?"

"One thousand three hundred and forty, around a hundred and twenty of them very promising."

"That's the entirety of our large-scale search operation."

Babak nods. "Those are the names that Lassie compiled after the attack in Leipzig."

Britta stares at him with wide-open eyes. "A hundred and twenty candidates—that's an army."

They've often speculated, in jest, about what would happen if instead of placing individual candidates they united them into a group. A person who has finished with life possesses the potential of a fragmentation bomb. If well managed, he can cause tremendous harm. How many suicide attackers would you need to put the whole country in a state of emergency?

Babak, now on his feet, is looking out the window at the streetlights of the pedestrian zone, thwarting the night's will to darkness. "Empty Hearts," he says to the reflecting windowpane, and Julietta begins to sing softly: "'When the future has passed, the past will return. One day you'll be asked what you did, baby. Full hands, empty hearts, it's a suicide world.'"

"How easy is this to decipher?" asks Britta.

"Show it to me." Julietta takes the magazine out of her hand and knits her brows as she gazes at Babak's dots. "Pretty easy, I'd say." She runs a finger over the pattern as if it were braille. "Child's play, really, when you get down to it. Every letter is allotted a fixed combination."

"I wasn't trying to reinvent coding science," Babak says at the window.

"I'd scan the pattern and use a tool, a little program, to examine it for frequencies," says Julietta. "I could write the tool in two days."

Britta glances at her in some surprise. She always forgets that Julietta can do more than treat herself like garbage.

"They were trying out something in Leipzig," Babak says slowly.

"And now they have the material to really get down to business," Britta says, completing his thought.

"Maybe Leipzig was only meant to put Lassie to work. Maybe it was a provocation designed to make us react and gather the data sets they wanted for them."

Britta doesn't answer him. They both know she was the one who insisted on the large-scale search after Leipzig, while Babak urged her again and again to lie low. The pain of having been taken in by such a simple ploy is so great that, for a moment, it drives out Britta's fear.

"Who's the guy in the photo?" asks Julietta.

"The client we wanted to place you with," Babak replies.

"You think they killed him because he was supposed to hire me?"

"How can we know the answer to that?" Britta snarls.

"Britta!" Babak admonishes her. "It's not her fault."

"Let it go, Babs." Julietta shrugs, sticks her earbuds back into her ears, and lets herself fall backward onto the mattress. Babak moves away from the window and back into the room. They look at each other a while.

"The photograph is a message," says Britta, and Babak nods.

"Then we agree?" Britta asks, and Babak nods a second time.

Chapter

The concrete cube stands darkened on its gravel bed, not looking like something you can open with a key. Since Vera is sleeping at Cora's tonight and Richard will stay at his Hatz-fest until at least one o'clock, Britta has dared to pop over to the house for a little while. Babak and Julietta have taken a walk into the city to get a couple of bicycles, maybe from somewhere near the train station but of course out of range of the surveillance cameras. They don't have a bolt-cutter, but Babak owns a set of pliers in various sizes, which will have to do somehow. They're all scheduled to meet in the city park in ninety minutes. No cell phones, no tablets, nothing with a wireless connection.

Inside the house, she's greeted by a special kind of stillness. The furniture is as silent as party guests who have just been talking about the new arrival. Britta has a feeling she mustn't touch anything. How little it takes to become a stranger in your own home!

Because there's no attic, she goes first to the attached build-ing that was planned as a garage but is used as a storeroom.

She finds her old backpack, the one from her student days. When she pulls it out of its corner, it looks a little faded, but clean; Henry has instructions to tidy up everything, including what may look like junk. A feeling of melancholy comes over Britta at the sight of the empty backpack. There was a time when it accompanied her on holiday trips, to Greece, Bulgaria, Hungary, and then later for half a year to Taiwan. When she traveled from Leipzig every other weekend to visit her parents, the backpack transported her dirty laundry, which she washed in her mother's machine. Sliding her hand into the side pocket, she feels the same mix of pencils, hair ties, tampons, small change, and little tins of cream that was in there twenty years ago.

She goes to the bedroom with the backpack and stuffs a few articles of clothing into it. In the kitchen, she takes some canned goods from the shelves: ravioli, peas, and peeled tomatoes, plus two packages of pasta and a few little cartons of Vera's multivitamin juice. Next she looks for the camp stove she believes she still owns but fails to find it. She has more success locating two fleece blankets that can be rolled up very small. Back in the garage, she gathers several more objects from shelves and boxes: flashlight, pocketknife, insect spray. The fuller the backpack becomes, the more confident Britta feels. Now it can stand alone—if she balances it correctly—and looks like something a person could live out of. Twine, paper towels, duct tape. As there's still some room, she adds a pair of work gloves. Then she heaves the full bag onto her back and relishes the familiar pressure of the straps on her shoulders. Britta's almost out of the house when she realizes she's also going to need money and a toothbrush. Once she's in the bathroom, she remembers toothpaste, a bottle of shower gel, and a face towel. Moreover, it occurs to her that she must leave some kind of note. The thought startles her, as though she has only now grasped that packing the backpack was a serious matter. She takes a notepad out of a kitchen drawer and looks for a pencil. And has no idea what she should write. *Dear Richard, dear Vera.* That sounds like a holiday postcard. But she doesn't have time for deep reflection just now. She bends over the notepaper and writes:

> *My dears, an emergency at work is forcing me to go on a business trip for a few days. Don't worry if you don't hear anything from me for a while. I'll explain everything as soon as I get back.*

She pauses briefly, and then she adds, "*I love you both. Yours, Britta/Mama.*"

None of that sounds like something she could have written.

The deserted park is softly whispering to itself. No nocturnal yoga classes, no twenty-four-hour joggers are disturbing the peace. Britta sits on a bench and lays an arm across her backpack, which hunkers next to her like a friend. Together they eavesdrop on the darkness, listening to the rustle of anonymous little animals, to the taciturn trees, to the strident cries of nocturnal predators. We're all constantly in flight, Britta thinks. Man and beast. Flight is the normal condition; one tends, however, to forget it. There's something comforting in that thought.

The whirring of the bicycles can be heard from a distance. Babak and Julietta materialize like silent shadows from the leafy blackness of a clump of bushes, he on a massive girl's bike, she on a mountain bike that's too low for her and must have belonged to a child. They stop in front of Britta's bench and look at her expectantly. They look like students coming back from a party, without jackets or handbags, their wallets shoved into the hip pockets of their jeans.

"Where are we going?" Julietta sounds like someone looking forward to a fun trip.

"You'll see," says Britta. "Get ready for a nice long ride."

They haven't discussed any further plans, but even so, they know what the situation requires. Things go well for the first thirty minutes. They glide through the city center, heading north, riding at a brisk pace on the illuminated streets. The monitors at the intersections report on the stock market, the weather, and the sixth Efficiency Package, the time display reads 1:30, they encounter only a few isolated cars. Britta finds that the movement does her good. Her muscles warm up and work rhythmically, her breath flows deep into her lungs, her head with its complicated thoughts isn't important anymore; her legs have assumed command. The riders pass under the A 392, and then the A 391. Britta can hear Julietta's soft, dreamy voice humming and singing behind her, "'One day you'll be asked what you did, baby,'" a child enjoying a family outing, "'You say you do nothing 'cause nothing is left, but one day you'll be asked what you thought, baby.'"

The houses drop away first, and then the street illumination. Britta has underestimated what it's like to ride at night on a dark country road. The light on her bike stopped working months ago; she wanted to have it repaired, but then she didn't get around to it. The groaning little generator on Julietta's mountain bike produces a trembling beam that flickers in front of them, and on Babak's bicycle there is no light at all. A few trucks veer over into the other lane at the last moment and zoom past them with horns blaring. The bright lights of oncoming traffic dazzle them into total blindness; the slight climb along the Braunschweiger Aue saps their strength. Lighted villages provide some relief, but after Hülperode there are fewer and fewer of them too.

They stop in an unlit rest area. The hair on Julietta's temples is drenched in sweat; Babak's holding tight to his handlebars so as not to fall over from exhaustion. Although Britta's the one carrying the heavy backpack, she's in better shape than the others. Her regular bicycle riding is paying off. She figures they're less than halfway to their goal. The general mood darkens when it turns out there's no drinking water in Britta's bag.

"How could you forget that?" asks Julietta. "Water's the first thing you think of."

Although the question doesn't sound provocative, Britta rejects it harshly. Maintaining the hierarchy will be the single most important element in dealing with what lies ahead.

They make slow progress in the following hours. Britta calls for numerous breaks, plans the journey in short stages, has the others stop and stretch and massage their leg muscles again and again. Thirst becomes a nuisance, then a pang, and finally a howl that drowns out every other thought in their heads. As they're passing an open service station, Britta forbids the purchase of drinks, even though she herself gets positively dizzy at the idea of a big bottle of orange juice. No one questions her decision, no one mutinies. Babak and Julietta follow her like a little army.

By the time they reach the house in Wiebüttel, Britta's impression that she's leading troops has vanished. The shoulder straps on her backpack are constricting her blood circulation and neural pathways; the palms of her hands tingle as though they've gone to sleep. She can tell by looking at Babak that his legs can hardly hold him up. Julietta, on the other hand—ever since the exertion degenerated into masochism—seems to be feeling well again.

Although the house has neighbors on only one side and the property across the street is undeveloped, Britta directs the others to remain in the shadow of the hedges until she can find the key. She picks up three flowerpots; the key's under the fourth. It's hard for her to believe that only a few days ago, she stood here and watched the girls run jubilantly into the garden. Now it's as though that two-family excursion took place in a different universe. At the time, she hadn't noticed how thoroughly all right her world was. Instead of romping on the lawn with Vera, she got agitated by a remark one of the girl's teachers had made about Molotov cocktails. Instead of raising her face to the sun and sharing Janina's delight in the country house of her dreams, she thought up a dilemma in which people could be sent to kingdom come by pressing a button. She didn't pay attention to Vera or listen to Janina because she thought she could do that anytime. How long has she been forgoing beautiful things because she takes them for granted?

When the door finally opens, she practically tumbles into the hallway, drops her backpack on the floor, and only with the greatest effort manages to haul her bike up the front steps. She waves to Babak and Julietta to follow her into the house. They carry their bicycles up the steps together and lean them on the wall inside. Britta shuts the door, and then they stand there, the three of them, in the absolute blackness of a windowless entrance hall.

"Where are we?" Julietta's voice comes out of the void.

"The place is called Wiebüttel."

"How far did we ride? A hundred kilometers?"

"A bit more than forty."

"Intense," Julietta says, although her brief hesitation reveals that she doesn't think forty sounds so impressive.

"Don't!" Britta cries when she hears Babak groping along the wall for a light switch. "Light can be seen from outside."

"Okay." Babak sounds weak. "And water? I'm dying of thirst."

"The kitchen's on the right, if I remember correctly. Just stay here."

She feels her way, bangs her shin on one of the bicycles, and stifles a cry, even though sparks fly before her eyes for a moment. When she finds and opens the door, her surroundings become a little brighter. Some light is coming through the kitchen window, maybe moonlight or the first light of dawn or the vague residue of light pollution that exists even in rural areas. In one corner of the kitchen stands a white enamel coal stove with a thick cooking plate, curved legs, and pretty handles, reminiscent of the days when there were world wars and smallpox. The blue and white kitchen floor says, "Peel potatoes and look out the window. Everything will be fine." But there's no sink and no faucets.

Britta feels her way back down the hall, bumps against Julietta, who giggles softly, and finds the bathroom, in which the old tiles are chipped and broken and have not been replaced with new ones. A brand-new, still shrink-wrapped bathtub, as yet uninstalled, is standing against the wall, and next to it hangs a washbasin with a mixer tap. When Britta turns the lever for cold water, the pipes start to moan, the sound spreading out deep inside the bowels of the house. Not a drop.

"The water's turned off," she calls into the hall. "We'll take care of that tomorrow."

"Babs is a total wreck," Julietta calls back.

With a little effort of the will, Britta again ignores that idiotic "Babs," along with the fact that Julietta would rather speak for him than for herself. "Take it easy," she says. "Just come with me."

Down in the stream, the water's flowing fast and cold. They have to lean over very far to scoop it up in their hands. Britta suppresses the idea that this water is alive, that tiny, tiny living creatures are wriggling in it, little worms and fishes and maggots and leeches, not to mention bacteria and microbes, all of which are descending into her body as she so greedily drinks. All three drink as much as they can, because they have no bottle, no can, not even a bucket they could use to bring a supply of water back to the house.

Tomorrow they'll get organized. Every house, even one that's standing empty, contains useful items. There are cellars, attics, toolsheds in which miscellaneous stuff can be found, flowerpots, tools, leftover firewood or coal, crates and boxes that can be used as tables and chairs, preserving jars you can drink out of, an old wheelbarrow, maybe even pillows or blankets and the main water tap. Now bright streaks in the eastern sky are clearly visible, and Britta and the others run back to the house through the garden. They all flinch, scared half to death, when three cats come skittering toward them at the door. Britta and Babak hold tight to each other, panting, feeling silly and light-headed after drinking so much so fast. Julietta squats down and extends a hand. And the cats actually come closer, first the gray one, then the black-and-white one, and finally even the striped one; they thrust their heads forward warily, sniffing at Julietta's fingers, and then with erect tails press themselves against her knees.

Inside the house, the outlines of objects are visible by now: the bicycles, the backpack, and in the background a staircase leading to the upper floor. Britta instructs the other two to go upstairs and lie on the only bed, which has a double mattress. She dismisses Babak's protest with a wave of her hand, though not even she has any idea why she's doing that, why she doesn't go up there herself and lie down on the mattress that smells like a grandmother, under the light fixture with the painted cats, up there, where she and Janina rested and were happy without knowing it. Babak could stretch out next to her, and Julietta would have to roll herself up in a corner of another room, commander and soldier, but instead Britta insists on playing the heroine, on sleeping alone without a bed, as if it might serve any purpose whatsoever for her to punish herself.

In the hall, she puts her arms around the backpack and heaves it up, it's nearly as heavy as a seven-year-old girl. She carries it into the kitchen and empties everything out onto the coal stove's cast-iron plate. She folds the fleece blankets lengthwise and lays them on top of each other, then rolls the face towel into a pad she can use as a headrest. The floor feels hard and cold under the thin blankets. Britta stares at the rectangle of the window as it steadily gets brighter and thinks so despairingly about Vera that her heart beats like a fist against her breastbone. She's absolutely certain she'll never ever be able to fall asleep, and then she falls asleep.

When she wakes up, she doesn't immediately know where she is. The sun's shining in her face, she can hardly see anything, a glittering substance fills the air: dust, she's inhaling dust, dust covers everything, dust is accumulating in her hair and penetrating all her pores. Britta sits bolt upright and gags; she's been sleeping on the blue and white tile floor, and everything around her is covered with filth. Her first thought is to climb on her bicycle, ride home, yank open the door, and shout at the top of her voice, "I'm back!" In her imagination, she can see Vera running to her, she can feel the impact of the little body when the girl throws herself into her arms. But she can also see the empty worktable in the practice and the photo of G. Flossen's dead body. With some difficulty, she gets to her feet. All her bones ache from lying on the hard floor. She'd give a lot for a look at a clock. From the position of the sun, she figures she's slept for three hours, no more.

Dazed though she is, she can make out her treasures on top of the stove. It's incredible how few things there are, compared with how heavy the backpack was. And she seems to have packed only useless items. When you don't have a can opener, a tower of canned goods is sheer mockery. The same goes for pasta without a cooking pot and a properly functioning stove. What she might get up to with work gloves and duct tape is a complete mystery to her. She greedily rips open one of the little juice cartons, drinks the contents in one gulp, and then does the same with a second carton, the multivitamin juice causing voluptuous little explosions on her gums. After some brief reflection, she sticks the remaining four cartons into the empty backpack, crumples it up, and shoves it between the legs of the coal stove. She shakes out the fleece blankets, swirling up yet more dust, throws the face towel over her shoulder, picks up toothbrush, toothpaste, and shower gel, and goes outside. An orange cat tries to get close to her, but she shoos it off with hand claps and loud hisses.

After she has overcome her reluctance and wet her face and arms with the stream's contaminated water, and after she's brushed her teeth and even washed her hair, she feels like a different woman. She tells herself that she's a person with a brain in good working order; whatever the problem, she'll find a solution. Sunlight glitters between the leaves of the trees, birds are splendidly twittering, and all at once, Britta can comprehend why people lie in a neglected meadow and look at the sky for hours on end. The mild breeze carries off the wretched feelings of the previous night, strokes Britta's damp arms, cools her face, dries her hair. *That's Nature,* she thinks, *it always just keeps going, no matter what happens.* Should she suddenly fall to the ground stone dead, the event would merit, as far as the sparrows were concerned, at most a brief, surprised pause before they returned to their sparrow business. As long as the sun sends energy, there will be fluttering, running, and creeping, mating, brooding, hatching, hunting, and fighting. Why should Britta stand here in despair, when her state is of interest to nothing and no one but herself?

Chapter

22

The bedroom is sunny and bright. Babak and Julietta are lying on the wide bed, their backs to each other, not touching. The gray cat's asleep at their feet. All three look as though they've been sleeping there every night for a long time now. Britta stands in the doorway a while, observing the still life, listening to the regular breathing. She feels something, something strong, but she can't tell whether it's beautiful or sad.

Actually, she wanted to wake up the two of them, but then she didn't have the heart to do it. She's burning to discuss the situation with Babak, but the truth is it can wait. Everything can wait. No more hurry. She has temporarily withdrawn from the popular society game called "Stress," which requires players to pack a day like a suitcase, striving to fit in as much as they can. Britta has nothing to eat, almost nothing to wear, no music, no Internet, and stupidly enough, she hasn't even brought anything to read. What she suddenly has, in abundance, is time. For a moment, this realization makes her slightly giddy.

Which could also be attributable to low blood sugar. She

absolutely must find some tool she can use to open the cans of food.

She remembers from her first visit that the cellar is relatively dry but doesn't recall what's down there. She tucks her head between her shoulders and slinks through the low vaults, entering one room after another, resolving not to think about spiders and not to be disappointed. She discovers a couple of wobbly wooden racks, on which—apart from dust—there is only an assortment of old preserving jars; some broken wooden crates, with which—however she may wish to—she can do nothing; and a shovel whose shaft has been sawed off. The preserving jars are so dirty that at first she doesn't dare touch them, but then she does anyway, carries them upstairs, and deposits them in the kitchen before continuing her search in the attic. The sight that confronts her up there is no better: a large, dusty surface area; light coming in through the gaps between the roof tiles; and a mound of old textiles, which smell moldy and are out of the question as a sleeping pad.

In the garden, her recollection that Janina's dream house includes neither a garage nor a toolshed nor a chicken coop proves correct. But Britta has no intention of letting herself be discouraged. She goes around the house to the area where an overgrown hedgerow conceals the neighbors' property from view. She pushes the long shoots aside, ignoring the tickling and the scratches on her skin, until she finds a place where she can force her way through the undergrowth. Crouching down, she remains hidden in the hedge. The neighboring lot features a country house, a sort of dacha, with green shutters and a shed whose door is propped shut with a diagonally placed wooden beam. The grass has been mowed in patches, and a child's swing hangs from one of the trees. But the dacha's shutters are tightly shut, and the garden breathes the peaceful atmosphere of disuse. This is a weekend property. Britta lets several minutes elapse in which absolutely nothing happens. There are no human voices to be heard; nothing moves except the birds in the branches. Eventually, she creeps out of the hedge, runs crouching to the shed, and silently rejoices when a swift hand movement suffices to dislodge the beam. The bottom of the door is stuck fast in the ground, so Britta has to lift it and drag it forcibly across the thick sod until a crack wide enough to slip through appears. When her eyes adjust to the dim light inside the shed, she almost weeps for joy.

Approximately an hour later, Britta sinks down onto her new bench, a construction of fruit crates that she's put together in the kitchen. Her entire body is sticky with sweat and dirt, her fingers black, her disheveled hair festooned with little twigs and leaves. But she no longer minds that; she's exhausted and proud of what she has accomplished. She crawled through the hedgerow at least ten times, being careful to take a new way every time so as not to tread down the grass too conspicuously. Next to the toilet in the bathroom, there now stands a bucket of water from the stream, and on the other side, a small stack of paper towels lies ready in a flat little box. In the kitchen, there are a couple of wine bottles, rinsed in the stream and filled with water, and beside them some cleaned-up preserving jars for drinking vessels. In the living room, she's put two sawhorses, on which an unhinged door can be laid to serve as a table, though she'll need Babak's help for that job.

Britta is especially proud of a little stock of tools, including a hammer, a pair of pliers, screws, and nails, along with a screwdriver, with which she intends to tackle the canned goods. In addition, she's found a somewhat tattered broom with its accompanying dustpan, plus a few pots and pans, which in the absence of a stove will be good only for storing their modest possessions. For decorative purposes, she's even brought along an old rug, beaten clean in the garden and rolled out in the kitchen. The fruit-crate bench has been paired with a fruit-crate chest of drawers, which holds her meager wardrobe, and on top of which is a washbasin filled with fresh water. Toothbrush and toothpaste stand in a preserving jar; next to it lies the neatly folded face towel. She has fashioned a comparatively comfortable bed from a set of pillows and cushions normally used on garden furniture.

Sitting on the bench under the window, Britta stretches out her legs and is about to doze off when she hears a muffled thud, followed by boisterous laughter. Either one of them has fallen out of bed, or they're tussling with each other for fun. A second later, footsteps come pounding down the stairs, Julietta calls out, "Hoo-hoo!" and Babak "Britta?" and then they're both standing in the kitchen as if it were the most natural thing in the world, and perhaps it really is.

"Wow," says Babak, looking around. "You've settled in very nicely."

"Looks great," Julietta adds, and Britta lets herself be infected by her housemates' good mood, although how they've come by it is a mystery to her.

Britta guides the two through the house on a little tour, explaining what she's managed to bring in and construct. While Babak nods with moderate interest and indulges in a few discreet yawns, Julietta proves to be enthusiastic; she praises the tools, the furniture, and even the water bucket next to the john.

One's half-asleep, the other's feeling adventurous. Britta envies Babak and Julietta when she recognizes that they don't have to worry about parents, friends, life companions, or children. Their location, whatever it may be, is not very important to either one of them. A few days in exile, no contact with the outside world, uncertainty as to whether or not someone's closing in on them, the notion that they ought to flee farther away, maybe even to another country—all that may cause them some difficulties, but certainly no existential problems. Living like this must feel like a video game.

Britta and Babak lift the living room door off its hinges and lay it across the sawhorses. Then they sit on their fruit crates around their new table, their heads not much higher than the table's edge, and even though they have to laugh at this scene, there's still something solemn about it. The table makes them a group, maybe a family: people who eat, bicker, and discuss things together.

"Now for a great big breakfast," says Babak.

"Is the coffee ready yet?" asks Julietta.

"I wish," says Britta.

"I'll go and take a look at what we have." Julietta stands up to go to the kitchen, but Britta holds her back.

"The kitchen is my territory. Nobody enters that room but me."

Julietta, conciliatory, raises both hands. "No problem. Then I think the best idea would be for me to get on my bike and see if I can find a village baker somewhere around here. Or a gas station."

"Nobody leaves the house. If you need exercise, run up and down the stairs."

"Britta," says Babak. "She doesn't mean any harm."

Britta disappears into the kitchen and comes back with a bottle of water, three preserving jars, and a little bowl of dry pasta. These things, together with the improvised table they're served on, look like a caricature of hospitality.

"You can't be serious," Julietta says.

"Apparently, you still haven't grasped the situation."

"Then let's discuss it," Babak interjects. "How great is the threat?"

Britta reaches into her bag, which has been constantly attached to her body since yesterday evening, takes out the photo, and throws it on the table. The corners of the photograph are bent already, the formerly glossy surface is dull and cracked. All three look at it in silence.

"If the Empty Hearts want to take us out, why haven't they done it long before now?"

"Because they wanted something from us. We were supposed to let Lassie run and process masses of data until a number of useful names remained. We did that. As soon as Babak's code is broken, we're at best a burden to them, maybe even a danger."

"How did they know about the picture with the dots?"

Babak and Britta look at each other and shrug.

"Maybe they had a suspicion. At any rate, some of them were in the program."

"The one whose pants were too big was Philipp," says Babak.

"You recognized him in the video?"

"You didn't?" He sticks a dry noodle in his mouth; the crackling sound between his teeth sounds ridiculously loud. "Five or six years ago. Very nice guy. Determined to die for the women's movement."

In Britta's mind's eye, the vague contours of a man appear, a young man who nodded affirmatively as he spoke, as if he had a constant need to confirm that whatever he was saying made sense.

"The one with anxiety disorder," she slowly says.

"One of the few who withdrew at Step Five," Babak adds.

"Once he got Ativan, he suddenly started doing extremely well."

"He thanked us back then, remember? With tears in his eyes."

"And now these rats are teaming up against us." Britta slaps the table hard, overturning a water glass. Julietta runs into the bathroom and comes back carrying the little box with the paper towels.

"Are you nuts?" Britta snatches the box away from her. "This stuff is precious. Or do you want to wipe your butt with your hand?"

"'Teaming up against us' isn't quite right," says Babak. "They're following a plan. It doesn't necessarily have anything to do with us—except that they're using our resources."

"But what sort of plan?" Britta asks.

"A robbery," Julietta suggests.

"Not a bad thought." Britta gazes at her appraisingly. The gray cat silently enters the room and runs without hesitation over to Julietta. It sinks down on its haunches, takes aim, and in one fluid movement springs onto Julietta's lap. The girl's experienced hands begin to stroke the animal, which lolls and stretches under the fondling.

"Such a mega-thing," says Julietta eagerly. "Mega-fighters, mega-planning, mega-dough."

"Can you please stop saying 'mega'?"

"The gold reserves in the European Central Bank," Babak suggests.

"Or a few savings banks," says Julietta. "They're sitting on a whole lot of money."

"All of that's conceivable," says Britta. "So let's say they're planning a massive attack and a big haul. And they're taking the people they need to pull off such a strike from our program."

"Not from the program," Babak corrects her, "but from the preselection. They have the data on one thousand and forty-three candidates, most of them with an average suicidality value of six points. Normally, that wouldn't even be high enough for them to get an invitation from The Bridge. A hundred and twenty got a score of around nine points. Of those, forty, more or less, would have made the short list, and even in those cases we don't know what kind of progress they would have made in the program."

"The Empty Hearts don't give a shit whether the people are actually suicidal. They're just looking for men who want to join them. Who want a little testosterone hogwash, accessorized with an English name, a tattoo, and God knows what kinds of rituals. They're not interested in taking great care, they're interested in firepower."

"Maybe it would be better if we talked about what's going to happen next for us," says Julietta.

In the ensuing silence, the cat's loud purring is clearly audible, like the motor of a perpetual contentment machine. Stroking the cat with one hand, Julietta lights a cigarette with the other. Britta's surprised to see how smoking rounds out Julietta, how cat and cigarette make her a complete person. Smoking probably means to her what a bed, sufficient food, and a working shower mean to other people.

"Why don't you go to the police?"

When Babak laughs, Julietta turns to him. "You have the break-in, the surveillance camera video, the photo of the dead man. That's enough for the cops to bust these Hearts dudes."

Babak continues to laugh softly to himself, but Britta makes him stop with a wave of her hand. "We can't go to the police," she explains. "We're not the good guys."

"In that case, how about a counterattack?" Julietta's slowly getting going. "Your algorithm can identify the head of the group."

"Lassie's not God Almighty," says Babak. "Besides, she's not here."

"Don't be so lame, Babs! If they're really recruiting a hundred and twenty people, that'll make a mighty big cyber-noise. It can't be so hard to pull out the right lines and put them together."

"And then?" Babak asks.

"What? 'And then?'" Julietta shakes her uncombed mane. "And then we build an explosive vest or something of the sort, I go marching in, and . . . BAM!"

BAM!—problem solved. Britta finds herself thinking about Vera so intensely that her eyes grow moist. She wipes her face with the balls of her thumbs.

"The Bridge never carries out attacks on its own," Babak says. "We're just intermediaries. Service providers, not terrorists."

Of course, Babak is right, but there's something tempting in the idea. *It would be self-defense,* says a little voice in the back of Britta's head.

"You would do that for us?" she asks.

"What?"

"Go to war for us. Instead of animal protection."

Julietta says nothing. In her enthusiasm, she has let herself get carried away for a moment. Britta watches the girl as she's initially assailed by doubt and then gives herself over completely to reflection. Something is stirring in Britta too. Deep inside her, a hatch opens, and behind it lies hidden a vast, dark space she hasn't entered for a very long time. She imagines a sign next to the hatch: "Principles Storeroom—Restricted Access—Authorized Personnel Only!" She has always persuaded herself that this room was entirely empty, and therefore there was no reason to inspect its inventory from time to time. While Julietta struggles with her dilemma—not an invented one, a real one, the kind you confront only when you have a clear idea of life—Britta feels an urge to take a quick look inside her own inner storage space. It suddenly occurs to her that the source of her constant nausea may be found there. But then Julietta looks up, and the hatch slams shut.

"I'm sorry," the girl says regretfully. "I'm afraid I can't do it after all."

Chapter **23**

After the meeting, Britta orders that the rest of the day is to be spent fixing up and settling into their new location. They guess the time to be about one thirty in the afternoon. Julietta and Babak receive permission to go to the stream to wash up. Britta tidies the conference room and sets about subjecting the kitchen to a thorough cleaning, as far as that's possible without a cleaning product. At two thirty subjective time, she gives the order to open a can of ravioli. They all gather around the table at once.

The operation is harder than expected. The screwdriver slips off the can, and hunger intensifies impatience until it's unbearable. Babak has a go with the hammer, while Britta and Julietta outdo each other with good advice. Everyone wants to grab the hammer and try it for themselves. The first hole opens with a bang; red juice spurts all the way up to the ceiling.

"Watch out you don't cut yourselves," Babak cries. "Actually, do we have any bandages?"

When Britta replies in the negative, Babak rolls his eyes, but the waspish comment she wants to make gets cut off, because at this very moment, Julietta manages to bend the lid of the can up a little way. As they have neither spoons nor forks, they let the cold, slippery dough pockets slide directly into their hands through the opening in the lid. Red sauce drips on table and floor, and soon it looks as though they've murdered somebody. Britta insists that Julietta also must share the meal, and so each of them receives a disappointingly small portion that piques their hunger rather than assuages it.

Afterward, they clean and wipe the whole ground floor together, getting rid of dust, spiderwebs, and dead flies, until Britta feels that she can move through the rooms without trepidation.

Around four p.m. subjective time, just when they're about to go on yet another expedition to the toolshed in the neighbors' garden, they suddenly hear voices on the other side of the hedgerow and return to the house with pounding hearts. They lock the door from inside and lie on the floor of the entrance hall in case anyone tries to look through the windows. They lie there for a long, long time while nothing happens. At last, Britta sounds the all clear and gives the group permission to stand up.

It quickly becomes plain to her that from now on, there is absolutely nothing more for them to do. The water buckets next to the toilet are full, as are the reserve bottles of drinking water. The floor is swept, the beds made. Fixing up and settling into the new location has been concluded. Britta estimates the time at around four thirty in the afternoon. They have no smartphones, no tablets, no netbooks, no televisions, no LifeWatches or digital eyeglasses; Julietta doesn't even have her old-fashioned iPod with her. No newspapers, no books, no pencil, no piece of paper. It's four thirty on a fair-to-middling summer day. Before them lies the void.

Britta goes into the kitchen and pulls the door shut behind her as if the room were her study, and she'd like to be alone because she has something important to do. With her back to the wall, she sits on the fruit-crate bench and tests the stillness. Waits to see what will happen if she just sits there. Thoughts immediately start racing around and around in her head. They show her Vera, Richard, and her spick-and-span concrete house. Then she sees the burgled rooms of her practice, G. Flossen's corpse, and Guido Hatz's mustached face. The stillness murmurs; Britta hears voices, stands up, and opens the window, but there's nothing there. A beeping begins in her left ear—in her school days, the kids would always say, "Somebody's thinking about you!"—except that now it won't stop, it's in her right ear too, the beeping gets louder, and Britta's heart is knocking against her ribs. *This is tinnitus, it never goes away, it'll drive you crazy, you'll go mad,* and she springs into action, searching the room, looking for whatever may be causing this beeping, but there are no electronics and no electric appliances, not even a toaster, and besides, she's already turned off the power in the cellar.

Britta keeps returning to the window and looking out, checking to see if it's getting dark, but the sun is still high in the sky, apparently time isn't passing, or maybe her estimates of the time have been totally wrong and it's only early afternoon or midday or morning, maybe the settling in, the ravioli, the meeting, and the housecleaning didn't actually require more than an hour and a half. Britta would give anything to have a look at a clock; she's lost without a map in a wasteland outside time.

Her stomach hurts so much that, against her will, she pulls out the folded backpack and drinks the last two little cartons of multivitamin juice. But that just makes her stomachache even worse; she throws her arms around her body and doubles up in pain. Lying on the cushions, which are constantly sliding away from one another, she closes her eyes and tries to think about something else. The first thing she sees is a plate of pasta with gorgonzola prepared the way Richard does it, steaming linguine covered with thick sauce: peeled tomatoes, two flat blocks of gorgonzola, fresh chives, a cup of cream.

Next she sees Julietta, dressed in black, walking along a street in the morning light, her movements decelerated as though shown in slow motion, her upper body broadened by the suicide vest she's wearing under her jacket. She throws her hair from side to side like someone in a shampoo commercial, she's gliding rather than walking, she swings her arms elegantly at her sides: a marvelous sight. Julietta enters a room in which several men—a tall thin one, a little squat one, and three others—stand up from their chairs and stare at Julietta, all five of them with turned-up shirtsleeves and open collars, so that their "Empty Hearts" tattoos can be seen. Julietta turns around and smiles at Britta, and then she detonates the bomb. In slow motion, everything flies apart, Britta sees the horror on the men's faces, which immediately thereafter explode into pieces, limbs flying around, flesh liquefied, pulverized, turned into the merest biowaste. A flood of happiness surges through Britta, a feeling of relief, euphoria, love for mankind.

Something touches her face. She jumps, she screams, she's lying on the floor, having slid off the cushions, she was actually asleep, she flails her arms, finally manages to sit up, and sees a cat duck into the corner next to the door and bare its teeth in a threat display. The little bastard was hiding somewhere. When she opens the door, the cat darts out of the room. Britta's heart is racing as though someone has tried to kill her. *I can't do this,* she thinks. *I can't stand it here anymore. I can't cope. I want to go home*. She reels across the hall in the direction of the bathroom, uses the toilet, and inadvertently knocks the little box with the paper towels onto the floor. By doing so, she discovers, under the stacked sheets, a crushed medication package, Ativan, two wide strips of it, and only three tablets missing; Julietta must have packed a supply before they fled the city. *This is Julietta's baggage, it's the sum of her possessions.* Britta picks up the package of pills gleefully, because now she has the girl in the palm of her hand. If Julietta's as hooked on those things as Britta suspects she is, after two days of withdrawal she'll be ready to give up on animal protection.

Britta hides the pills in the firebox of the antique stove. Then, with a groan, she lies down on the makeshift mattress again. Exhaustion drones inside her skull; the weakness in her arms and legs is painful. She can't sleep. Her whole body itches. No doubt, there are vermin in the house, mites, ticks, fleas, something that will eat her alive if she doesn't keep moving. *It's still not really dark yet, it will never be dark again, is it maybe dusk? Is it a little darker outside than it was before, or at least less bright? There's nothing to do. Absolutely nothing to do.* Britta kneels in front of the stove. She takes out the little cardboard box, presses out a pill, and puts it into her mouth.

The next thing that wakes her up is a hand, a hand shaking her shoulder. And then a voice: "Come. You have to see this."

It's Babak's hand and Babak's voice. Half-asleep, Britta struggles to her feet.

"What time is it?"

Babak laughs. He goes down the hall ahead of her. It's night, pitch-black night. One behind the other, they climb the stairs. There's a light on up there. *That must be my flashlight,* Britta thinks, *they were in the room with me and took my flashlight,* but right away she sees flickering, and then the lamp itself: a gas lamp, hanging from a hook on the wall.

"Where did you two . . ." she begins, but then she's in the doorway, with a clear view of the bed. Julietta's sitting on the edge and beaming like an artist at her gallery opening. Britta sees, artistically arranged on the bed, three bags of chips, a cylindrical can of Prinzen Rolle sandwich cookies, three bottles of soda, several little packets of little gummy bears, and a large paper bag, in which, Britta presumes, there are bread rolls and croissants. While she looks, the others remain silent.

One of them left the house; judging from the looks on their faces, it was Julietta. She disregarded Britta's orders and rode her bike somewhere to buy things. Britta ought to yell at her, reprimand her, maybe even throw her out of the program. But she's got so much saliva in her mouth that she can't speak. Before she knows it, Julietta has pressed a cookie into her hand. Britta takes a bite. She's quite aware that she should eat slowly, preferably a bread roll rather than a cookie, she should chew thoroughly and swallow cautiously, but she polishes off the first cookie and stuffs three more in her mouth and reaches out a hand for the fifth. Babak is scooping chips out of a bag with both hands; Julietta sits next to him, eats nothing, and smiles proudly. She lights a cigarette and begins to tell the story while Babak and Britta chew and chew. She rode pretty far, she says, all the way to Celle and an Aral station there. She was the only customer, and the boy at the night window had put her order together with the most perfect indifference; her case was clear, because the stuff she bought looked like provisions for the final act of a party, when nobody who's left feels like drinking any more alcohol. As for the time, it was shortly after two when she made the purchases, so now it's probably getting close to four, they should enjoy this moment of knowing what time it is, and in fact, Britta enjoys this knowledge almost as intensely as she does the chocolate cream in her mouth.

Julietta goes on talking, she says she hid her face as well as she could from the surveillance cameras in the gas station, but without conspicuously turning away, and after all, nobody's looking for her, nobody knows anything about her, and even though Britta's aware that these assertions aren't completely correct, because anyone who's familiar with The Bridge and observes its activity for a while will know that Julietta's one of its candidates, she—Britta—tacitly admits that there's little possibility of the Hearts' stumbling by chance upon a girl who's riding a bicycle around a commercial zone in Celle late at night. Britta doesn't begrudge Julietta her joy over her successful feat; there's something touching about her enthusiasm, which reaches its peak when she says, "You two are the Red Army Faction, and I'm your support base," and they all have to laugh at that.

After eight cookies, Britta's hunger is sufficiently satisfied for her to regain self-control. She stands up, slightly swaying from the sugar rush, and takes her leave to lie down a little longer.

Julietta follows her to the head of the stairs. "Have the tablets made you feel better?" she asks, and she sounds so innocent, so free of reproach, ridicule, or irony, that Britta can do nothing but nod mutely.

"Let's divide the supply fairly," says Julietta, and she briefly touches Britta's shoulder before turning around and returning to her room.

Chapter **24**

The very next morning, Britta gives revised orders. From now on, Babak is to ride his bicycle to Braunschweig every night. He'll make his way to Lassie's secret location, bring the server online, and start searching for the Empty Hearts' recruitment efforts. He must be back before daybreak, which means that he has to travel forty kilometers in each direction, and every time in considerably less than two hours. In no case can he stop on the way, speak to anyone, or drop into a service station. Food procurement is Julietta's responsibility. On her much-too-small mountain bike, she will seek out appropriate shops, stores, etc., within a twenty- to thirty-kilometer radius, without ever showing up twice at the same place. Both Babak and Julietta will leave the house when darkness starts to fall; both are happy to have a job to do.

They give extensive thought to the question of how long Lassie's online search activities can continue before being noticed. Babak says it depends on whether the Hearts have an IT expert in their ranks and, if so, on how capable he or she is. Even if Lassie should create a stir, it would still be no easy task to draw conclusions about her well-secured location, and so they can figure on having several days left, maybe even a couple of weeks.

Britta takes on the heaviest burden. She can't leave the building; she keeps the household in order, washes and dries socks, sees to it that the water supply is full, the table clear, and the food stocks adequate, all of which takes her barely an hour. She spends an afternoon shampooing the rocking horse in the living room with shower gel, cleaning its saddle and bridle, and polishing its amber eyes. When the rocking horse is white again instead of gray and smells of vanilla, time stretches out before Britta into infinity once more.

For the most part, Babak and Julietta sleep until late in the day after making their nightly rounds, while Britta slinks through the house, conscientiously performs her modest duties, and tries to keep her aggression in check. She has used twine and duct tape to bind together the cushions that serve as her bed so that they don't slide apart anymore, and thanks to her daily Ativan ration, she manages to sleep a few hours every night. Her unrest, however, doesn't leave her—it's as though her system were conducting a permanent, hopeless war of attrition against itself.

She gives Babak two little notes to deliver. No envelopes, no return address, no signature. Despite such precautions, the risk is irresponsibly high, because they have to assume that known locations will be under surveillance. But Britta can't act otherwise, and the others stifle any comments.

The first note reads, "I'm fine. I love you."

The second, "Operative pause. Stand by."

Babak drops the first note into the concrete cube's mailbox, after crouching in some bushes for twenty minutes and making sure that no human person is anywhere around. He gives the second note to the night porter at the Deutsches Haus hotel and tells him it's for Jawad and Marquardt. After that, he spends an hour riding his bicycle all over the nighttime city, checking every minute to see if he's being followed, before returning to headquarters.

Afternoons are the worst, viscous blurs of time that refuse to move on. Summer remembers what it's capable of and abuses the badly insulated house with merciless solar radiation. Dust and heat unite into something that barely deserves the name "air" and doesn't allow itself to be breathed very well. When the heat becomes unbearable, Britta uses one of her garden furloughs to lie in the stream for a quarter of an hour. The sparrows make a ruckus in the cherry tree, the flowing water is pure relief, and for a few moments, Britta can leave everything behind her. She peers into the blue sky and promises a God she doesn't believe in anything he wants if he will only get her out of here alive, and be quick about it.

Julietta has bought Ping-Pong paddles and balls at some gas station, and now the two of them, she and Babak, kneel on the floor upstairs in the afternoons and hit a ball back and forth, which produces a nerve-racking noise. Britta bears it as long as she can, and then she charges into the hall, bellows "Quiet, dammit!" and withdraws again, while upstairs, Babak and Julietta grumble audibly. Before long, there's usually a knock on the kitchen door, and one of them requests something to eat or asks some senseless question meant only to lead to an argument. Then they accuse each other of being to blame for their present situation. Britta calls Babak a loser; Babak calls Britta a tyrannical control freak, and if Julietta tries to interfere, the other two, in unison, forbid her to speak. Britta threatens to reduce Julietta's daily Ativan ration, and Julietta asks Britta if she intends to blow up the Moltke Bridge by herself. Quarreling with one another is dreadful, and at the same time it feels good, like an insect bite you constantly have to scratch.

Babak often deflects reproaches or questions with an "I don't care!" that makes Britta so furious that she follows him through the house and lectures him until he holds his hands over his ears like a little child. She wants him to break down, and because he doesn't, her despair grows to such proportions that she herself starts bawling. At some point they back away from each other out of sheer exhaustion, crawl back to their respective corners, and wait for night to fall; Babak and Julietta, so they can leave the house, and Britta, so she can take her pill and go to bed.

When she's lying on her cushions, Britta frequently recalls a film about the far-left 1970s RAF, the Red Army Faction, that she saw years ago. The film shows how the underground fighters slowly but surely go crazy. How they begin to distrust one another, gall one another, hate one another. When she first saw it, Britta thought the RAF terrorists must have been weaklings; in their place, she was sure, she herself would have done better.

Out of boredom, Britta does something she hasn't done for an eternity: she reads newspapers. She's told Julietta to bring her the most recent editions of the only two papers that still have a decent circulation, the *Darmstädter Allgemeine Zeitung* and the *KULT*. For years now, the *DAZ* hasn't found fault with the CCC and instead provides a statistical foundation and intellectual trappings for its right-wing, nationalistic edifice. The inveterate Christian Democrats of the *KULT*, on the other hand, never tire of glorifying the past under Angela Merkel. All the other papers offer a mix of ticker-tape copy, regional news, and soccer results, content so cheap they don't have to sell advertising anymore. The few remaining thinkers have retreated to blogs, where in a combination of self-accusation and recrimination they continue to argue about who's responsible for the triumph of the CCC.

The newspapers' print layout and smell transport Britta to another time. How proud she was when, as a middle school student, she started reading newspapers! It meant she was observing the world through grown-up eyes. Britta acquired opinions and tried them out on her parents, studied argumentation patterns and practiced the vocabulary of indignation. She unhesitatingly joined the community of citizens who tasked themselves with defending democracy, not in the Hindu Kush, but at home in living rooms, in open-plan offices, and around barroom tables. Later, when she was at the university, Britta still felt like a part of the extended democratic family, even when the front lines grew indistinct and the sense of community began to erode. In those days, Trump wasn't yet a daily reality, just the odd scandal; concepts like pluralism, equality, and integration still had meaning. Reading the newspaper was like a membership card; it gave a sense of belonging. As astonishing as it seems to Britta now, in those days there was something she believed in.

Lying full stretch on her stomach with the cool kitchen tiles beneath her, Britta ignores the fact that the sunlight has once again tracked down clumps of cat hair in the corners. Alternating newspapers, she reads articles from the *DAZ* and the *KULT.* The pieces in the *DAZ* are long and unaccompanied by any pictures: the concept of the nation and of the national; cultural morphology; an outline for a new weapons law. *KULT* still runs thick headlines—hands off free trade, five reasons why Angela Merkel was right, and so forth—along with soccer news and half-naked female soccer players. The longer Britta reads, the greater her discomfort grows; it turns into an ache, first mental, then physical, so strong that she must interrupt her reading, roll onto her back, and breathe into her stomach, and while she lies there and breathes and looks through the window at the sunlit green of the trees, she understands, all at once, what's happening to her, what's hurting her, why there came a time when she stopped reading newspapers and reflecting on the world. The cause is "paradoxical pain," the agony of paradoxes. Nonvoters disgruntled with democracy run for office and win, while committed democrats stop voting. Intellectual newspapers work to get over humanism, while populist rags hold on to the ideals of the Enlightenment. In a world made of contradictions, thinking well and speaking well cease to be options, because every thought cancels itself out and every word means its opposite. In the midst of paradoxes, the human spirit can find no place; Britta can't be a voter or a citizen anymore, or even a customer and a consumer, but only a service provider, a member of a service team that supports and supplements the collective journey to the abyss. In such a world, one can be against political violence and still head an enterprise like The Bridge.

The resulting pain has never left her. It has sealed itself and sunk deep into the cellar of her personality. Britta would like to draw a black border around every single newspaper page, for each is an obituary, the epitaph of a deceased friend. *Rest in peace, public discourse, you were the greatest host of all time. There was always room at your table, you were ever available for animated dinner discussions or pub visits, you could be battle and sport, but also homeland and destination. We remain behind, unconsoled, isolated, distraught.*

During the night, Britta has a nightmare. She dreams of riots. She watches through a tinted car window while several people are beaten to death by a group of men in Braunschweig's Cathedral Square. The police don't intervene, and the mob moves on. Britta doesn't understand what they want, she only hears them chanting, "Full Hands Empty Hearts Full Hands Empty Hearts." She knows they'll be coming for her next, for her and her family, and she races through the city in her car, rushing home to protect Vera and Richard, innocently asleep in their beds. She wants to grab them and flee with them before the mob reaches their neighborhood, but she can't find the house, she can't even find her street, Braunschweig is spinning around and around, Britta drives faster and then faster still, her frenzy grows, time's running away from her, she's going to fail, she'll lose everything, she awakens with a cry.

She lies on her cushions, breathing heavily, fighting the urge to take another Ativan, telling herself that the panic will subside on its own, that it does no harm to the body, even if it makes your heart ache and cuts off oxygen, that she's experiencing nothing more than a physical overreaction, the sort of thing she learned about in her training. She gets up and opens the window. The cool night air is a gift; it strokes her body like an affectionate touch. It's so quiet that Britta can hear the bats hunting in the garden. The soft flapping of their wings, like fabric moving in the wind—no human could devise it, and yet it exists, totally independent of human imaginative power. The bats plunge through the darkness, and should their flight have a message, it goes like this: *Don't be afraid.*

Chapter

Britta spends the rest of the night waiting for Babak. The seconds pass like minutes, the minutes like hours. Julietta has bought three children's watches at a gas station, and one of them—bright green in color—is lying next to Britta's makeshift bed. Living without a watch was torture, but now even just staring at the dial is becoming a torment. In spite of the Ativan, she hasn't had more than two hours' sleep. The thought that the pills might stop working causes Britta heart palpitations and respiratory distress, which she regards as proof that the pills don't work anymore, an assessment that makes her heart beat even faster, until her chest hurts so much that she has to stand up and open the window again to get some air. During the psychiatric clinic stay prescribed in Step 5, almost all the candidates are treated with Ativan. Dependency sets in after fourteen days, and withdrawal from the drug is said to be as brutal as withdrawal from heroin. Julietta needs two tablets a day in order to remain capable of functioning. Since she doesn't plan to outlive her Ativan supply, she's indifferent to the dangers of addiction.

Shortly before five, Julietta returns and hands over her purchases—food, newspapers, cigarettes—which Britta sorts into her resources management system, and which will be distributed according to fixed rules. Julietta's so exhausted she can hardly stand up. Every night she has to go a little farther, without knowing where and when she'll come upon the next gas station with twenty-four-hour service. Tonight she went beyond Celle and had to summon up all her remaining strength to get back to the house in good time. She asks Britta if she can start going back a second time to gas stations she's already stopped at, making sure that a sufficient interval of time has passed between visits. Britta replies that she'll put the matter on the agenda for discussion at the next status meeting, scheduled for three p.m. sharp. When she asks where Babak is, Julietta shrugs and goes off to bed.

Britta remains in the kitchen, standing at the window. The first daylight is dissolving the darkness. At this hour, there are no animals to be seen—the nocturnal ones are already asleep and the diurnal ones haven't gotten up yet. Any minute now, Babak must appear. He'll be frustrated from his efforts to make Lassie produce the desired results, even though the algorithm for an alternative search pattern is ready for implementation. Britta has grown accustomed to not knowing where he spends the nights. Even if he's in some damp, nasty cellar, hunched in front of a screen, she envies him. *Anything's better than this house.* With every passing minute, her aggravation increases. She has decreed that he absolutely must be back before five a.m. at the very latest; now it's already a quarter after, and no trace of Babak. Anxiety makes it impossible for Britta to lie down again. She paces around the house, peering out every window, watching the light redden the treetops on the east side of the garden, flinching when she hears the first songbird. Why can't

Babak simply do what he's told? Even Julietta gives her all to be back on time. Britta will have to reprimand him, and then he'll tell her once again that she needs to control her paranoia. That she gets a kick out of bossing people around because she has no other way to feel loved.

It's five thirty. Britta's boiling with rage. She's sweating so much that her T-shirt is glued to her back. The dust drives her crazy, the cats drive her crazy, there's no escape, the heat will get hotter, the cats will continue to lie on the chairs in the conference room, on the window bench, even on the rocking horse, and on Britta's pallet if she forgets for just one minute to close the kitchen door, it absolutely doesn't matter how many times she chases the wretched creatures away, they always come back, always, changing colors, dwindling and then multiplying again, another pointless day is beginning to turn, slowly, excruciatingly, on its axis, only to arrive at its starting point, at another sunrise, always another sunrise, and in the midst of this imploding universe, which is held together only by laws, by rules, Babak doesn't stick to the rules, he comes and goes when he feels like it, as if they were on a family excursion here, as if he were still incapable of recognizing the seriousness of the situation, as if Britta were the only rational being in the world, his tardiness makes her feel unbearably alone, *if the Hearts have grabbed him,* she thinks, *I'll kill myself.*

It's shortly before six when the front door opens. Babak carries his bicycle into the entrance hall and simply lets it fall to the floor. He doesn't seem to care whether Britta or Julietta is sleeping, or whether the crash can be heard on the street. Britta's standing as though paralyzed in the conference room, where she's been walking around the table for the past several minutes.

"Good morning," says Babak.

He's pale. He leans heavily against the wall. He's trembling. He is pure accusation, reproach made flesh, something she'd like to knock over with both hands so she wouldn't have to see it anymore. The sight of him intensifies Britta's wrath.

"Are you drunk?"

"Don't be ridiculous." Babak wearily shakes his head. "But you look pretty weird," he goes on, smiling a crooked smile.

Britta looks down at herself. She's wearing nothing but underpants and a T-shirt. And yet she's sweating. Dirt's sticking to her skin, she needs a rinse, that's all, she has to wash up, and then she'll be like new.

"Don't change the subject," she says. "You're too late."

"Do you have any idea how much I hurried to get home?"

"Not enough, apparently."

With a sigh, Babak crumples, gives up trying to talk to her, shakes his head again, and tries to get past her and up the stairs.

"Stay put, pal."

Never before has Britta called anyone "pal," but these days she's doing many things for the first time. When Babak keeps walking away from her, she grabs at his arm, catches the sleeve of his T-shirt, and hears the sound of tearing fabric, which must be absurdly delicate, because she didn't have a very tight grip on it. A cloud of male scent rises up. *We all stink,* Britta thinks, *we're all dirty, we've lost the war on grime.* In the harsh morning light, she can see how unshaven Babak is. Julietta brought him razor blades and shaving cream from a gas station, but there's no mirror in the house. *We aren't human anymore—any animal is cleaner. Hygienically, we've hit bottom.*

"You tore my sleeve off." Babak sounds shocked.

"You're too late," Britta murmurs, examining the piece of fabric in her hand from all sides.

"Let's be serious, Britta." He tries to take hold of her, but she bats his hand away. "You have to get yourself under control. If you keep on like this, you're going to drive us all to ruin."

"Me? You two?" She laughs. It does her good to laugh like that; it's the best joke she's heard in a long time. "I make the rules. I bear the responsibility. I'm holding the whole thing together."

"Britta."

Babak tries once again to touch her. Britta backs away and collides with the wall.

"Something's not right with you," Babak says. "You're slipping away from us. You're slipping away from yourself."

"Stop it!" She points an index finger. "Please don't talk to me like that! You can't even tell what time it is. No! I'm talking now." She really has to say something. The thoughts she's formulated over the course of many sleepless nights must finally come out in words. Her insights have been numerous; even just today she lay on her cushions and perceived various connections, while the objects in the room stared at her instead of vice versa. Among her realizations were things that had to do with Babak, now she must verbalize them, even though she's having difficulty concentrating for some reason. "You want me to feel bad. I was feeling bad already, before we came here. And now, all of a sudden, no matter what I do or say, you think everything's shit."

"Britta—"

"Shut your trap!" She doesn't care how loud she's getting, she has a right to be loud, this is her house, there's a preliminary contract and a notary appointment, terms that make her start to laugh again. *As if such things had any meaning whatsoever.* "Ever since we got here, you've shown your true face. You've never been my friend. You just needed somebody. A sister, a mother, a babysitter. Now you have Julietta, and so you treat me like dirt." There it is again: *dirt.* Surprised, Britta pauses for a moment. Everything has to do with everything else. Babak's leaning on the wall, right at the foot of the stairs. His head's resting on his chest; he knows she's right, this is the reaction of a person who's hearing some truth.

"When this is all over, I'm throwing you out. Your time with The Bridge is up. I don't want anything more to do with someone who can't manage to get home by five o'clock."

Babak lifts his head. He's crying. "I've—" he begins, but Britta doesn't let him go on.

"Maybe you aren't really going to Lassie. Maybe you're meeting your lovers and going out partying. While I sit around here racking my brains, you're hanging out at the I-Vent and laughing your head off at me."

"Today it took longer, because—"

"It's always been like this, I always did everything myself, you never had to make any decisions or bear any responsibility, you let me pull you along like . . ." Her strength fails her, she can't go on, she braces herself again, she has to bring this to an end. "Like a cart through dirt."

"The trail leads to Berlin," says Babak. "Chaussee Street. It's probably Guido Hatz."

Chapter **26**

When she wakes up, she feels something tickling her face. She wants to cry out, "Richard, stop that!" and tries to reach out a hand, but finds she can't move. Under her is no firm mattress, just sliding cushions. Then she realizes she's not awakening *from* a nightmare, but *in* a nightmare. She opens her eyes without seeing anything; either it's pitch-dark, or she's blind. Every time she tries to move, her body hurts, and so she lies still and listens. Someone's in the room. Something cool is laid on her forehead, a wet cloth. It feels good, and Britta drifts off again.

The next time she awakens, she knows immediately where she is. When she tries to sit up, she's pressed back down onto the cushions. She struggles and feels her own weakness, she's stuck like an insect in a drop of resin. Surrender brings relief. Britta's not sure who else is in the room, she hears a voice, female, friendly, then comes the cold cloth, which calms her down. When she'd get sick as a child, her mother would sit on the edge of her bed and cool her forehead. *Mama,* Britta thinks, *why did you leave me, none of this would have happened if you had been here.*

She dreams the Hearts have grabbed her. She's sitting on a chair, and someone is busy sewing her eyelids to her brows so that she'll be able to follow the impending torture unblinkingly.

Scream, scream, scream. Someone's holding her down, something big is being thrust into her mouth, a stone or a walnut, then comes water on top of that, *Step 6,* Britta thinks, and immediately panic sets in, she defends herself with arms and legs, water flows out of her mouth, *You must swallow,* someone says, at some point she swallows, painfully, the stone forces its way down her throat, and then it's over, she sinks back down onto the cushions, she sleeps.

Now she can see. It's daytime; the sun is shining, making little dust particles glint and dance in the air. A gray cat is sitting in the middle of a patch of sunlight, comfortably opening and closing its eyes, an image of peace, and Britta's so happy that she can't even bring herself to hate the cat. She tries to sit up, but a hand pushes her back onto her pallet.

"You look better. But stay in bed, don't get up."

It's Julietta, who's sitting next to her on the floor with another cat in her lap. She smiles. When she leans forward, strands of her hair graze and tickle Britta's face. Julietta gives her a pill, not so large as a walnut, but also not exactly small.

"Ibuprofen," Julietta says. She supports Britta's head, helps her drink water. After Britta swallows, Julietta strokes her hair and soothes her. "I had to force the first ones down you. You fought me like I was trying to kill you." She smiles and nudges Britta's nose with a finger. "You had a fever. Over a hundred and four. We were really worried about you, you know?"

Britta tries to say something, but nothing comes out. She shuts her eyes for a moment.

"You're constantly torturing yourself," says Julietta. "You think you can vomit up the emptiness inside you. But emptiness can't be vomited up. It has to be filled." Water splashes in a bucket, and then the cool cloth is on her forehead again. Britta's vision begins to blur, Julietta looks distorted, her voice swells and falls, Britta's not sure anymore whether Julietta's actually speaking or her words are sounding only inside Britta's head. A hand strokes her hair, the pressure on her chest decreases, a deep breath expands her lungs. There's a sudden movement, and Britta's eyes snap open. Julietta's still sitting beside her with the gray cat on her lap. But now she's holding a large stone in her right hand.

"Watch this," she says.

The hand with the stone whirls through the air and strikes the cat on the head. The animal makes a gasping sound, starts to writhe and howl. Julietta presses the cat against her leg, deals several more blows in quick succession, and then it's over. Silence. She lifts up the lifeless cat so that Britta can see it clearly, hanging limp as a rag from Julietta's hand. Her face is spattered with blood.

"Are you crazy?" Britta manages to say before she turns over on one side and retches. This time something comes up, a bit of mucus; she spits on the floor and rolls herself back onto the cushions. Julietta's smiling, her eyes sparkle, her loose dark hair covers her shoulders like a curtain. She's holding the dead cat, she's surrounded by a halo of light, and Britta's not sure she's really seeing the scene before her.

"That's just sick," she whispers.

"I thought you hated cats," says Julietta.

"But that's no reason for you to—"

"You see? You know the difference between right and wrong."

Britta's coughing, maybe also weeping, she wants to do something, to get up, to check and see whether the cat is still alive after all, but she's too weak even just to raise her hand.

Julietta bends over her; at first Britta wants to ward her off, the cat murderess, but then she breathes in Julietta's scent, her smell of unwashed hair, cigarettes, and sweat, a redolence so delightful that Britta suddenly understands how a man can be capable of loving a woman with all his senses, to the point of senselessness, to the point of insanity.

"You're not empty," says Julietta softly. "You carry everything inside you. You just have to let yourself listen to yourself."

Britta's body grows heavier as Julietta hums a song, "'You say you don't think 'cause thoughts don't make sense but one day they'll ask why you ran, baby,'" and Britta would gladly say that she has understood.

Trampling, as of a hundred feet. An army is deploying. Britta springs up from her pallet and is standing before she can wonder whether her legs will support her. Dizziness spins her against the wall. The world closes in upon her, the heat, the dust, the smell of cats and mice. Through the window, Britta can see the sun shining extravagantly, late morning, she guesses, and even though she has no idea what day of the week it is, the color of the light makes her think of a Sunday. Peace. Quiet. Birdsong. Her eyes glide through the room, searching the floor for the carcass of a dead cat, but nothing's there, no spots of blood, she has no time to think about that now, the tumult is starting again, footsteps, excited whispering. Britta shifts her weight forward, gently pushes herself off the wall, sets one foot in front of the other, and feels abrupt euphoria when the exercise is successful. She's standing upright, she's moving, her head's at the right height. Stepping lively, she goes across the hall to the living room. The whispering becomes a fierce hiss: "Get down! Shit! Get down!"

Britta needs a few moments before she understands what

she's being told to do. There's so much to see. Her friends are cowering under the window. Julietta has raised herself high enough to peer outside, her line of sight just over the window bench. Babak's staring at Britta with wide, fearful eyes. On the floor next to them: chair legs, rope, several fist-size stones.

Thoughts promenade in single file through Britta's head. *Beautiful weather. Something has happened. These two have armed themselves.* She hadn't thought about weapons. Usually she thinks about everything. She wants to tell them how fantastic she finds their initiative. Babak creeps toward her on all fours, seizes her wrist, and tries to pull her down to the floor.

"Get down, goddamn it!"

At that moment, Britta directs her gaze to the window. A white Hilux is parked on the street in front of the house. The driver's door opens and a man steps out, a tall man with a black mustache. He examines the house closely, looking for signs of life. When Britta moves, his eyes swivel to her and a smile lifts his mustache. His right hand goes up, he waves, and Britta waves back. Babak and Julietta groan loudly.

Guido Hatz, Britta thinks.

Only when her brain says the name does the reaction come. *The trail leads to Berlin. Chaussee Street. It's Hatz. Who just said that?* The sweat glands on her head begin to prickle, her stomach gets hot, the nape of her neck cold.

"Shit," she whispers. Outside, Guido Hatz is taking a few quick steps in the direction of the front door. Britta goes down on one knee beside Babak.

"I'm sorry," she whispers.

"Maybe it's not so bad," says Julietta, keeping her voice down. "I believe he's alone."

"Okay." Babak crawls back to the little collection of objects and takes a chair leg and the rope.

"Stand up," Julietta says to Britta. "Go out into the hall. When he knocks, wait until Babak and I are in position. Call out to him, say 'Just a moment!' or 'Coming!' At my signal, you open the door and let him go past you into the house. You have to let him go first, you understand?"

Britta nods. There's a knock. Julietta picks up as many stones as she can carry, ducks her head, and creeps down the hall. Before Babak follows her, he pokes Britta. "Just a moment!" Britta calls. "Coming!"

Chapter  **27**

When Britta was a child, her mother frequently listened to a pop song about God. *No one laughs at God in a hospital / No one laughs at God in a war.* Once Britta asked what the lyrics meant, and her mother explained them to her. At dinner that evening, Britta returned to the theme: "Why are there people who believe in God?"

Her parents looked at each other, amused and proud that their daughter asked such intelligent questions, but also a little uncomfortable.

At last, her father said, "Life is simpler for many people if they have a god."

"Why?" asked Britta.

"Because then they have someone they can pray to," said her father. "If they're in a war, or in a hospital."

"And because then they know why they're on earth," added her mother.

"But we don't believe in God, do we?"

"I don't," said her father.

"Do we know why we're on earth anyway?"

"But of course, sugar."

"So why?"

The parents' discomfort grew; they looked as though they really would have preferred to withdraw and consult with each other before continuing the conversation.

"Look, darling," said her mother. "You're basically asking about the meaning of life."

"A difficult problem," said her father.

"What's the meaning of life?" asked Britta.

"Everybody has to decide that for themselves," said her mother. "Would you like some more soup?"

"And what have you two decided?"

"Or more bread?"

"What's your meaning of life?"

The parents exchanged looks, laughed a little; her father shrugged his shoulders and then spread his arms out to his sides to stretch his back. Her mother finished her wine.

"It's so nice that we're sitting here together and we're doing fine," said her father. "As far as I'm concerned, that's the meaning."

"But that's just the way it is," said Britta.

"Exactly." Britta's mother leaned forward to caress her head. "And we can be thankful for that."

"And if we weren't so fine anymore, would life be meaningless?" asked Britta.

"No, of course not," said her father. "We'd simply not be so fine anymore."

A moment passed in which nobody knew what to say.

"When you're grown up," her mother said at last, "you'll find out for yourself what you'd like to live for."

"That's called freedom," her father added.

. . .

"God, am I glad to see you," says Guido Hatz after they take the tape off his mouth.

He doesn't look like someone with a reason to be glad. When he entered the house, Babak and Julietta fell on him from their hiding places on either side of the door. Babak caught Hatz's legs in the rope, and Julietta whacked him on the head with a stone, not hard enough to knock him out, but sufficiently hard to raise a bump on his forehead that swelled quickly. They then bound him hand and foot with duct tape. Julietta went through his pockets and produced a crypto phone and a ballpoint pen. No weapons, no papers.

It wasn't easy to transport Guido Hatz down the cellar stairs. Letting him walk down himself was not to be thought of, and so they dragged him, not handling him particularly gently as they did so; they merely saw to it that his head didn't strike the stone steps too hard.

When illuminated by the flashlight, the low-ceilinged room looks pretty spooky. It smells like the oil tank that must have been here once. There are no windows; the broad daylight outside is immediately forgotten. Britta and Julietta can barely stand up straight; the slightly taller Babak must hold himself at an angle and keep his head down. Guido Hatz is sitting on a fruit crate, looking deathly pale in the flashlight beam, which Babak aims directly at his face.

"Where are the others?"

"Which others?"

"You surely haven't come here alone."

"Of course I came here alone."

When Julietta picks up the chair leg, Hatz instinctively ducks away from her. The fact that he's actually afraid of them surprises Britta at first; it almost seems as if they were just acting out parts—Hatz's role is the frightened victim, theirs the grim-faced perpetrators. But then she notices how his eyes are darting around the room and realizes that his fear is genuine. She sees herself through his eyes: a woman who has spent ten successful years in the terrorist business, an expert in the techniques of torture and interrogation who regularly has her henchmen rough people up before subsequently sending them to a martyr's death. A woman who at the moment is pallid, dirty, half-naked, with rings under her eyes, accompanied by two associates who don't look any better than she does. They're not the friendly service providers of a capsized century; they are themselves among the endangerers.

"How did you find us?" asks Julietta.

Hatz laughs. His laughter sounds a bit false. "You leave an energy trail that shines in the dark."

"Bullshit." Babak points a finger at him. "You kicked up a lot of racket on the Internet precisely because you didn't have any movement data."

"Why do you ask questions if you already know all the answers?"

"I found you only after it occurred to me to look for the people who were looking for us."

"The service wasted a great deal of time on Leipzig and Berlin," Hatz explains. "I said right away: Braunschweig and the surrounding area. The energy fields were speaking quite clearly. But never mind—everything has turned out all right in the end."

"Turned out all right?" Finally, Britta also has something to say. "What the hell has turned out all right?"

Guido Hatz gives her a fleeting smile; there is sympathy as well as fear in his eyes. "What's turned out all right is that I'm here. Before the others, I mean."

"Which others?" asks Julietta.

"The ones you all are hiding from." He moves cautiously on his crate, looking for a comfortable position, which is hard to achieve with bound hands and feet. "I'll be honest with you." Britta registers the change in his tone of voice; he's trying to take an active rhetorical stance. "The thing with you—well, mistakes were made, on my side as well. Nobody figured you'd go underground, or if you did, not so fast. Or so professionally." Another smile, this one with a touch of admiration, he's doing his job well, sitting there tied up in front of three shabby-looking figures and telling them something about professionalism. "Your disappearance came as a complete surprise. We weren't ready for it. From the beginning, I wanted a cooperative strategy, and I'm as certain as ever that we'll reach an agreement. If we'd had one already, that stupid break-in wouldn't have been necessary. But the others got cold feet because time was getting away from them."

"Which others?" Julietta's harshness is unsettling; she's the youngest and slightest of the three, but apparently also the one with the shortest fuse. Guido Hatz has been aware of this for a while; he observes her from the corner of his eye and makes a placating gesture with his head in her direction. But before he can formulate his next words, the chair leg slashes through the air. Julietta swings it like a baseball bat and lands a well-aimed, powerful blow on Hatz's shin. He groans, doubles up in pain, nearly falls off the crate, and has to struggle mightily to maintain his balance. No one comes to his aid, no one helps him straighten up. They simply watch him with a mixture of sympathy and revulsion. They can hear the whimpering noises coming from his throat, sounds of agony and self-control.

Britta shoots a glance at Babak and recognizes that he feels the same way she does. She urgently hopes that Hatz will do nothing to provoke Julietta further. Should she go at him again, none of them would be prepared to stop her.

"That was really completely unnecessary," Hatz says through clenched teeth. "I'm here to make up for failings, not to get you in trouble."

"And we have to know whether you're alone," Julietta says. "If I beat you to a pulp and nobody rescues you, then we can be sure you don't have any backup."

"I'm alone, goddamn it!" Hatz bawls. "I just want to talk with you!"

His distress seems real, and when Julietta turns around to face Britta, the two of them nod to each other. Soldier and commander.

"You bear the responsibility for any little games you play with us, no matter what kind," says Britta. "I should think you would have grasped that by now."

"Okay, okay." He groans once again and spits on the floor. "We'll start over from the beginning. Do you remember your first operation?" Babak and Britta mentally draw closer. Of course they remember. They remember Dirk, their first candidate. And the escalating discussions at every step of the evaluation process. And the cautious initial contacts with different groups. The torment of waiting for the action to be carried out, and the relief of seeing the first pictures of the stricken whaling vessel. Ever since then, an echo of those thrilling days has marked all their operations.

"I was the officer in charge, and I immediately took the matter in hand."

"So you really do work for the BND,"[1] Babak says.

---

1 Translator's Note: The BND (the *Bundesnachrichtendienst* or Federal Intelligence Service) is Germany's foreign intelligence agency.

"You can imagine for yourselves what I work for. Pick the agency you find easiest to digest. Whichever you choose, you'll be reasonably correct."

"Since when do the services employ water diviners?"

"The services employ people who can do the job. As the years passed, did you ever ask yourselves why the authorities left you in peace?"

"No," says Britta. "We always assumed that our work served the public interest."

"There's a confident reply." Guido Hatz laughs. "Maybe also a little megalomaniacal. Actually, someone—namely me—has been holding a protective hand over you for the past eleven years."

"Surely not personally," says Babak.

"The farther things get from state control, the more personal they become." Hatz smiles, lost in thought. "I've always stayed in the background, you've always remained inside your parameters, it was like a tacit agreement between us. Then the Leipzig attack happened." Hatz makes a face; something hurts, either the memory or his shin. "We knew at once it wasn't you. The machinery shifted into a higher gear. Our job isn't to stop things from happening, it's to know what's going to happen."

Britta glances quickly at Babak; he's thinking the same thing she is. Leipzig was an anomaly that unsettled the balance of power. Britta's been right from the start. A fact that brings her no satisfaction in this basement room.

"Do you remember Enrico? Enrico Stamm?"

When this name is pronounced, a shape appears before Britta's mind's eye, a man who seemed to have been put together out of disparate parts: heavily muscled body, upper arms the size of hams, broad, thick chest, powerful back, and on top a little head with a buzz cut and metal-rimmed spectacles, the look of a first-semester philosophy student. Enrico entered the program a good while ago; Britta can only estimate how far back, maybe eight years, it couldn't have been long after Merkel's resignation. Enrico was a fanatical Merkel supporter: he talked about her incessantly, in a slightly whiny voice that seemed too small for his body, just like his head. Apparently, what bound him to the former chancellor was a full-blown mother complex. He didn't want to live any longer in a world that had driven out his idol in such a humiliating fashion. His traumatic experiences included the forced special election, the "Merkel must go!" cries from the furious crowd congregated outside the Chancellery, and the moment when Angela, after the results of the election had been officially announced, stepped in front of the cameras and took responsibility for the CCC's strong showing. She formed a rhombus with her fingers and explained, in her cool, slightly lisping way, that she saw in the day's election results not only a catastrophe for Germany, but also the wreck of her own personal career. Amid the booing of some journalists who were present, the ex-chancellor's controlled facade finally collapsed. A tear ran down her face as she cried into the microphone, drowning out the hecklers, "I wish our country, I wish us all good luck!" Then she left the podium, her shoulders hunched, suddenly looking like an old woman.

Enrico Stamm had watched this scene again and again. He'd developed an excruciating fixation on the moments of Merkel's departure, he spoke of nothing else, and he begged Britta to help him put an end to his life as quickly as possible. Britta had tried her best to help the muscleman acknowledge his real motives, had put him through all phases of the evaluation process with excessive thoroughness, and yet had never gotten him past harping on Angela Merkel. Enrico was one of the few candidates to be dismissed from the program on the basis of an outside psychological assessment. The psychiatrist commissioned by The Bridge certified that he had a severe narcissistic personality disorder but did not consider him to be suicidal.

When she revealed the psychiatrist's conclusions to Enrico, his eyes blazed with pure hatred. For a long moment, Britta even believed that he was going to attack her physically. In the end, however, he merely spat on the floor, yelled something like "You'll see, and soon!" and left The Bridge's offices. Since then, she's heard nothing from or about him.

"The very same." Hatz nods as if he's overheard her memories. "After he got the ax from you two, he gathered a few fellow sufferers around him."

"People don't get the ax," Babak corrects him. "After a thorough evaluation, they receive a reference number that—"

"Yes, yes!" Hatz would have liked to put up both hands. "In any case, Stamm had met a few other candidates in The Bridge's program, and he stayed on the ball, did research, contacted more and more people. Before long, he'd put together a group of men who still thought they wanted to die for a higher cause even after they'd had to face the fact that they weren't good enough for The Bridge."

"It's not a question of whether the candidates—"

"Let it go," says Britta.

"Over the years, Stamm has built up a parallel structure."

"The Empty Hearts."

"That's what they call themselves since they entered the operative phase."

"And the services knew nothing about all this?" Britta asks.

"We knew about some things, we didn't know about other things, and we let many things happen." Hatz shrugs his shoulders, a gesture possible for him even though he's bound. "The Hearts communicated discreetly and were inactive for a long time. Until the Leipzig attack."

"The most idiotic crime in history."

"On the contrary." Hatz laughs. "Enrico Stamm is either a genius or the epitome of the 'dumbest farmer with the biggest potatoes.' The explosive devices Markus and Andreas had on them weren't live. Furthermore, shortly before the attack took place, the authorities were informed that it was about to happen."

"Stamm betrayed his own people?"

"For him, it wasn't a question of blowing up the Leipzig airport. Leipzig was a red herring for you, an invitation for us, and a baptism by fire for his own troops." Hatz shrugs again. "From Stamm's viewpoint, everything went off perfectly. We all have to admit that. You provided him with the data he needed, and he got a visit from us."

"What's that supposed to mean?"

"There was no time to infiltrate his group. After the Leipzig affair, we approached him openly. He'd gambled on our having common interests, and he was right."

During the last several minutes, the atmosphere in the basement room has grown more relaxed. Babak's aiming the flashlight at the floor so he won't blind anyone. Julietta's carrying the chair leg over her shoulder like a walking stick. Britta's leaning against the wall with folded arms. Sitting in the midst of them, Hatz no longer seems like a torture victim, but rather like a teller of tales. No one speaks for a while; they give themselves up to their different and yet somehow shared thoughts. A car drives past outside, bearing witness to a thoroughly normal day, the kind nobody down here believes in. Britta doesn't even try to organize the wealth of information she's just received.

She realizes that she's atrociously hungry, and that Hatz must specify at once exactly what those common interests are.

"So what are those common interests, then?" asks Babak.

"The Empty Hearts are planning a putsch," says Hatz. "They want to remove the CCC government and reinstall Merkel."

After this sentence is spoken, a different form of silence prevails. The explanation is strikingly obvious and at the same time hard to believe. Babak is the first to recover his power of speech. His radiant smile shows how much he likes the new revelation.

"A putsch," he says. "A coup d'état. Super."

"Merkel's over sixty," says Julietta.

"Adenauer was seventy-three when he assumed office," says Hatz.

"And what comes after that?" asks Britta.

"Good question," Hatz says. "Chancellors and ministers can be replaced, and so can senior administration officials. But the people who matter are the intermediate authorities." He pauses and looks at each of the others in turn; his eyes are shining, as if envisioning the Holy Grail. "Everywhere in the administration and the military, there are, still today, supporters of the old political parties, dyed-in-the-wool democrats who have suffered for years because they've had to work for Regula Freyer and her people."

"In the services too?" asks Julietta.

"We don't serve any government, we serve a principle. Our mission is to defend democracy, to protect the continent, to preserve the achievements of past decades."

"With the help of a putsch, if need be?"

Hatz starts straining and pulling at his bonds. If he's to speak properly, he needs his whole body. "When the CCC is finished with the Constitution, only an empty shell will be left. Europe will definitively break up, and the alliances with Russian, Turkish, and American autocrats will catapult the world back into the nineteenth century. There's a constitutional right to resist."

"All the same, the loons are the ones who get elected," says Britta.

"For example the National Socialists, or have you forgotten?" Hatz laughs bitterly. "Besides, you have to wonder what a democratic election is worth when it's massively controlled from the Internet. Political opinions have long since become commodities, capable of being produced and sold. Democracy isn't as romantic as it was fifty years ago. What's wrong with you?"

It's only when he asks this that Britta notices she's clinging to the wall, her scalp feels ice-cold, and the cellar room is rotating around her. She gags and tries to speak at the same time. Julietta's the first to reach her. She holds her tight with both arms, so Britta can inhale the smell of her body, living and good, the scent of a person who sat on her bed with her while she thought she was dying.

"She's hypoglycemic," says Hatz. "Give her water and something to eat, you nitwits. And put some clothes on her."

"Hungry," Britta whispers. "Hungry," and then a piece of chocolate is suddenly in her mouth and makes her taste buds explode. Someone holds a glass of water to her lips, someone else pulls a sweater over her head and helps her into her pants. The cellar stops turning around. Julietta lets her go, and Babak pats her on the shoulder in his awkward way, as if people were creatures it wasn't really permissible to touch.

"Feeling better?" Hatz asks, and she nods. In spite of his restraints, they're slowly becoming a team; Britta doesn't know whether that's good or bad. Things are probably going optimally from Hatz's point of view. He clearly has the upper hand.

"Now I'd very much like to discuss the next steps." Again he looks around at them, as though he were at a business meeting. His tone of voice is self-assured and at the same time respectful; he speaks to Britta and her people as equals, one more little step and they'll feel like allies. "Stamm has spent the past several days exerting a lot of pressure to recruit fighters selected from your lists, and as far as we can determine, he's been extremely successful. We estimate that the group includes more than fifty by now. His people are tattooed, briefed, and if necessary trained, all on the fast track. If the Hearts strike with over fifty men, it will be like an earthquake. The capital isn't ready. Nobody has any countermeasures in place against suicide attacks."

"What's the plan?" Babak asks.

"Chancellery, party headquarters, parliamentary offices, all the ministries."

"Wow," says Julietta. "With a little luck, they can take out most of the CCC's elite leadership."

"Exactly right." Guido Hatz smiles broadly. "After that, things just have to move fast."

Now they're all smiling. Ten white utility vans drive in a convoy through Berlin's streets, attracting notice but going unchallenged. Once they reach the government quarter, the mission splits into its individual components, and the vehicles scatter and vanish down narrow streets between big buildings. Three men wearing casual clothes and showing press passes register at the gate of the Reichstag building. Four others, dressed in suits, disappear among the tall columns of the Chancellery, where a cabinet meeting is taking place this morning. Other vans stop in front of CCC headquarters in

Charlottenburg, the Ministries of Foreign Affairs and Internal Affairs, the Aliens' Registration Office, and the Federal Agency for Mainstream Culture. Some passengers are wearing business suits; several are dressed in blue workmen's overalls, in cleaning crews' uniforms, or in the jeans-and-sports-jacket outfits favored by representatives of the media. Badges around their necks display identity cards, building security passes, visitors' passes, lobbyists' passes. The men smell noticeably of aftershave lotion, which masks the odors of adrenaline and testosterone; they're carrying briefcases or toolboxes, shouldering backpacks, or pushing handcarts with cleaning supplies. In most cases, their torsos look a little swollen.

Britta can see it all, down to the smallest detail. At ten o'clock sharp on the morning of a glorious summer day, the first shots ring out. Secretaries scream, research assistants and interns throw themselves on the floor in the halls, a sprinkler system gets everything wrong and fills lawmakers' offices with water. Three policemen reach for their weapons; their shirtsleeves ride up and reveal the jagged letters of the Empty Hearts logo. On their way through corridors and into the center of power, men chiefly concerned with causing sufficient noise and panic fire at lamps and windows and spare the lower-level workers, here and there eliminating security officers, everything goes incredibly fast, they know the layout of the buildings, they've received precise instructions, they all have their respective targets clearly in mind, they move rapidly without running, and in the end every team opens the door to a specific room, where the people inside look at them with eyes bulging in fear. The explosions shake the capital. Britta, Babak, Julietta, and Hatz see the clouds of smoke, dust, and glass shards that burst from the windows. They hear alarms, sirens, frenzied security systems, they observe groups of people massing in the squares, they watch as traffic comes to a standstill, communications networks break down, and tanks roll through the streets of Berlin.

In a few minutes, the explosions are over, but the hysteria continues. A state of emergency is proclaimed, the Internet and phone networks switched off. Policemen give notice that certain areas are off-limits, evacuate the government quarter, send people home, impose a curfew. Peace, however, has long since settled over the corpses and the rubble. Tattooed bodies are lying everywhere, in individual parts or with their heads blown to pieces, in conference rooms and offices. Meanwhile, the silent takeover begins. Black limousines glide through the city, well-dressed men and women get out of them, show their credentials, enter buildings, assume responsibility. They form something they call an interim government. They're friendly, composed, professional. While expressions of sympathy from world leaders are coming in and the press is talking about a war footing and offering speculations on the origins of the Empty Hearts, the state apparatus, unnoticed, well-oiled, keeps on functioning, purges itself, eliminates excess, dismisses members of the CCC and recalls the faithful from the old days, collects taxes, awards construction contracts, marries couples, distributes electricity and water, puts trains, buses, and garbage trucks back into service, and announces new elections, which will be held at some indefinite future date.

They see it as something that has already taken place. Logical, obligatory, inescapable. Intoxicating in its consistency. Britta feels the blood in her veins begin to prickle. Sweep away, smoke out, tidy up. An operation of historical dimensions. The uprising of the righteous, the terrorism of the good, spring cleaning for democracy. She imagines how a storm of renewal will blow through the country, carrying off not only the CCC elite but also its supporters, those notorious grumblers who have been undermining the foundations of democracy for years with their resentment and their narrow-mindedness. Who have transformed the Internet into a venue for sludge slinging and rumormongering. Who are happy only when they can look down on other people. Who put themselves and their childish needs above all else. Who would rather believe simple conspiracy theories than come to grips with the complicated truth. Who constantly demand that something must change and lose their minds when someone offers proposals. Whose ingratitude is exceeded only by their self-centeredness, so that, even in conditions of the maximum prosperity, they are capable of envying everybody else. Whose greatest joy lies in anonymous hate. That sedimentary deposit of bad-tempered post-democrats who are in the process, thus far successful, of sacrificing the greatest civilizing achievement in human history to their own personal inferiority complexes. *To hell with them!*

"Awesome," says Julietta.

"Lunacy," says Babak.

"Okay," says Hatz. "Now you understand what we're talking about. What I want from you couldn't be simpler. You have to keep a low profile. Suspend the program, and do nothing at all. I should have put my cards on the table from the start; it would have spared us all a lot of trouble." He gives them a remorseful shrug. "You can imagine that the secrecy level of such an operation doesn't make it easy to lobby for reading in outsiders. From the very beginning, Stamm was for eliminating you as soon as he got hold of your data banks. But that would have caused too much commotion, political as well as physical. And apart from that . . ." For the first time since Hatz was hauled to his place on the fruit crate, he's searching for words. Now he's looking at Britta only and speaking directly to her. "There's every possibility that you'll never understand what a guardian angel is. It has something to do with love, and you're not in a position to recognize when others feel something for you." The silence in the room deepens, taking on another color. "I wouldn't allow anything to be done to you or your people. You ought to know that. Your disappearance, when you went underground, was a terrible time for me." He straightens himself as best he can, sits upright, and seems, perched there on his fruit crate, to grow. "But good, that's in the past now, from this point on we work hand in hand. It will take us just a few days, a week at the most. I suggest that you stay here in this place—it's shown itself to be relatively secure. Naturally, I'll upgrade your supply situation and have the property put under inconspicuous surveillance. We'll get you some communication technology and you'll take a few days' vacation."

"What about me?" Julietta asks.

"You'll be given an operational role with the Hearts. If you'd like that. You'll march in the front rank. How would that be?"

"I want to die for a good cause."

"This is the best cause in the world!" Hatz turns to Britta again. "After the change, The Bridge won't be able to go on as before. The world won't be the same. But I can personally guarantee you that you'll find your place in the new system. A good, well-paid, interesting, and effective place. People like you and Babak will be more than urgently needed. You're the salt in the soup of the coming order."

Guido Hatz's monologue has ended. What will come next is completely clear. Britta will go up to him, something solemn in her slow steps, and cut him loose so that they can shake hands. Hatz will stand up and stretch his back; maybe they'll even exchange a brief embrace. Then he'll get back into his car, and things will take their course.

Britta bestirs herself. Hatz looks at her, in his eyes the affection of a father seeing his daughter again after a long time. Britta returns his gaze. She gently places a hand on his shoulder while bending down to reach the rolled-up pair of socks lying next to the fruit crate. With a single, swift movement, she shoves the socks into the space between Hatz's upper and lower teeth, which are parted in an open smile, and wraps duct tape around his head, once, twice, three times, all the while pressing his upper body against her own. She checks to see whether he can breathe through his nose and releases her hold on him. He immediately falls to the floor, rolls back and forth, rages, heaves his body around like a fish on dry land. The sounds he produces through his nose during his fit have nothing human left in them. He tries to speak, to shout, to reach Britta, who takes a step back when his scuttling, writhing body propels itself across the floor and gets too close to her feet. Julietta and Babak, shocked into silence, follow the spectacle.

"What are you doing?" Babak asks.

"The opposite of what Hatz wants."

"And why?"

"Because it's the right thing to do," says Britta. "Give me the phone."

Julietta needs a few seconds before she understands the request. Then she hands Britta the crypto phone she found in the pocket of Hatz's jacket.

Britta takes her time, examining the correspondence of the past several days. When she's sure she has internalized the context, she writes a text message to "Heart": "Vixen on board, expect additional family members, given names Butterfly, Boar, Ferret, meeting eighteen hundred hours, coordinates requested."

Before even a minute has passed, the reply comes in. Latitude and longitude, all the way to the fourth decimal place. Britta commits the numbers to memory, gives the phone back to Babak, instructs him to keep an eye on Hatz, puts the key to the Hilux in her bag, and leaves the house. Julietta goes with her.

The sunlight dazzles them. A gray cat is sitting on the topmost of the front steps, consuming some luckless prey.

The hum of the needles produces a special kind of tranquility, like crickets chirruping or birds twittering on a summer evening. Concentrated silence otherwise prevails in the room, something between surgery and handicraft, with exhaustion to boot. For the first time in weeks, Britta is able to relax.

After they left the house in Wiebüttel, Britta and Julietta drove in amazement through a completely normal day, a Sunday, actually, as became evident when they encountered weekend excursionists on the B 214, all driving perfectly normal vehicles among which the Hilux no longer stood out, nor did the people in it, two young women in a big SUV on their way back to the city.

When they passed the sign for Braunschweig, Britta, against all reason, decided to make a little detour. She turned off the highway and entered the quiet residential district where she lived. She steered the Hilux through the narrow streets, parked it, conspicuous and oversize as it was, with the bicycles and family cars, asked Julietta to wait, and hurried over the paved walkway to her house. When Richard opened the door, she leaped into his arms with whatever strength remained in her emaciated body. Next she swung Vera through the air, savored her happy shrieks and cries of "Mama, Mama!" and embraced Richard a second time. His wide-open eyes were like labels on a big bag filled with questions. Britta reassured him that it would all be over soon, that she would come back, that their lives would change but go on together, that he shouldn't worry, that everything was going to be all right. Then she ran off, accompanied by Vera's tears and Richard's horror, jumped into the driver's seat, and drove away again.

Anxiety overcame Britta on the way to the Deutsches Haus; she'd had no contact with the candidates for days, and she couldn't be certain they were still staying there. But her worry proved unfounded; both were in their respective rooms, had not budged from the place, and had patiently awaited further instructions. Marquardt greeted Britta with a hearty handshake, his face was almost fully healed, he looked good, and he was ecstatic at the news that now, finally, things were set to move forward. Jawad too was happy to see her: "*Wallah,* Frau Britta, why you leave us alone so long?" The two men climbed into the rear of the Hilux and leaned forward between the front seats to high-five Julietta.

At a gas station, Britta bought three cell phones for her commandos. They each presented valid identification cards and made sure the station attendant recorded their data correctly so they could be certain they would be under uninterrupted surveillance from then on. Back in the SUV, Britta instructed the three to carry their new devices with them always and to leave them switched on at all times. In succinct words, she informed her troop that external circumstances had necessitated a change in plans, alterations in the assigned deployments, new clients, and—for Jawad and Julietta—an immediate transition to Step 12. Marquardt looked delighted; Jawad declared, "Whatever you say, Frau Britta"; then they fell silent, and Britta loved them for that.

Now they're sitting on folding chairs lined up against the wall, leafing through the available magazines or examining folders full of laminated pages with different designs, from tribal patterns to colorful mermaids. The studio seems to be located in a universal dead zone; here time has stood still, Kurt Cobain is groaning "Come As You Are" through the loudspeakers perched under the ceiling, advertising posters for erotic fairs and trade shows from the 1990s hang on the walls, and the place smells of cannabis and patchouli, an aroma that takes Britta back to her own childhood. She sees her mother's too-large pants and too-small T-shirts, her father's ripped jeans and worn-out gym shoes, she sees the square Volkswagen bus they drove to Kraków and Prague after the Wall came down, and she's surprised to think that they were happy back then, that there was actually a decade in which people felt something like happiness.

Julietta keeps her eyes shut as she holds out her arm to the tattoo artist. She has taken off her long-sleeved black shirt and is sitting on the revolving stool in her undershirt. Her thin body shows all the ribs in her rib cage; they stand out like handles you could use to lift her up and carry her away. A man with a gray ponytail has laid her forearm across his knee. His belly rests on his thighs when he bends forward to see better. Britta has told him they're in a hurry, it mustn't take more than sixty minutes per person, and he replied that such speed would be possible, provided that he had an extensive, monochrome surface area to deal with. In everything that's to come, Britta thinks, large surface areas and single colors will probably matter. The writing on Julietta's arm is already complete in outline; to fill in the empty spaces, the gray-haired man changes needles. "A big tool for the innards," says he, and you can tell by looking at him that this is a point where his clients usually laugh.

Britta sits upright in her chair and yields to the urge to close her eyes. Three hours to go before their meeting with "Heart." She's checked the coordinates of the meeting place online; they designate the premises of The Bridge, which Britta finds both cheeky and brilliant. For the moment, she's in complete equilibrium. Her stomachache has disappeared, and Britta is reasonably sure it won't be coming back. She'd forgotten that there's a condition beyond pain. It's called Paradise.

She sees Vera's face and hears her voice: "Bam!—problem solved." Mega-Melanie and Mega-Martin circle each other in a whirlpool. A gray cat floats toward Britta, it seems dead, but then it lifts its head and waves a paw at her. *You carry it inside you. Just listen.*

"Okay. Next, please."

The tattoo artist's voice makes Britta jump. When Julietta stands up and fishes a cigarette out of her pocket, Britta follows her outside. For a while, they gaze mutely at the cars going by, and it's the loveliest sight there is. Then Britta starts to talk. She explains her plan in a few words, and it takes no longer than the duration of a cigarette to make clear what she has in mind. Julietta occasionally nods, draws on her cigarette, and says "Okay" several times. She looks neither surprised nor disappointed. *She's an amazing girl,* Britta thinks, feels warm affection for her, and at the same time sudden pain at the thought of what's in store. She must restrain herself from embracing Julietta.

Instead of doing that, she says, "I had to think about my parents while we were in there. About the nineties. Back then, we often took car trips to Eastern Europe. My parents were all hot to see what was behind the Iron Curtain. I was still a child, but I clearly remember the long drives. And the music, and the upbeat mood. And the magic of the word 'Europe.'"

"How beautiful." Julietta flicks her cigarette away and lights herself a fresh one. "I'd give a lot for such memories."

"In those days, there was a beacon that lit up every horizon. Europe, world peace, democracy. My parents believed that everything would work out for the best. That the era of world wars and arms races was at an end, and that they themselves were setting out into a better future. But soon after the turn of the century, they stopped talking about that. They became downright silent."

Julietta watches the traffic, squints, and listens. A group of "Sport Is Public" joggers trots past, giving the smoking girl dirty looks. They make Britta want to light a cigarette too.

"All of a sudden, there was no better future anymore, no place we could set out for together. All that was left was the possibility of building a wall around yourself and hoping that things wouldn't get too terribly bad."

Julietta nods while showing the joggers her middle finger. Britta has to smile.

"For me, it's like a stone in the pit of my stomach."

"What is?"

Britta considers. "Democracy. I've never voted for the CCC, never grumbled about Europe and the powers that be, never participated in an online firestorm. I simply decided to do my own thing. For years, I thought I was too good to follow the newsfeeds." She shakes her head and pushes her hair back with both hands. "People like me are to blame for the current state of affairs, not the CCC extremists. Regula Freyer won her election through the ballot box, whereas my best friend decided, at least hypothetically, that she would exchange her right to vote for a washing machine. And I looked down on her decision too, because I thought I had better arguments for standing by and doing nothing."

"And now?"

"Now I know that right and wrong exist only after you make your decision. Before that, all your efforts to avoid mistakes are just a charade, they make no more sense than a soccer match without a ball."

Julietta nods and mimes striking something with a closed fist, maybe with a stone, but it's possible that Britta's mistaken about that too.

"The voters who put Freyer and her crowd into office have to vote them out again," says Britta. "We're still a democracy."

"I get it," says Julietta. "I'm with you."

"But it contradicts everything you wanted."

"That's where you're wrong."

Julietta turns her head and looks her in the eye. An extremely serious, thoroughly adult look. "A good cause is the part that's important to me. This is one."

"How do you know that?"

"I don't know it, I feel it. Hatz is wrong."

"Don't the CCC assholes have to go away?"

"Of course they do. But not like this." Julietta smiles. "It's good that you've made your decision, Britta. Now you're a human being again."

They gaze at each other. And Britta takes her in her arms after all. They hold each other tight for several minutes, they know it's the last time.

. . .

Shortly before eighteen hundred hours—six p.m.—Britta parks the Hilux on the rear side of the Kurt Schumacher Apartment Blocks and walks, followed by Julietta, Marquardt, and Jawad, the rest of the familiar way to her practice. On Sundays the Passage looks even more deserted than usual, even the eternal dental laboratory opposite her office is closed, the blond robot's place vacant. You can tell by looking at the concrete slabs of the pavement that no shoe sole has touched them for many hours. Something has come to an end here. As if not only The Bridge, but also the whole Passage, this whole part of the city, has entered a new state, an afterward, an end time, in which human will has no more dominion, and command is only in the long, slow breath of things.

The door is slightly ajar. A first glance into the half-light shows that nobody has entered the premises in their absence. That's why Britta likes this city; in Berlin or Hamburg, an unlocked office would have been plundered long ago by young hooligans, and after that junkies would have spent nights here, and then high school kids would have thrown a bonfire party.

The practice feels like a museum. Lassie's missing, Babak's dot picture is gone. What's left is a dusty still life of worn-out furniture and useless junk. It's as if The Bridge's heart has been removed. The rooms are already beginning to smell unoccupied.

Julietta, Jawad, and Marquardt drop onto the living room suite. Jawad's tattoo crosses his shoulders and the nape of his neck; he bends slightly forward in his seat, because he can't lean back against anything. On Julietta's and Marquardt's forearms, the letters of the words "Empty Hearts" stand out as though in relief, swollen, surrounded by inflamed skin, and shiny with Vaseline.

Britta goes downstairs to make coffee. The dregs in the dirty cups in the sink have dried and formed a layer, as hard as lacquer, that no effort can remove; the sugar has gone lumpy; the milk in the refrigerator is sour. Britta doesn't know how many days have passed since she last flipped a switch or opened a cabinet in here. *It's incredible how fast objects turn their backs on you if you stop busying yourself with them.*

She looks in the cabinets but finds no clean cups, and the bottom of the coffeepot is coated with dried grounds too. Not long ago, such a sight would have made her gag, but now she takes a sponge and resolutely scrubs the pot, finally enlisting her fingernails in the effort, until it becomes clear to her that it's no use, and that she's keeping it up only because she doesn't know what she ought to say to her fighters upstairs, because she's afraid of having to endure silence. She gives herself a shake, turns off the boiling water, and goes up the spiral staircase.

"I'm sorry, but no coffee."

No one reacts. The three look tense, like a band before they hit the stage. Britta sits in a chair and tries to be quiet in a similarly self-possessed way.

At six o'clock sharp, the door opens and Enrico Stamm comes in, as casually as if he were entering a greengrocer's shop. Two faithful followers enter behind him; Britta knows at once that she's never met them. *These guys must be new, two of the names from Babak's dot picture,* Britta thinks, and she's impressed that Stamm has taken care not to appear with any former candidates, so as not to confront his men with their former commander. No doubt, Britta still has power over some of them, if only because they hate her. The two young men are not older than twenty and considerably less self-assured than Stamm. The tattoo is prominently displayed on the back of one's shaved head. In spite of the summery temperatures, both are wearing jackets, from which Britta concludes that they're armed, a fact that in this case she finds rather more heartening than distressing. The more weapons, the more specific the plan; and the faster everything will unfold.

Outwardly, Stamm hasn't changed since she last saw him; all that's new is the tattoo visible under his open shirt. As in the past, his bulked-up body moves somewhat laboriously, as though its own strength stands in its way, while his small, sharp-eyed head is in constant, jerky motion. He has assessed the situation with lightning speed, and he seems to like what he sees. When he notices the fresh tattoos, he instinctively starts nodding.

"Britta, how's it going?"

"Excellently well," Britta says, glad that her answer corresponds so closely to the truth.

"I guess Guido was right. He wanted to talk to you all from the start."

Stamm spits on the carpeted floor, aiming between the coffee table and the sofa. That this does not disturb her in the least makes Britta aware of how much has changed.

"I've brought you my three best candidates," she says. "Marquardt has gone through the entire evaluation process. Julietta and Jawad have yet to complete it, but they're close, and they're definitely ready."

"Fuck your evaluation." Stamm spits once again. "We're an army, we want to fight."

"My people want that too."

"Then they're welcome."

Only now does Stamm subject the three to a closer inspection. He gives the wiry Marquardt an appreciative once-over, gazes rather disparagingly at the somewhat flabby Jawad, and then turns to Julietta. "This one's the star," he says.

Julietta gazes up at him. Her hair falls in her face, and under it her eyes smolder like the eyes of a predatory animal.

"She belongs on the very front line."

"That decision is up to me."

Stamm bends forward, brushes Julietta's hair to one side, and observes her face, as if she were a bauble that he might buy. Julietta's expression remains impassive. Britta couldn't say for sure what Julietta thinks about Stamm and his behavior, but in all likelihood she's totally indifferent to him and it. She doesn't even bother to push his hand away while he's running his fingers over her hair.

"She'll draw maximum media attention."

"Oh, Britta. You still think you're the only one who knows which way the wind blows."

Stamm turns away and says a few words, sotto voce, to his men, who nod and move their jaws as though they suddenly have chewing gum in their mouths.

"You can go now," says Stamm to Britta.

This is still my office, she wants to shout. *I pay the rent. The carpet you're spitting on is mine. Take your filthy fingers off Julietta, she's mine too.*

She sits there for a little while, rigid, as if in shock. Only now does she grasp that this is the end. A little chain of last moments. Her last sight of Marquardt and Jawad. A last smile from Julietta, who nods encouragingly. The last seconds on this chair, the last steps through the practice to the door. She will never see anyone or anything in this room again.

It costs Britta an enormous effort. She has trouble moving, as though her body suddenly weighs a ton. She forces herself to look no one in the face. Not to say good-bye. To ignore Stamm's complacence.

Everything feels wrong, the time, the day of the week, the

weather. It should be a cloudy winter morning with depressing light. With cold, damp air that creeps under your clothes. But instead, it's a radiant summer evening, as if made for a long walk, for a mild night in a beer garden or a cookout with friends.

Britta goes. She gives her body orders, her hands open the door, her feet step out into the Passage. She doesn't even turn around. As she passes the dental lab, her cheeks are wet with tears.

Chapter **29**

Knut and Janina come over at six.

Cora and Vera embrace, squealing as though they haven't laid eyes on each other for months, although during the course of the past several days, Vera has been spending almost every afternoon at Cora's house. Janina's carrying a bowl of pasta salad, which, together with a bag of veggie burgers, will serve as the evening meal. Richard's in the kitchen, trying his luck with a crème brûlée. Babak's sitting at the table with a glass of beer whose foamy head has collapsed, though he hasn't drunk a bit of it. He looks like a person who hopes he might be allowed to chop a few vegetables. When he stands up to greet Knut and Janina, he bangs his knee against the table leg, murmurs an apology, and gets tangled up with Janina, who tries to hug him as he holds out his hand to her. Although Babak knows the other guests, he behaves as though he's inadvertently stumbled into a family gathering.

"Children! Stop screaming so much!"

"What are you making there?"

"The key is to make sure the caramel layer is absolutely perfect. Brown sugar doesn't work, it burns too fast."

"He must have read that online. He's making it for the first time."

"God, Britta!" In the middle of the kitchen, Janina pulls her tight and hugs her long and hard. "I've missed you so much."

Britta returns the embrace. Giddy with happiness at being home again, she lifts her friend off her feet and turns with her in a circle, as though she were her personal savior. Then, slightly embarrassed, she busies herself with transferring the pasta salad to a big ceramic bowl painted inside and out with ants, pill bugs, and other insects.

"Get yourself a beer," Richard says to Knut. "And pour the girls some prosecco."

Knut opens the refrigerator, takes out a can, immediately pops the top, and puts a bottle of prosecco on the kitchen table.

"Have you heard that Freyer wants to ban the import of foreign beers?" Knut drops his chin and imitates rather perfectly the chancellor's way of speaking: "German beer is German tradition."

"That means no more Staropramen."

"Or you'll have to buy it on the black market."

"Cheers." They tap beer cans and then hold them out toward Babak, who quickly lifts his glass and takes a sip of the now-tepid liquid.

"How was your vacation?" Janina has sat next to Britta at the table, while the men are standing around the countertop. The girls have disappeared into Vera's room, where they're playing a game Britta doesn't recognize. It apparently involves reciprocal hitting—slapping sounds can be heard, followed by screams of "Owww!" and laughter. Britta pours prosecco into the glasses, raises hers in a toast to the others, empties the glass in one swallow, and pours herself another.

"Sorely needed," she says, whereupon Janina laughs in agreement.

Britta has told Richard she was going through a collapse, probably burnout, a kind of nervous breakdown that was ultimately the very thing Guido Hatz had predicted. Between one moment and the next, she'd found that she couldn't go on, she needed a break, she had to get away fast, away from everything, so that she could have time to reflect and to find her way back to herself.

Richard has accepted all this. He hasn't asked why she didn't simply call him to explain. Or why she'd said in her note that she had to go away for business reasons. He's uttered not so much as a word about her ragged clothes, her unwashed hair, or the fact that she's lost at least fifteen pounds. Only his reserved attitude expresses his disbelief. She thinks highly of him for not trying to drag the truth out of her. She knows that he suffered from unbearable anxiety, which he had to repress so as not to worry Vera, and that he's almost as exhausted as she is. In spite of everything, they're not arguing, and she knows it's because they've made a tacit agreement to live with a lie— Richard naturally assumes she has her reasons—and this fact provides further proof that all the decisions she made with the aim of protecting her family were correct.

"So where were you?"

"In a little place outside Celle, not all that far away. A family-run boardinghouse with just a few rooms. I was the only guest. There's a wellness spa nearby, and also a few hiking trails, but I stayed in my room and didn't even turn on the TV. I have no idea how the time passed. Apparently it needs no help doing that."

Knut and Janina laugh. The more Britta tells the story, the more credible its details sound.

Babak gazes at her with friendly approval; he likes not having to talk.

"Why did you tell Richard you were on a business trip?"

"I didn't want to answer any questions. I didn't want him to be worried."

"Well, I was a little worried, all the same," says Richard, playfully aiming his kitchen torch at Knut, who threatens him with a knife and cries, "Much to learn you still have, young Jedi."

"And how are you feeling now?"

Britta smiles. "Much better." She empties her second glass of prosecco and pours another. "A few decisions have been made." An expectant silence falls, and all eyes turn to Britta, as if this were more than a spontaneous, come-as-you-are gathering, as if they've all come here because Britta wants to announce something.

"I'm giving up the practice."

Knut and Janina stare at her, dumbfounded. For a few seconds, they're too surprised to say anything. Britta sits between her friends with a grin on her face. She has pulled off a coup.

"You can't be serious!"

"Are you trying to fool us?"

"I don't believe it."

"This is simply the right moment." Britta's eyes meet Babak's, and they nod to each other. "The time is ripe for a change."

It's clear from looking at Knut and Janina that they can't imagine Britta without her practice. Their faces reflect a question she's been asking herself for days: What will be left of her when The Bridge no longer exists?

"As long as Richard's so busy with his work, I'll just take it easy at first. Afterward we'll see. Something's sure to occur to me."

"Well, then." Knut raises his glass, a little hesitantly. "Congratulations. Or is that wrong?"

"It's exactly right."

They clink glasses. While Britta downs her third prosecco, she feels with every fiber of her being that everything is, in fact, exactly right. Although she's been home from exile for only five days, she's already adjusting to her new life, and it feels good to her. She has let Henry go and is enjoying the privilege of doing her own housecleaning. She gets up early in the morning, makes breakfast for the family, takes Vera to school, and then calmly dedicates herself to housework. Around ten thirty, Babak blows the Hilux's horn outside her front door and Britta climbs in beside him for their daily trip to Wiebüttel, where they—as they say—"feed the cat."

When they went to see him for the first time, he began to bellow as soon as they took the tape off him. Babak tried to put the water bottle to his lips, but he was yelling so loud that they had no choice but to stuff the gag back in his mouth.

"Let's just wait," Britta said. "After twenty-four hours without water, he won't resist when we try to give him some."

For a while, they observed the spastic convulsions Hatz was having on the floor. These grew weaker as his rage subsided and his mood deteriorated to dull despair.

The next day, things went better. When they removed his gag, he didn't throw another tantrum; on the contrary, he'd been waiting for them, he watched them, and he swallowed, mutely and greedily, everything they held to his lips. They made a toilet out of a chair without a seat, shoved a bucket under it, and let Hatz, his legs still bound, squat down. When he's finished, they dispose of his excrement. A distinctly unpleasant activity, but more unpleasant still are the daily dialogues, which repeat the same, unchanging pattern. Because they feel sorry for him, they tell him lies, even when doing so is pointless.

"What are you going to do with me?"

"Everything's turning out the way you wanted. Julietta and

two other fighters have joined Empty Hearts. The Bridge is ending all its own operations and getting out of the game."

"Then why are you still holding me here?"

"For your own safety."

"But that's bullshit!" This is the point where Hatz talks himself into a rage, every time. "It makes no sense! My people will find me! They'll get me out of here!"

"It's only a question of when," says Britta.

To gain time, Babak takes care to move the Hilux regularly. He uses Hatz's crypto phone to write messages to "Heart" as well as to two other numbers that he and Britta believe are those of contacts in the intelligence services. "Everything under control," or "All going according to plan," or "New assets placed under Heart's command." Julietta, Jawad, and Marquardt have instructions to carry their new cell phones with them at all times and to send occasional messages to Hatz's crypto phone, in military-style shorthand: "arrived at HQ," "orders received," "acquisition of equipment begun." The last message was received the previous day, so Britta knows it can't be much longer now. Julietta's been instructed to fix the time of the action herself. There's only one criterion: soon. The tension grows daily; it's like old times, when they were waiting for the start of their first operation.

"And what's going to happen with . . ." Janina breaks off and blushes.

"With Babak?"

"To be honest, I was thinking about our house."

Britta puts a hand on Janina's arm. "Not to worry. Our deal's still good."

Janina tries not to look too relieved. Britta tries not to imagine how one day she'll drink coffee in that house of horrors, in the kitchen on whose floor she spent the worst hours of her life. She imagines Hatz sitting in that cellar forever, shrunken, isolated, vitiated, while the girls romp around upstairs and Janina serves homemade carrot cake.

"Babak's about to start working with Swappie," Richard announces. "He's going to develop the algorithm that will make us the market leaders."

An embarrassed Babak demurs while Knut and Janina applaud and demonstrate, with many "ohs" and "ahs," that his future is just as important as theirs. Babak and Britta exchange an intimate smile. They've talked a great deal in the past few days, partly about old times, but also about how things will be, starting now. They've agreed that big changes won't be necessary, that they'll still see each other regularly, and that Babak, since he'll be working with Richard, will remain in the family. They've held hands and embraced each other a good deal. They're thoroughly aware that something is coming to an end, and that nothing in the world will replace what The Bridge was for them.

Babak's presence this evening raises the number of diners to seven, so Richard pulls out the table in the dining area. Vera and Cora come storming in and want to help set the table, a sure sign that they're hungry. Under Britta's supervision, they distribute more dishes from the insect series: plates with earwigs, cups with millipedes, small bowls with cockroaches.

"Perfect!" Richard cries from the kitchen. "Simply perfect!" Britta's happy his crème brûlée has turned out well, as happy as though the dessert were some sort of oracular sign.

The meal runs its course, problem-free. The company chatters about this and that and makes jokes about the threatened beer embargo; Knut mimics Regula Freyer again, and everyone laughs. Talking about politics doesn't bother Britta anymore. The girls annihilate their pasta salads in seconds and ask if they can watch an episode of *Megamania,* which broadcasts before the television news on Friday evenings. When Britta consents, the two charge into the television corner, shrieking for joy, whereupon Richard yells after them that they must not be so loud.

Janina tells the others about a teacher who starts to sing when she gets angry, probably to keep herself from screaming.

"Take your see-eats, take your see-eats, and be still, and be still," Janina sings, to the tune of "Frère Jacques," while the others bend over with laughter. Then they amuse themselves for a while by singing instead of talking—"Pass the sa-halt, pass the sa-halt, thanks so much, thanks so much"—and go from one laugh attack to the next. It does good to laugh like that, senselessly, foolishly, fueled by a few glasses of prosecco and a gathering of people who want nothing more than to be merry.

"Awesome, babe!"

"Helicopters!"

"Hey, look at that. Are those tanks?"

"Soooo many!"

"Mommy, come see!"

It's Babak who gets up first.

"What's going on?"

"They broke into the series," says Vera.

The government district in Berlin. If the television report were in black-and-white, it could be mistaken for historical footage—a world war, the building of the Berlin Wall, something from the twentieth century. A convoy of armored vehicles drives through the Tiergarten park. Crouching soldiers run across the patch of grass in front of the Reichstag and surround the building while helicopters fly in circles overhead. When the picture changes, a special forces team, dressed in black, can be seen storming the CCC's party headquarters on Savignyplatz.

"As if by a miracle, no one, except for the suspected terrorists themselves, seems to have been hurt," says the voice of the female news anchor. "According to the police, three suspects are dead, one woman and two men."

"So what happened?" Richard asks.

They're standing in a huddle on the star-shaped rug pattern, five adults, staring at the TV screen while the two little girls bounce excitedly on the couch.

"A string of attacks in Berlin," Britta says. "Apparently, different government buildings were targeted, but without success." Babak, who's standing right next to her, gives her a poke in the side as a reminder that she can't know more than the television does.

"I can't believe it."

"Is this intense or what?"

"It's a goddamned movie or something."

Knut, Richard, and Janina vie with one another to express their consternation, which is mingled with a trace of avidity for more information, more egregiousness, more scandal.

"We hear from reliable sources that this operation was in all likelihood an attempted putsch against the CCC government."

"Putsch?" cries Janina.

"What's a putsch?" asks Cora.

"An attack on the leaders," says Knut, in the tone of a parent machine programmed to answer children's questions.

"Mark Zudowski in Berlin, what details can you give us about what happened there today?"

"It was Mr. Meyer, for sure," Vera crows.

"Who's Mr. Meyer?" Richard asks.

"The arithmetic teacher," Britta says.

"Bam!" Cora cries. "Problem solved!"

"Be quiet! Or you go to bed!"

"There are some indications of an extensive plan," says Mark Zudowski, who wears round eyeglasses, although he's clearly not shortsighted. "The three culprits all had tattoos that refer to a larger group."

And there they are. The pictures were taken by Britta in the tattoo parlor; Babak uploaded them to the Internet so that the broadcast networks would have something to broadcast. The news editors haven't taken the trouble to pixelate the faces, maybe because there wasn't enough time, or because dead terrorists have no personal rights, or simply because it would be a shame to cover up Julietta's face. She looks fabulous, her hair wild, her eyes penetrating. Marquardt gazes expressionlessly at the camera, his shirt so wide-open that part of his new tattoo is visible. Jawad is pictured from the side in order to show his tattoo as well; he's intentionally projecting a rather fierce image, and only those who know him can see that he's having fun playing the terrorist.

" 'Empty Hearts' is allegedly the name of an alleged terrorist organization whose alleged objective seems to consist, or to have consisted, in carrying out a large-scale attack on governmental institutions."

"Mark Zudowski, what went awry in the terrorists' plan?"

"Precise information on that subject is not yet available to us. There may have been a division within the group or a simple operational misunderstanding. We're just being notified that the police are carrying out a large-scale raid." Zudowski puts two fingers on his ear to press the transmissions from his radio unit deeper into his ear canal. "Arrests have already been made."

Zudowski's image is replaced by a photograph: a man with

broad, powerful shoulders and a strikingly small head, screwing up his eyes as though blinded by the sun.

"That was fast!" cries Babak, and this time it's Britta who nudges him.

"They're showing photos of suspects, just like that?" Knut asks.

"Well, they're public enemies," Janina says.

"How could the people behind the attacks be identified and taken into custody so quickly?" asks the news announcer, while Zudowski is getting more information from his earpiece.

"Apparently, the suspects operated with extreme carelessness," Zudowski reports. "Cell phones were found on all three of them, and the movement profiles in the phones led investigators directly to the group's headquarters."

Babak and Britta secretly clasp hands, only for an instant, and then they let go again.

"How can people be so dumb?" Richard murmurs.

"What did you say?" Britta asks.

"Imagine if they'd been successful." A wide grin adorns Knut's face. "They would have gotten rid of all the CCC creeps at once."

"A lovely idea," says Richard. "You wake up in the morning, and the nutcases are all gone."

"Room for a new beginning," says Janina.

"Then the old guard comes back!" Knut enthusiastically raises a finger. "It's a hundred to one that the intelligence services are behind this. Those offices are still full of Merkel's people."

"That would be terrific," Janina raves. "To have a proper government again."

"Are you really listening to yourselves?" asks Britta. All at once, it's so quiet that Zudowski's voice can be heard again.

He's currently showing photographs of the weapons. "First you go years without voting, and then you think it would be great if the government district would get blown up?"

The embarrassed silence persists. Mark Zudowski has acquired more information about Julietta: name, age, family background, education. He calls her "the pretty young woman" and draws parallels to Ulrike Meinhof and Gudrun Ensslin.

"Maybe it's just a tempting fantasy," Richard finally says.

Britta keeps quiet and stares at the TV. She takes everything in, the changing images, the changing correspondents. Commentaries, background information. Appeals to the population. Analyses, interpretations, prognoses. Speculations and hypotheses. The others talk some more about what might have happened had the attackers acted less stupidly. They discuss whether there can be such a thing as a democratic coup d'état, whether and when political violence is justifiable. Britta's familiar with the scenarios they're sketching out. She herself has dreamed of them. Such a discussion doesn't elicit any reaction from her anymore. The longer she listens to the others, the surer she is that she did the right thing.

At some point, Knut, Janina, and Cora go home; at some point, Richard puts Vera to bed. After that, the three of them—Richard, Britta, and Babak—sit in front of the TV a while longer, until Richard starts to yawn and says good night. "Tomorrow at eleven?" he asks, and Babak confirms that he'll be coming to the company offices for their first concept meeting at that time.

"Don't stay up too long," says Richard before he disappears.

When they're alone, Babak says, "We have to think about letting Hatz go."

"We'll drive out there early tomorrow morning."

"Will he be arrested?"

Britta shrugs and shakes her head. Then she says, "People like Hatz don't go to jail."

They remain seated, zapping through the channels, watching news reports that only repeat the same information.

"Was she . . . contented?" Babak asks at some point.

"She was happy."

"But it wasn't what she originally wanted."

"Nevertheless." Britta strokes his back. "She loved us. In her way."

Babak starts to cry. Softly at first, and then harder and harder. Britta holds him close. After a while, his sobs grow weaker, and he raises his head.

"You realize, don't you, that the CCC will emerge from this putsch attempt stronger than ever?"

Britta nods.

"In the next elections, nobody's going to have a chance against Freyer."

Britta nods again.

"I'm not sure I understand why you did what you did."

Britta smiles. She thinks about the gray cat but says nothing. They don't talk anymore. They watch the next analytical segment and another report. They wait to see Julietta's picture again. And again, and then again.

A NOTE ABOUT THE AUTHOR

Juli Zeh's novels include *Eagles and Angels, In Free Fall,* and *Decompression.* She has worked at the United Nations in New York, taught at the German Institute for Literature in Leipzig, and currently lives in Brandenburg, where she is an honorary constitutional judge. She has been awarded numerous prizes for her work, including the German Book Prize, Carl Amery Literature Prize, the Thomas Mann Prize, and the Hildegard von Bingen Award, and several of her novels have been adapted for film and television. In 2018, she was awarded the Order of Merit of the Federal Republic of Germany for her outstanding contribution to literature.